MW00640217

ENTITLEMENT

ENTITLEMENT

RUMAAN ALAM

RIVERHEAD BOOKS

NEW YORK

2024

RIVERHEAD BOOKS
An imprint of Penguin Random House LLC
penguinrandomhouse.com

Copyright © 2024 by Max Revision Ltd.

Library of Congress Cataloging-in-Publication Data
Names: Alam, Rumaan, author.
Title: Entitlement / Rumaan Alam.
Description: First edition. | New York: Riverhead Books, 2024.
Identifiers: LCCN 2023056645 (print) | LCCN 2023056646 (ebook) |
ISBN 9780593718469 (hardcover) | ISBN 9780593718483 (ebook)
Subjects: LCGFT: Novels.
Classification: LCC PS3601.L3257 E58 2024 (print) |
LCC PS3601.L3257 (ebook) | DDC 813/.6—dc23/eng/20240102
LC record available at https://lccn.loc.gov/2023056645
LC ebook record available at https://lccn.loc.gov/2023056646

International edition ISBN: 9780593854068

Printed in the United States of America
1st Printing

BOOK DESIGN BY MEIGHAN CAVANAUGH

for David Abbott Land,

with my love

But money lights your world up. You're
trapped, what can you do?

—David Berman

I t was a strange, sultry summer, the summer of the Subway Pricker, but Brooke Orr had decided not to let that interfere with the business of life in New York. She and everyone in the city carried on, ignoring the debilitating heat and the lunatic at large who was jabbing unsuspecting commuters with a hypodermic. The *Post* had dubbed this man (well, it must have been a man) the "Straphanger Sicko." That moniker wasn't the one WNYC used. They spoke to an expert on air who speculated that this man derived some sublimated sexual thrill at poking into strange women. A layperson could have figured that out. There were three victims thus far. But a prick was an innocent violence, a timid violation, nothing much. Life must go on: errands to run, places to be, jobs to be done.

So Brooke was, where else, on the subway. You'd have known it was Monday. Some sobriety in the air, some frankness in the light. There was a feeling of beginning. A man in a shapeless suit and too-wide tie frowned at his cellphone. A woman, all pointy joints and neck, leaned with idiosyncratic grace over the edge of the platform, yearning to catch the light of an approaching 6, recalling a flower contorting for sun. A skinny boy in glasses wore an NYU T-shirt. A gaunt and bedraggled person was likely homeless, but might have been one of the last of the bohemians, a cohort supplanted by coeds and millionaires. At the top of the stairs, a girl in a blue smock handed a free tabloid to anyone willing to take it. Inside the station, a few sweating New Yorkers pointlessly fanned themselves with its insubstantial pages.

Brooke could feel the damp at the back of her neck coalescing into a drop, which would eventually descend, at its geologic pace, over her spine's uppermost moraine. She was aware of the musk of her body beneath the many remedies used to disguise that smell. She had that specific twinge at the temples that only caffeine would mollify. No matter. The train's conditioned air would dry the sweat, her deodorant (scented of thyme) would do its work, and there was time—she always left a cushion—to procure an iced coffee before walking the blocks crosstown to the offices of the Asher and Carol Jaffee Foundation.

The train arrived with a clatter that could damage the human ear. Its silver carriage might once have seemed optimistic, though now it was dingy and pockmarked. The open doors were accompanied by an unintelligible announcement, but most riders did this by rote: the same station, at the same hour, sometimes even served by the same conductor with his signature pitter-patter—the forecast or a thank-you for riding with the MTA or a general wish for good cheer as the train scooted along its merry way. The seats were citrus colored, the floor warped with bubbles. You had to choose to find it charming.

ENTITLEMENT

The crowd would overwhelm at the next station, but for now,
plenty of seats. As the train moved, it was sometimes possible for
Brooke to catch her reflection in the window opposite and she took
the opportunity for appraisal: skin dewy, teeth clean, hair tidy, jew-
elry simple, shirt and blazer spotless. The normal workday consid-
erations, the more important as this was a significant one. Today,
Brooke would meet Asher Jaffee, the big boss, the man in whose
name she worked, the deity for whom she and her colleagues were
intermediaries in the exalted task of giving away his earthly fortune.
First impressions mattered.

Union Square was thick with impatient nine-to-fivers. The doors
took a moment to open, a beat so automated grates could slide forward to bridge the gap between train and platform. This brief hesitation drove people to frowns, grimaces, near despair. Once upon a
time, Brooke would have leaped from her seat, back of her hand
against the door instead of on the greasy bar, pushed through the
crowd, and transferred to the express train that would carry her into
the Bronx. There was still that muscle memory of the commute she'd
navigated for nine years as a teacher at the Endeavor School, and it
was a relief that this was no longer her fate.

Brooke pulled limbs into herself as a heavyset woman eased beside her. She lost sight of her own reflection as people filled the car.
Commuters grasping for the bar took that opportunity to glance at
wristwatches. They shuffled bags from one shoulder to the other. A
muscular man wore a tank top that left his tawny nipples peeking
out. There was a bewildered family of tourists, eyes searching for
some confirmation that this was the way they sought, but the universe offered them only another garbled announcement. New Yorker
born and bred, Brooke was adept at noticing as well as ignoring all

of this. The very reason she didn't fear a subway pricker. She was impervious.

Someone in the car was playing Candy Crush with their phone's volume turned up. Brooke closed her eyes. The game's electric racket reminded her of the bell at Endeavor, which would be sounding even then, beginning the school day. That bell no longer dictated her life. There was no signal necessary to remind her that she was due in the conference room of their too-large suite soon, to shake hands with Asher Jaffee. Adults did not need prompting, reminding of their obligations, and this job made Brooke feel, perhaps for the first time, truly grown-up.

She opened her eyes because the train had stopped short of Twenty-third Street. The people around her frowned and sighed and looked heavenward, though everyone knew such interruptions were to be expected. Brooke took out her phone, because what else was there to do with these found, fallow moments? She looked at the headlines, anodyne that day, the good luck of a boring moment in the world's long history, Obama's placid America. She put the phone back into her canvas tote bag, looked from left to right much as those flustered tourists had, sure there was some explanation in the offing. A minute might pass this way but two, even three, and you understood, if you knew the city, its rhythms and signs, that something was wrong.

"Attention, attention. Because of a police investigation at Forty-second Street, all uptown four, five, and six trains are experiencing delays." The sunny conductor repeated this boilerplate. People talked back, almost jeered, sucked teeth, and reached into bags and pockets for phones, hoping for a signal so they might inform receptionists, bosses, clients, and colleagues that there was *some problem* on the subway. We are important people, they were saying or hoping. But what could you do? This was life and so it went.

"It's that sicko," a woman seated opposite said to the woman beside her. Brooke could not tell whether the two were friends or simply allied by the common cause of irritation. Brooke didn't think it was *that sicko* because Brooke didn't believe in him. She thought the pricker like Santa Claus or the tooth fairy, real only if you believed him to be. Three women felt something touch their bare skin, reported some alien sensation. Come on. Brooke respected imagination's power. She'd read about a gaggle of tenth graders who, through admirable mental focus, stopped their menstruation, swelled with nothing at all, five pretend pregnancies, a pact of sorts. Forget positive; the power of thinking at all! A nefarious unseen man armed with a syringe? *Give me a break*, she thought.

A minute went by and then another. Then two further minutes, then three. The train's hum quieted, its air-conditioning paused, and the people around her began to panic. Fine, she began to. The only reasonable response to being trapped beneath the earth in an old machine, of all days a morning she had an important rendezvous. That stab near the eyes as she thought of the iced coffee she'd promised herself. She could almost feel its damp weight in her hand. She looked at the time on her phone, though this provided no comfort.

The conductor returned, again invoking that police investigation. Brooke, angry now as the rest of the people around her, pictured beefy, baby-faced men standing about with yellow tape, hands on lethal pistols as the imagined assailant slipped into the stupid optimism of a June morning. She could get off at the next stop, several blocks short of where she needed to be. She could hurry, but this would bring out the sweat, which might defeat the slick of stick in her armpits, though this would muss her white shirt and wrinkle her gray blazer, though her face would not be dewy but wet. Fortunately, white people—and her office was all white people—could never quite tell when a Black person was flushed.

After twenty-one minutes, an eternity, the length of a sitcom, the train huffed out of its slumber, propelled forward almost by the collective will of the people within. The passengers were relieved but still displeased. Brooke gathered her things, queued with the other souls who were abandoning ship, stepped from the stale air of the car into the stupefying heat of the Twenty-third Street Station. Too late, now, to bother with an explanatory email to Eileen, her boss. Brooke had to get to that unremarkable building, not far from Penn Station, where the Asher and Carol Jaffee Foundation had its offices. She could not think about the coffee she wanted. A scrum of bodies overwhelmed the stairs to Lexington, like those scenes of salmon leaping into falling water, determined to spawn, powered by the impulse toward life. In Brooke's little more than half an hour underground, the sun had asserted itself. The sky hazed with that distortion field of palpable heat. She hadn't worn flats because of first impressions. The report of concrete under her heels reverberated into her calves. Brooke, all sinew, all muscle, all focus, ignored the pain and the sweat and, at Twenty-sixth Street, the oncoming traffic, because she had a place to be, she had work to do.

There was no attendant in the chessboard lobby of 256 West Thirty-sixth Street. Brooke fumbled with the key. In the month since that had been issued to her, she'd yet to master the lock's quirks. The elevator awaited; of course it did, the building was largely vacant. The foundation's only eighth-floor neighbors were a chiropodist nearing retirement and a shop that rented formal wear. The elevator juddered and Brooke took the moment to inhale and exhale as a yoga teacher had instructed would be useful in class but also in life. She ran a crumpled tissue across her slick forehead.

The hallway lights flicked on as they sensed her presence. The cheap tile ended at the doors to the suite, which was laid with dusty, thin carpet. Twenty-nine minutes late, Brooke stepped purposefully past the never-used conference room, walled in glass like a natural history museum's diorama, another empty room with a smudged window in the direction of Mecca, various dark interior spaces, closets holding nothing at all, dead ends. At the far end of the office was what they called the living room (to imply they were a family, perhaps), and the kitchen, and the executive offices, including Eileen's, which adjoined a conference room. There, she knew, Asher Jaffee and the staff of his eponymous foundation wondered what had become of the new girl. Brooke went inside. She tried to communicate penitence with her body.

There was a man standing at the table's head. There were four people at the pill-shaped table, fidgeting in their too-high chairs like children in pews. Brooke knew him though she'd never met him. The office's walls were hung with dozens of photos of Asher and Carol Jaffee alongside Kissinger and Morgenthau, Redstone and Bronfman, Bill Cosby and Nancy Reagan and Andrew Lloyd Webber: grins, dated hairstyles, long-out-of-fashion clothes. Leave aside the snapshots; they talked about him all the time—*Asher likes* or *Asher would say* or *You know how Asher is*. "Asher," Eileen had said, during Brooke's interview, "is very involved." This was a promise, this was a pledge, but maybe this was also a joke, maybe even it was a warning.

The room was quiet. She had interrupted.

"Well, I've quite forgotten—" Asher Jaffee sounded amused, though he did not smile.

"There you are." Eileen said this mostly to herself. The woman had some ineffable quality: she seemed efficient. Eileen was doing the work she was born to, with her grasp of modern leadership (the carrot, never the stick), her unfashionable dress, her competent speech.

"I am so sorry. To interrupt. To be so late." *Because of a police investigation at Forty-second Street, all uptown four, five, and six trains are experiencing delays.* But that was only an excuse, something a child would tender.

8

"Asher Jaffee. This is Brooke Orr. The new program coordinator." Her tone said that Eileen considered the matter of Brooke's tardiness settled.

Asher Jaffee was an old man, and had beaten the majority of men the world over by making it to eighty-three. He saw this a victory on par with, indeed maybe related to, the four billion or so dollars he'd amassed. No, money didn't buy time. Same, as everyone said, for happiness. But he had the trifecta. The money itself flowed through his veins. The money held him high, no trace of stoop. The money was steady and so there was no tremble in his hands. Even his eyes. Look past the folds and see those were still the same (naughty) as they'd been when he was a child. There were spots on his hands but they were as capable as ever they'd been. Neither jam jars nor the ghost keypad of his cellphone stymied. Most important, his mind, humming reliably. Asher Jaffee read the papers, watched the market, bought and sold, and conducted business as usual as he had for the previous sixty years. Needless to say, Asher Jaffee continued to succeed, to thrive, to bet smart, to earn. He took his seat at the table's head. Asher was unimpressed by tardiness, but kept his silence, understanding, after a lifetime inside them, how to comport himself in a conference room.

"Mr. Jaffee." Brooke had planned on a shake, but there was no hand outstretched. She took the seat beside Kate, the office's youngest and therefore most junior employee. Next to Kate, with her girlish upspeak and the fruity scent of her shampoo, her soap, her lotion, her chewing gum, Brooke could only appear smart and interesting, even if she was sweaty and ill at ease, her tote bag on her lap as if she were preparing to leave.

"Maybe this is a good time to talk about de Blasio. I still think it would be useful to identify someone in the administration we can work with directly." Jody was not masculine but boyish, some essential femininity peeking out of the edges of her butch presentation. She was so slight she wore blazers and khakis from Brooks Brothers' kids' section. The effect was of a woman in disguise, but all workplaces demand pantomime from their inhabitants.

"De Blasio." Asher made a face. Candor was permissible in front of these people because they worked for him. He disliked the mayor. "Even Mike Bloomberg couldn't do much about the lumbering machine of the government. And de Blasio is no Mike Bloomberg."

"This was something we talked about before your trip," Jody reminded him. "I feel strongly that someone from the city could—"

"When you're in City Hall, you're part of the problem." Maybe he'd have been the exception! What might have been? "Think what I could have done. With no deputies and commissioners and whatever. Just a room full of people like you." But even Asher Jaffee knew that he was too old, now, to run for office.

Brooke could see what her boss was getting at. This was how people had spoken of George W. Bush: equipped with folksy charm and an MBA, he might save the state from itself. Maybe, reflexively, the thought of that president, whom her mother had hated with more fervor than any other in her lifetime, made Brooke roll her eyes.

"You don't agree?" Asher fixed his attention on Brooke with that teacher's instinct to spot the troublemaker, the clown, the ne'er-do-well: first the girl was late, now she was mocking.

"I'm not sure—" If Brooke was being asked her opinion, she would offer it. Perhaps she could recover from her embarrassment, impress with her acumen. Perhaps this man was testing her and she had to rise to a challenge.

"You've been brainwashed about *democracy*." Asher Jaffee understood how liberal arts girls thought. It was not that interesting to him.

Eileen didn't have children of her own but was this office's exasperated mother, charged with keeping the number one son focused. "I think what Jody is saying is true. If you're willing to call the mayor. Get him to identify a contact person. From there, Jody and I can manage the heavy lifting. Your point about government inefficiency is well-taken, but we must deal with the world as it is." She tried to put a smile in her words.

"We're changing that world, Eileen. Aren't we? I mean that's the fundamental mission." Asher was very clear on this.

Eileen bristled at the mention of a mission. Jody had spent months urging Asher Jaffee to draft a statement of purpose for his family foundation. The billionaire refused to comply. He'd made a fortune by diversification; he would give that fortune away by the same logic. The environment, education, health, the arts, civic engagement, a better society by every measure. "We all agree on that, Asher."

No one spoke because there was nothing to say. Every meeting in every conference room in the city went precisely this way. Such gatherings were the inverse of Quaker ceremony. The rite was in everyone's saying something. Once quiet had settled, the thing was concluded, everyone involved nearer God. Brooke could tell that Kate, a Penn graduate whom the rest of them thought, nonetheless, a little dumb, was in fact holding her breath. There was some fragile peace.

"Natalie!" Asher leaned back in his chair and the woman he had summoned appeared almost immediately. Pallid and spectral, hard dark eyes vigilant behind gold-rimmed glasses, Natalie had spent

half a century answering Asher's telephone and opening Asher's let-
ters and guarding Asher's time. She came when he called; often she
sensed the summons before it had been issued. Asher did not bark her
name, though. There was tenderness there.

"Mr. Jaffee." Natalie never put a question mark in her dealings
with the man, just as she never referred to him by his first name.
Some mysteries were so holy they had to be preserved.

The old man gave a child's sigh. "I need to speak to the mayor."

"Of course." Steel trap, Natalie didn't write down her tasks. "If
you're finished here. You do need to call Catherine Hendricks, Mr.
Jaffee." Natalie's single objective was to help Asher Jaffee live his
life. "I'll get the mayor, and I also have a few more calls for you to
make. Eric Stone, Ben Hammond, then someone from the Rubin-
stein Group was wondering whether you had ten minutes."

He might have sighed again, but he did not. Asher Jaffee was not
much of an actor. He couldn't pretend that he didn't enjoy being in
demand. Asher Jaffee loved being loved. "We're done here," he said,
and that made it true.

N ot a bad day, in the scheme of things, but not a good one. A great mystery how time moved by its own logic. A Monday was not meant to slip by, but that one did. Brooke's office routine: a cup of tea, the writing of emails, idle chat, that day on the subject of her tardiness.

"I ride the four all the time. It's freaky!" Kate had grown up in Grosse Pointe, suburban girl reared on fear.

"It's just the media." But Brooke knew that WNYC was not prone to hysteria. What she wanted to say was that nothing bad could ever happen to a girl like Kate.

There was another meeting of the staff. There was a trip to Starbucks. There was the voice of Asher Jaffee from elsewhere in the office. That was it. Brooke had made plans to wow the guy with her initiative, her competence, no, her brilliance, but God did what he always did: ha ha ha. She was not disappointed or mad, but irritated at herself, which was worse.

There was, at least, dinner to look forward to. For Brooke's mom, Maggie, the empty nest occasioned not crisis but renaissance. The woman who once had Taj Mahal, Peking Garden, and Sal's down the street on speed dial—what's a single mom to do?—had enrolled in cooking classes and now found diversion (even joy, maybe transcendence) in the kitchen. A roast chicken with crisp coins of potato; vinegared cucumbers over a scoop of rice; a Mercurochrome-colored curry, cubed tofu bobbing in the brew. You never knew what she'd come up with next.

The apartment that Brooke and her brother, Alex, still thought of as home was within walking distance. The shoes were an issue but she didn't have to run. It didn't matter if she was late. A mother would not mind. The Polish staff had known Brooke since the day Maggie had brought her home. Tom (really Tomasz), Chris (really Krzysztof), Joe (really Jarek), and the rest were deferential but distant, smiled but did not waylay with niceties.

The thickset Poles in the lobby kept the world at bay, so there was no need for a key in a lock. This door, passage to her childhood, Brooke had long mastered. Her body understood the heft of the thing, the arc of its swing, the amount of force to apply, as she could see, before stepping into it, the dark foyer, with its bamboo-framed mirror, the wall-mounted hooks for tote bags and umbrellas, the waist-high demilune with its unsteady pile of junk mail and catalogs.

There was the helicopter whir of the blender in which Maggie was preparing gazpacho and, beneath this, feminine voices. Naturally. Maggie had always collected women and Brooke's life was ruled by a central quartet: Maggie and Sayo and Paige and Allison. When Maggie became a mother, by adoption, that *choice* women of their generation were so keen on, the coalition became what they would have called a family. A form filed in the school office attested that Auntie Sayo was able to fetch the kids from their classrooms. Maggie's last testament appointed Auntie Paige, in the event.

Allison was doting, heavy, sweet smelling. Sayo was distracted, benign, but ever present. Paige was glamorous—which was to say tall and thin and ineffable—but had derring-do, a tomboyish fearlessness. She wore Yohji Yamamoto and always had fat bouquets of tuberose in her apartment, but Paige vacationed in Antarctica, forswore makeup and perfume. For Brooke's eighteenth birthday, Auntie Paige, in some fashion Brooke's father figure, had slipped a Cartier bracelet onto her niece's thin wrist, where it remained. "It's what a woman needs," Paige explained. Brooke considered that moment her official entrance into adulthood.

The voices lifted to compensate for the appliance. It was Auntie Sayo, most constant companion, these days. One of those four-generations-in Japanese from California, Sayo had an accent East Coasters thought incongruous, a voice instantly recognizable to Brooke. A tennis player, a golfer, the ruddy-faced widow of a plastic surgeon so successful that he owned polo horses, there were photos of pregnant Sayo beaming with infant Brooke in her arms the day she arrived in this very apartment. Her own daughter, Kim, born three months later, was essentially Brooke's cousin. "I thought it sounded interesting."

"I suppose it's better than that fiasco with that school. A teacher?" Maggie switched the blender off. Maggie had been single so long that she was accustomed to unburdening herself to each of her friends. "I could have predicted that would end badly—"

"She has to find herself." This was the kind of thing you were reared on in California. Sayo didn't understand the problem of a way-ward child.

"For nine years?" There was no need, between old friends, for Maggie to mask her irritation. There was something familiar about these complaints; she'd made them before. Mothers worried, and there was nothing so unusual in Maggie's concerns for her older child, im-perfect as the rest of us.

"They're different, this generation. They're not us."

"It's beneath her, Sayo." Maggie decanted the chunky soup into a bowl. "It's *administrative*."

Brooke lingered in the hallway, weighing the thrill of overhear-ing a candid conversation against the words that were being said. By instinct, she held her breath, believing this might erase her, as chil-dren imagine that when their eyes are closed they cannot be seen.

"I spent a small fortune on Vassar and she's a secretary to some zillionaire." A mother's sentiment could power cities. It defined every-thing. It was, always, the decisive word. A wooden spoon clattered in a porcelain sink.

I'm not, Brooke had some instinct to say, a secretary. And *to* Asher Jaffee? She had only just met the guy! She knew this would not help her case. She was not meant to ever have heard this. She stilled herself.

"It's a job. She's happy." Sayo considered happiness enough. Only Paige, among the aunties, would have risen to Brooke's defense. But Paige was rarely seen. Her chic magazine gig was a casualty of the 2008 economic convulsion. Clever Paige saved herself by marrying a Greek who lived on Central Park West. She said she felt like Mrs. Onassis. Then the Greek dropped dead and the apartment went to his ex and Paige was, strictly speaking, homeless. Paige consigned her Hermès bags and cashed out her 401(k). Paige, who had danced with Albert of Monaco and dined with Karl Lagerfeld, took a job manning the telephones at an orthodontics practice in a Rockville Centre strip mall. She rented a room in an exurban town house that belonged to a flight attendant named Mark.

There was the scrape of Sayo's stool on the glazed tile, a sound Brooke associated with herself and Alex abandoning milky bowls on the kitchen island, bounding off to feign the brushing of teeth. Brooke would, of course, have to pretend never to have heard this. She would have to lie. She moved backward into the foyer. She opened the door and knew just how to close it so that it made a noise. This report bounced off the close walls and reached the kitchen, and Maggie emerged, drying hands on a plaid tea towel and smiling at her only daughter. "There she is. I hope you're hungry."

An actress follows her cues, and Brooke let herself get swept into the spirit of the thing. A kiss on Auntie Sayo's well-sunned cheek and a glass of chardonnay so cold it tasted of nothing.

Maggie had cabbed to Murray Hill to buy spicy Indian snack mix. Sayo spooned some of this into the palm of her hand and tossed it back. "Tell me about your job again."

Brooke could see in this question the age-old conspiracy of adults v. children. Sayo was interrogating, hoping to either prove Maggie wrong or understand just how right her friend was. Brooke had explained all of this. She had, in fact, been so proud.

"He founded Jaffee Office Supply." Brooke knew the whole story. Asher Jaffee had taken over his paternal uncle's stationery shop. Asher registered at Brooklyn College to avoid being sent to Seoul, left before getting a degree, and opened an outpost in the Financial District, catering to office-supply managers instead of Flatbush schoolkids in need of pencils and rubbers. In time, there were trucks: Jaffee . . . In a Jiffy! *Advertising Age* called this slogan one of the greatest of the twentieth century. ("Its six syllables contain its entire promise.") It was written by Asher Jaffee himself.

Asher bought out his uncle. He married a girl named Barbara and expanded into a catalog business. Asher was seer: he saw the inevitability of the computer, and Jaffee could be relied on for magnetic tape. Asher was overachiever: he realized he was providing paper for others to print on, so expanded into that business. Asher was lucky: that subsidiary business of printing pages of mazes and word searches to be laid on the plastic trays at thousands of McDonald's nationwide made him a millionaire.

Asher and Barbara became parents the day Kennedy was shot. Linda Jaffee died at her desk at Cantor Fitzgerald thirty-eight years later. A whole life in the parentheses between American tragedies. By September 11, 2001, Asher was already a billionaire. Real estate, mostly: in the 1980s, he'd balked at expanding retail operations because his grandfather had taught him that it was wasteful to pay rent. By the magic of math, the malls he'd acquired in the name of thrift became more profitable than the ledgers and staplers still ferried about Chicago and San Francisco in yellow trucks emblazoned with the old-fashioned promise of *a jiffy*. His and Barbara's divorce occasioned a battle royale for custody of a Monet and the Eighty-first Street town house. (She got the painting; he got the mansion.)

He met Carol in one of those corporate photo ops men like him often had to endure. She was there to attest that Jaffee was an equal opportunity employer. That their first meeting was for the camera's benefit foreshadowed the tabloids' interest in the blonde from St. Paul, a gold digger who'd hit the mother lode, as they told it. Jaffee sold Jaffee before the recession destroyed the company. He was an informal economic adviser to the elder Bush's administration, invested (wisely: Microsoft), joined corporate boards, wrote a business book (*Paper Thin: Making a Million Out of Nothing*), monitored his money, and then resolved to give it all away.

The man's own words about the death of his daughter were an early viral sensation for his friend Ariana's new publishing venture. Some actuary had sat down and done the math! Uncle Sam tendered three million dollars of condolence. *In the face of reality*, Jaffee wrote, *money means nothing. The question is how to make a life with meaning.* So, he was declaring it aloud: he would get rid of his money until he was left with only peace. That, right there, was the mission statement Jody so badly wanted. There was disagreement, on the internet, as to Asher's net worth, but Brooke trusted *Forbes*, which put it around 3.7 billion dollars.

Brooke did not say most of this. "He wants to do good. I think it's a worthy cause." She knew what her mother and her aunt were thinking. That however meaningful the task of the Asher and Carol Jaffee Foundation, Brooke's contribution was something beneath her.

Auntie Sayo, a little tipsy maybe, nodded her head. "I think so. Worthy cause." She looked at Brooke's mother.

Maggie pushed away from the island. "What's that those Occupy protesters said? The one percent. It's clarifying to think of them that way. The megarich. They wreak havoc on the environment and refuse to pay fair taxes, then they get to decide what's a *worthy cause*, bless the rest of us with some of their leftover money."

Brooke had imagined bringing home to her mother the story of how she had impressed Asher Jaffee that day. A small recompense for the previous five years spent telling her mother how badly she

wanted a new job. Brooke assumed the older women would be tan-
talized by her frontline report on the if-not-quite-famous certainly
well-regarded Asher Jaffee. She had been excited to be the center of
attention. But Brooke could hardly tell the story of how her morning had actually gone.

Kim's arrival provided a recalibration. In the end, though people
asked, no one wanted to know how your day was. Any distraction
will do.

Kim was a stunner. You couldn't be for miscegenation just as you
couldn't be against it, but her Japanese mother and Black father had
collaborated on a masterpiece. She was so tiny you felt proprietary
about her, Brooke the more so: Kim the perennially much smaller
person at her side. Brooke had felt protective of her the entirety of
their lives. Two diapered creatures, Brooke dark and hard, Kim soft
and unable to hold herself up, melting into the body of her almost
cousin, not quite sister. Two nine-year-olds on a Central Park playground, the elder spindly and lean, the younger still cherubic. Kim
was like a living doll: slightly different, slightly better, sent to make
Brooke's life less lonely. She had always reckoned herself lucky for
that. Brooke and Kim had chosen the same college because they could
not imagine otherwise.

"I smell something good but what else is new?" Kim wore a cashmere sweater despite the heat. She seemed always to be trembling with
some chill.

"Mom's doing tapas, so you smell shrimp in garlic." The young
women touched knees, arms, wrists as they spoke, as twins, remem-
bering the confines of the womb, often do.

"You wore this today? Okay, Melanie Griffith." Kim had special
dispensation to tease.

"Some of us have to go to offices." Brooke, too, was able to rib. A fact but still a delicate subject: Kim didn't need work but ways to fill her time. She played tennis with her mother; she shopped; she helped out a fashion stylist, though this was more volunteering than anything, a worthy use of her good taste and flexible schedule. Kim had recently reached what her long-dead father had considered maturity, and with that came some sum, never named, pennies from heaven. Why age thirty-three? What had her father known? No matter: Kim was on the cusp of great change. She'd become the person she was destined to be, and that person would never have to go to an office.

Kim's laugh said that she herself was the subject of her own mockery. You had to have a sense of humor about these things. With the money from her father came an imperative to prove that her life still had some purpose. "I have things to do, too." Mock defensive. A little gag.

Brooke could rib, but knew the line between this and cruelty. "It's not like they'd miss me if I didn't show up at work." The job mattered but she didn't.

"Please. I'm sure they don't know how they ever got on without you. Hey, where is Alex? I never see that guy at these dinners."

Maggie served meals in the kitchen's ample nook so she could fuss at the stove and still participate. "He's busy!" Maternal pride.

"Like mother, like son." Sayo did not mean this as insult to Brooke.

Brooke would not hear it that way. She loved the guy. Yes, her little brother had been a white baby placed for adoption (it happened), and if you pretended, as many did, Alex looked rather like Maggie, pink-skinned and gangly. That left Brooke outside of something, but the judgment of the wider world had little to do with how she felt.

Maggie took this opportunity to talk about Alex's work then her own. A lawyer by training, she ran an organization dedicated to reproductive justice. She thought the big-name donors mostly money launderers. The Access Coalition provided cash and safe passage for women living in states with less-enlightened governments. Real change, real community, real results: bus fare, a spare room in which to recuperate, the indignation of the righteous. Often the unused bedrooms in that very apartment played host to some Kendra or Ashley, agog at her first sight of Manhattan. "Between his job and the wedding planning, you can imagine how busy he is."

In some private part of herself, Brooke had imagined that her mother might speak of her this way. There was common ground—Maggie's work was about, fundamentally, doing good. Brooke had followed in her mother's footsteps! But there was something particular between Maggie and Alex, maybe the usual jazz of mothers and sons. Brooke had a familiar feeling, ugly, best suppressed, and she disguised this with a veneer of smile, nod, downturned face.

Alex had interesting work, as an architect. Alex was going to marry a beauty: Rachel, Persian Jewish, with nut-brown tresses and flawless white teeth, a degree from Boston University and a job at the United Nations. Alex, little sibling, had an adult life in the offing. Brooke loved him and didn't envy him a bit, but she understood that the job and the fiancée meant that Alex was good, Alex was thriving, Alex was to be admired, that Alex was not—had Maggie used this word?—a disappointment.

Brooke woke up in the bed's very center. There was some rebellion in that. Historically, yes, she'd have been pitied: a spinster! As Brooke saw it, we spend most of childhood dreaming of adult liberty. Once that arrived, why wouldn't you want to hold on to the freedom just attained? Brooke was determined to enjoy these moments, especially having left behind a job that did not satisfy for one that did. The rest of her future was out there, somewhere distant. For now, she was going to spring for cocktails, order dinner in, make it to vinyasa twice weekly, buy the too-expensive trousers if she felt like it. Brooke wasn't interested in parsing the distinction between satisfaction and happiness.

Sure, she was aware that the apartment was shabby. Someone had put up an insubstantial wall, an attempt at making it into something other than a studio. But there was no need for privacy when you lived alone. The windows might be drafty but they were large.

A love seat was the only thing that would fit in what she had designated the living room but it was cozy. The burblings and sighs of the building's innards, once loud enough to keep her awake, had become as familiar as the thrum of blood in the ear when she put head to pillow. She had almost become fond of the indigent sleeping on the heating grates across the street. She felt proprietary, even, about the network of cracks in the plaster ceiling. They made Brooke think of those illustrations rendering constellations as connected dots.

This place wasn't meant to have been her fate, but as they said: be it ever so humble. The plan, ancient history now, had been to live with Kim and Matthew, dearest of their Vassar circle, a tidy and effective trio. But two-bedroom apartments were easier to come by than three and landlords were suspicious of kids just out of college. The solution they arrived at was that Sayo would be guarantor for Kim and Matthew's lease. Maggie would underwrite Brooke's move into a place all her own. It wasn't that her friends had chosen each other over her; it was logical. Her bruised feelings were forgotten because that was how time worked.

It had only been a month that she'd worked at the foundation and already her morning's routine felt like the only reality she'd ever known. Brooke made her bed first thing, a priority instilled by her mother. It was the proper way to begin a day. She brewed coffee and stood in the hot shower then considered her options, the bed an array of stacks of trousers and sweaters bought on the spree when she first secured this job. Kim had accompanied her to J.Crew and frowned, then they'd A-trained to Brooklyn to ransack Kim's wardrobe: What did she need with business casual?

If she lived with Kim and Matthew, Brooke would have someone to approve the day's outfit. She had to rely on the mirror she'd paid some Craigslist-man-with-a-van thirty dollars to fetch from the Paramus IKEA. Brooke sent Kim a cellphone photo of her own reflection. This had become a routine. Kim, up early to take the dog for its pee, wrote back immediately. Not the insipid intercourse of women in movies. No emoji, no exclamation point, no canned affirmation, no *You got this girl*. Kim wrote back: *yes*. All Brooke needed was that *yes*. All anyone needed was a *yes*.

This was backstage business. Once the apartment door was closed behind her, Brooke became some other person, or a real person, on the familiar walk to the subway. Brooke had that most common out-of-body experience, extrapolating away to see herself as the hero, the star, the protagonist of the real world. She loved this version of herself because she had put so much preparation into it: clothes, posture, timbre of voice, the lot of it a performance. It was a feeling of pure ego. Once at the office, this had to end. The individuals who worked for Asher Jaffee didn't matter; his money and the people it would help did.

That morning, Brooke was summoned to see Eileen and Jody in the living room, with its sofas and potted plants, its genteel air. Brooke couldn't help but feel like pupil called before principal. She ran damp palms across her thighs as she squished into the charcoal leatherette.

"We've been talking," Eileen began. Her breath smelled of old coffee. "You've learned the ropes. Maybe you're ready for your first independent assignment?"

It had been four weeks of sitting in on meetings she could barely follow, of chopped salads and lattes, of helping Eileen sort through cryptic financial records. Perhaps Brooke, listening along, sorting stacks of papers, had seemed like a secretary. But what secretary merited an *independent assignment*? Brooke sat up a little straighter.

"My idea," Jody said. "Credit where it's due." Jody had that way of joking—every punch line indicating some deeper feeling, some actual truth.

Eileen began to apologize then understood she was being ribbed. "What do you think of oysters?" she asked Brooke.

"It doesn't matter what you think of them," Jody reassured her.

Brooke vaguely remembered having heard some talk of oysters. It hadn't made any sense and it still didn't. "I don't know that I have an opinion." She didn't want to lie, and she didn't like sounding so noncommittal.

"That's the point," Jody said. "You do the reading. You talk to the people. You form an opinion. You come back and tell Eileen." Her advice carried her fondness for Brooke. Anyway, Brooke was in need of a challenge, and Eileen was in need of help. Consultants were expert at the obvious.

"I can do that." A relief. She knew how to read. She knew how to think. She had to remember that.

Jody saw the thing as settled. "Right. Then Eileen and I can focus on the fact that we have too much money." Jody was always blunt; she figured she was paid for her honesty.

Eileen didn't want to get into this in front of Brooke. "That's open to interpretation," she replied. "Brooke, I'll send you some emails. All the salient contacts and dates. If there's anything unclear—"

Jody had a subject and she wouldn't let go. "I'm here to help Asher get rid of his fortune, not oversee its growth. *Almost exponential.* You've been on the calls. If we're making more than we're giving away, we're failing. That's not a foundation. It's a business."

Brooke understood that she was dismissed, or that this was between the two of them. But what child could resist eavesdropping on the grown-ups? "I'll go take a look."

On her first day, Brooke had chosen her office at random. There were so many, all unoccupied. No hierarchy pertained, no one cared where she staked her claim. She had selected a little cell with a hollow-core door, an inexpensive desk, bad lighting. The room had a sense of private purpose, quite different from the classroom, a communal space, institutional and never quite hers. She had some instinct to text Kim again, report what she had decided was a triumph at work. But it wouldn't mean anything to Kim, or her approval of this did not matter to Brooke. This was private. Brooke opened the computer and began to read and felt again like a child in her mother's bedroom closet, playing office with marbled notebook and stapler at the ready.

Brooke would not have guessed that there were people with an enthusiasm bordering on mania for the humble oyster. All kinds in this strange world. The group's fervor was persuasive. The aim was to repatriate the oyster to New York Harbor. This would clean the waterways. This would repair a broken food chain. Beavers would return. You couldn't be alive in 2014 and not know that the earth was broken, but it was exhilarating to learn that it could be healed. What was needed was time. And oysters. And millions of dollars, which was where Asher and Carol Jaffee came in.

As she read, Brooke could feel her mind changing. No, she'd never eat an oyster again—a gelatinous accretion heavy with pollutants. These people had petitioned, and it was Brooke's job to hear their prayers. Brooke would relay her recommendations and maybe make the case to Asher himself. She would, in her own small way, change the world. That this was just all in a day's work was a blessing, was a thrill.

She wished she had a notebook. Jody carried one, was forever interrupting herself to jot some observation in the red-leather volume. It was the sort of thing professional people had. It was imperative for this work. It was the prop that would unlock her performance. On Amazon, Brooke found the very model that Jody used. It would be strange unless she bought a different color. But if Brooke had that book, she'd forever be jotting down ideas, reminders, insights. No one could take her for a secretary.

The website had made the transaction so easy it felt unreal. It was not until Brooke printed the receipt for her expenses that she realized her Amazon cart had had other things in it, waiting for her: a toilet brush, a paperback. She could take a Sharpie to the page, blot out the fact that she had a bathroom that needed cleaning, that she wanted to read *The Bonfire of the Vanities*. Brooke knew that Eileen only scribbled her initials on the first page, that Asher Jaffee could easily buy her a toilet brush *and* still help repatriate the oyster to New York's waterways, but there was a difference between right and wrong.

It turned out that beaver dams could affect the temperature of groundwater miles downstream, some complicated hydrological chain of cause and effect that was a net benefit in a warming world. Imagine! She was engaged enough that Natalie's rap at the door surprised.

"I'm so sorry to interrupt, my dear. I only wanted to say that I put something on your calendar. Lunch with Mr. Jaffee, today at one thirty." That nasal Brooklynese sounded put-on, tiptoeing to parody.

Not so: it was the last, pure gasp of something, a trace of a vanishing America.

Brooke was undefended, and her expression gave her away. "Lunch with—me?"

"Mr. Jaffee requested it. I've made a reservation at Keens. Walking distance. One of Mr. Jaffee's favorites." A sly smile to say that for decades she'd been booking him tables there.

Brooke did not ask why a billionaire would want to have lunch with her. Not her place to demand that answer. She thought of the oyster, invisible beneath the water, indifferent to human life, busy with its humble task. There was a lesson. Leave behind the guilt that she had failed as a teacher. Forget her own mother's skepticism. Make her an oyster! Useful, small, hidden, important, no, imperative. Let this be her purpose. Let her, unnoticed, make the world a better place. Because that was what they were doing, right?

Natalie did not quite understand the expression on the younger woman's face. Her hand at her throat, as though clasping a necklace she did not wear, Natalie leaned in a little, conspiratorial even from across the distance of Brooke's small office. "Don't worry, my dear. He's a very nice man."

sher and Brooke passed a Taiwanese costumed as a Tibetan, a gentle con artist tying bracelets to the moist wrists of tourists: a blessing for a dollar, what a bargain! Her handbag's straps crossed her chest like a car's safety belt. A block from the steakhouse where they were expected, there was a chrome diner. Asher marveled that the species endured, extolled their simplicity. Brooke thought this his way of suggesting it. "We should eat here," she said. He was amused. She'd be okay with that? A sandwich instead of a steak? Of course she would! She was game. She was a good time. She was eager to please.

The lone waitress was a much-mascaraed Greek who brought weak coffee in shallow cups. She called them *sweetie*. She committed their orders to memory, shuffled toward the counter, and recited them to the Salvadoran tough at the grill. The other patrons were a man gnawing a gyro and a woman crumbling saltines into Manhattan clam chowder, both staring into cellphones.

"Lunch with the big boss and it's only a five-dollar grilled cheese. I hope you're not disappointed." Asher Jaffee was the sort who could refer to himself as the *big boss* without irony, without a twist, without a wink. That was just what he'd been, for years and years.

"Not at all." Easier, wasn't it: no complicated salad, no worry whether it was expected or frowned upon to order wine. She could focus on small talk. "How was your trip?"

Asher and Carol had celebrated their silver anniversary with a monthlong jaunt. "It was fun." What a bore, Europe: buttered toast and foreign newspapers, shuffling through churches, trying to be appropriately cowed. It was impossible to stay on top of the college basketball finals. He loved Carol but they were impatient with each other. Asher was not himself without an office. "But I'm glad to be back. Brooke, how old are you?" He believed himself old enough to ask with impunity.

"I'm thirty-three." A personal question but one she didn't mind answering. Her mother had always crowed about her own age, never hesitated to pronounce it: forty-three, fifty-one, sixty-two. To be anything but proud of living however long you made it was empty vanity, one of men's tools for keeping women in check.

He nodded like this was the correct answer. "You're married?"

But surely this question was not legal. Brooke's instinct was to laugh but that would have been too much to explain away so she simply shook her head.

Asher had seen her roll her eyes at him in the conference room. She was a cool character. The waitress deposited their food. He picked up a single french fry, too hot to eat. "Pretend I don't know anything about you." A flash of lying in bed at the George V, squinting at a résumé on his telephone. But no one had mentioned that Eileen's girl was Black! Maybe you couldn't these days. Times changed, and you adjusted. He would never have said *colored* anymore.

Brooke thought of the trouble she'd taken with that single page. "I studied at Vassar."

Asher thought people put too much stock in college and said so. "My only degrees are honorary. Where did you grow up?"

"Here, in the city."

Outer borough kid still, Asher loved Manhattanites. He thought them sophisticated. "And what do your parents do?"

"My mother works in reproductive health. She's trained as a lawyer. But she's more of an advocate." How to explain a mother like Maggie? It was a particular burden to have an extraordinary parent.

She didn't bring up a father. The sort of omission you leave alone. "And since college you've been—"

"Teaching. In the Bronx. Endeavor. It's a charter." She elided the first, lost year of her adulthood. Two years after 9/11, the economy had been frail enough that Brooke had fled home, found a part-time stint at a shop that sold (yes) high-end yarn. The alumni office connected her to the Vassar grad who ran Endeavor. She had no education in education, but this didn't matter.

He could see her more clearly now. "You found yourself in some underfunded classroom and thought—there's got to be more."

People heard *the Bronx* and thought lead paint, asthma, trucks, and whores at Hunts Point. "Not underfunded." Endeavor's board of directors included a former secretary of state. Bloomberg let them use the fourth floor of a failing public school. Endeavor's bathrooms were stocked with paper towels and maxi pads, Endeavor's pupils wore white button-downs and red polyester ties, Endeavor's meal ser-vice (all vegan on Fridays!) was brought in from some unseen kitchen daily.

There was something she was avoiding and he wouldn't be fooled. "But you're not there right now."

How to choose: admit being a cynic or a failure? Brooke had gone in to teach *Animal Farm* but there were kids who struggled with Beverly Cleary. The kids—not *bad*, merely kids—did not trust her, and were right not to. One look at this Ms. Orr and they knew that respect was not warranted. She was barely an adult, had no training, nothing but the confidence of the suits who ran the school. To teach required more, though: a devotion, an understanding, a gen-erosity. "It became clear to me that I wanted a different career."

"Disillusioned," he diagnosed.

Oh, she had loved them: Ivy, Malik, Thomas, Nevaeh! Filmed with adolescent sebum, swollen with preteen braggadocio. They were loud and unruly and funny and on the precipice of becoming. Brooke had learned, quickly, that she was not equal to the task. But she thought she understood these kids and what they needed. Still, all she could do was observe, with the dreadful certainty that their lives would not turn out as they should, as they could, had every-thing that forged them been otherwise. Go back, she wanted to tell them. Be different. Change the circumstances of the lives of your parents, maybe your grandparents. Impossible. Rather than blame herself, Brooke found a scapegoat in that old standby: the system. "Maybe it's bureaucracy. It wears you down. You can't teach like that, you need to feel—it has to be a calling, I think."

A distrust of institutions, red tape, circular talk was one of

Asher's hobbyhorses. A girl after his own heart. "You're an ideas woman, you're saying."

She had an opportunity. That's what this meal was. She should simply tell him: No, she could not control her classroom. No, she could not communicate with the parents. No, her kids had not excelled at the regular tests. But Brooke was not without ideas! She had her art history major. She had something she believed in. Brooke asked for money to buy digital cameras. Brooke asked for money to visit MoMA. The kids looked at Carrie Mae Weems and made photographs. The kids looked at Jean-Michel Basquiat and made self-portraits. The kids looked at Jacob Lawrence and fixed their reality in primary colors. Geniuses! The lot of them, touched by God! She explained all of this. "That old cliché. It was the kids who taught me."

He was bored. "Fast-forward to now."

"The school only cared about STEM. Coding and that kind of thing." It was a decree from the board. She had gone to them for more money and was gently scolded. "It wasn't about what the kids needed. It was about what the school needed. Grants and funding would be easier to come by if they had a flashy promise." Endeavor was not interested in Brooke's methods.

"Learning about technology sounds prudent to me."

"I'm not saying it's not. But I found myself arguing over the purpose of school itself. They wanted to prepare the kids for the workplace. But what about their souls?" Ivy, Malik, Thomas, Nevaeh would never master coding, whatever that was. But it was hard to prove the value in rendering the self as a scribble on paper. The arts cost Endeavor ten thousand dollars a year, but this was no longer, she was told, in the budget.

"The soul?" This ambition touched him. Here was a person Asher wanted in his employ. "Are we, then, the foundation, I mean, in the business of souls?"

She wouldn't be embarrassed by her earnestness. "It made sense to me to leave." What she meant was that the foundation didn't depend on someone else's largesse; Brooke was one of the people, now, who controlled the money.

Damn right they were in the business of souls. "Well, we don't have org charts. Pointless meetings. The money isn't doing a damn thing if we don't give it away." He liked the way she spoke, even if mostly what he liked was that she was bound to answer his questions. Why not ask the biggie, the most revealing one: "So what do you want to do with my money?"

All Brooke could think of was oysters. "My job is to help you make that decision. To find—"

He shook his head. Wrong answer. "Jody thinks we need a mission. I don't like limits. Literacy. Gay marriage. The environment. Voting rights. Universal childcare. I want it all. That's the reason I was a success in business! Paper. Then catalogs. Then malls. Then real estate." Forget the fortune. Asher had made an ecosystem, money its essential element; no, a galaxy, each of its infinite stars money itself.

"I'm excited to be a part of it." Brooke had believed this since that first interview with Eileen but it felt strange to say it aloud.

He prodded. "You want to spend your Jesus year on the business of the soul." He saw something in her, or he was flattered by this sanctified talk.

"You want to go down in history for giving away a fortune, not being a kid from Brooklyn who made three billion dollars selling erasers." Brooke was accidentally quoting the internet. Maybe the whole subject was taboo. But how could you talk to someone with three billion dollars without picturing those dollars, piled up, as in a gangster movie?

Asher was used to being misunderstood. "Someone's been reading Wikipedia." His mouth was full of sandwich. "Also, it's four billion. I don't care about history. This isn't about ego."

It was perceptive of him to know she'd been researching him, and lazy of her to have mentioned erasers, a detail once specified by a publicist crafting the myth of Asher Jaffee that had since made it into every account of the man's life. But could he see her blush?

Asher went on. "I'll likely be dead before the end of the decade. I want to do something with however many years I have left. But why don't you tell me what you'd do."

Brooke could not forget that it would have cost Endeavor almost nothing to change her students' lives. "The arts enrich. Kids know that. They gravitate to it. Finger paint. Dancing." This was what she believed, but had anyone ever asked about that before?

"Say more." Carol would not approve of his greasy lunch. He shook salt over his plate. Just as he'd not thought about the rights of gays to marry one another until last year, he'd never before considered the question of finger paint.

As a rule, she liked listening more than talking. But this was an important man, a powerful man, and he seemed to want to hear it. "Art doesn't need defending. It belongs to everyone. Or it should. Markers and paper cost money. The schools put in metal detectors instead."

"The schools need metal detectors." Asher was sober. "This is the reality. Madmen burst in with guns and shoot kindergartners."

Brooke knew all this—the sickness of the culture, the violence of American life. "I can't think about that."

"The technology has outpaced whatever the Constitution promised us. But there has to be a way to preserve our liberty and, you know, make sure our toddlers don't get blown away."

"No one else—not Bill Gates or whoever—has bothered trying. I don't know if I think it can be done. You can't teach Americans to renounce violence, but you could teach some little kid that art belongs to them. You can't change the culture. But you can actually change that child's experience of the world." She knew that she had done well, that she had aced this test.

There was something in her or something between them. They called this chemistry but it was indifferent to the logic of science. A charge or a spark or a feeling, a magic thing that sometimes bound you to someone you didn't know. He should have this girl out to the house. Show her the Francis Bacon, the Childe Hassam, the Mary Cassatt, the David Hockney. She was an art lover and he had some desire to impress her.

She kept going. "Do poor children know this? That they're allowed to want to make something, or look at something, and feel a certain way? That it's beautiful and it's ours, all of ours."

He was right to have put his faith in Eileen. When he'd first met her, she'd run an organization that provided struggling mothers with free diapers. The statistics she spouted, their first meeting, had enraged him. She'd left that confab with a commitment from him to give a hundred thousand dollars and an offer, carte blanche, to help him change the world. He'd had a feeling about her. That she had hired Brooke affirmed that he was a good judge of people.

This woman, Brooke, Black, gorgeous, serious, passionate, was the sort of woman he wanted at the foundation, the sort of woman he wanted working in his name. It was electric, almost chemical. "So, find out who needs markers and paper, or ballet slippers, or guitars. Find someone who's teaching children that art belongs to them, too. Bring me a plan. Tell me what we can do."

It was as though this man she didn't know understood something about her, something that had, until now, eluded even her. Brooke had a sincere desire she had never given a name to. She had dreams as selfless as those of her mother's. She wanted to make the world a better place, and he had seen this. He had given her an opportunity. "What we can do," she said.

"Together," he said.

They'd been doing this forever. They were young enough that half their lives seemed an endless stretch. There was consensus that the best thing about Vassar was that it was where she and Kim had found Matthew. Brooke, Kim, Matthew in the dining hall with veggie burgers and bowls of Lucky Charms. The three of them in the one Poughkeepsie diner where they knew, unspoken assent, that two and a half Black people could congregate unmolested. The three of them tentatively puffing cigarettes in the coffee shop with threadbare ornate sofas and low tables that, in that unimaginable place, the past, permitted smoking. The three of them would endure, they knew. A cliché, two girls and their gay best pal, but Black people understood better than most that it was a waste of energy to mind. You couldn't worry about the ways you conformed (or failed to) to expectations. As Brooke saw it, she and Kim were continuing what their mothers had started: a most modern little family.

Matthew's work as a project manager at an ad agency meant

overseeing the complex dinner orders for fussy art directors forced to work late. Thus, he'd forged relationships with the management of many decidedly not charming restaurants on Park Avenue South who would happily comp his drinks. So when they went out like this, it was occasionally to one of these placeless places, high ceilings and indifferent staff, where tourists from Madrid tried to decide between the veggie lasagna and a sweet hunk of salmon. A martini, they told themselves, was a martini. No. It was the more delicious when it was free.

"Cheers. Thanks, Eeyore." Kim and Brooke still called Matthew this. The nickname remained apt. Matthew was a glass half full of barbs. This was gay bonhomie. The girls teased, but they loved this about him.

They sat at the bar, otherwise so empty that Matthew could spread his long arms on the counter with impunity. "My job's perk. The occasional free cocktail and subscriptions to every magazine our clients buy pages in." Matthew protested but he was a company man. It was destiny. His father had only ever worked for Bell Atlantic, his mother had only ever worked for the Cape Henlopen School District, and it often seemed possible that Matthew would spend the rest of his life as a project manager at his agency. He did not mind that likelihood. Thirty-second ads for hotels, billboards for cosmetics conglomerates. He didn't pretend it was moral. Matthew said, often, that most jobs were just sending email. The pay was good, and there were sometimes free martinis. What more could you want?

"Speaking of perks. I have these Miu Miu shoes for you." Kim thought Brooke so fortunate to wear a seven. She never got to keep the occasional, unwanted shoes herself, as they were all model size.

"You love to see it." Brooke, while elder, had inherited so much from Kim. "I got nothing, unfortunately. Perk-wise."

"You like it, though?" Kim had long known that she would come into a sum you could only call vast. This meant her young adulthood was strangely circumscribed, a flirtation with reality, like rumspringa. Your work was the first thing strangers asked about at a party. Maybe that was why she had been an assistant at the desk of an art gallery, then a quasi volunteer at a publisher that produced lavish books of paintings and photographs, and now her current gig as a stylist's assistant, though she was far too old for the apprentice tasks of steaming trousers or running to the Kmart in Astor Place for a three-pack of Hanes tank tops.

Brooke recited some of the facts she'd learned about oysters. She was being boring, but with old friends this was allowed.

Matthew was perplexed. "He has a billion dollars and he's farming oysters?"

"He's improving the world." Brooke said this with a wryness she didn't entirely feel.

Matthew was himself, as ever. "Oh, that's all."

"I mean, oysters, why not?" Kim was not stupid, but she had a tendency to sound distracted. She was more willing to believe than Matthew was. "It's charity. You're like your mom! Making the world a better place."

Had Brooke chosen both teaching and her job at the foundation because her mother felt that the only useful work was selfless? Children never clearly saw the source of their opinions, ideas, habits, biases. "We'll see. It's a job. Not a crusade."

"It's a slogan. It's a dream. It's a man with a guilty conscience." Matthew speared his olive and chewed it with a wistful look. "Anyway, I can't believe we're not talking about the fact that she is leaving me."

The two of them had spent more than a decade in that top-floor walk-up in Bed-Stuy. Kim knew it was the end of an era but tried to downplay this. She didn't like a scene. "I'm not leaving you, I'm—" She was unable to complete the thought.

"I'm going to be the only one in Brooklyn." Matthew mock pouted but he didn't like this. Kim's moving out was a reminder of time's passage. Late-night pad Thai at the desk once or twice a week, and Matthew had begun to notice his shirts pulled at their buttons. He had never appreciated his own youthful beauty and he knew that it was on the wane and he was disappointed.

"Move to the city, Eeyore." Brooke thought it just that simple, maybe because Maggie had covered the fee to the real estate broker and put up the two months' security deposit back when she'd had no job to speak of. "If you're patient. If you look. There are deals."

But Matthew had a churchgoing landlady who hadn't raised the rent in a decade out of some sense of racial allegiance. Matthew had a plan—employer-provided health insurance, model tenancy, and maybe, with luck, occasional indulgences: forty-dollar steak frites, the kind of fuck where the earth moved, a sweater from Barneys, Broadway tickets. This seemed so paltry beside whatever Kim would do, even Brooke who, despite her abortive teaching career and shitty apartment, had the secret weapon of a chic mother with a Manhattan apartment. He figured *compare leads to despair* and tried not to think of himself in competition with his own friends.

"I think I might have found a place, actually. You guys should come see it. I need the seal of approval." Kim knew it would be apparent, the first time her friends saw the apartment on Charles

Street, just how much money her dad had set aside for her, though they would never discuss it.

"Looking at apartments is to gay guys what watching football is to straight men." Matthew said that he was ordering another.

"So move into the city. We'll help you look," Brooke suggested. "The East Village. You could walk to work if you wanted."

Matthew made one of his meaningful pronouncements. "This is it, huh? How we know we're in our thirties. Talking about real estate instead of men."

"You make us sound old," Kim complained.

"Just an observation." Matthew had his hands up in protest.

Kim loved Matthew and their sweet apartment with its crooked floors and all that ornate painted-over woodwork. She'd even grown fond of the racket of the summertime streets: echoing bass, boozy shouts, the taunt of the ice cream trucks. But she knew that it was time to move on. The question of real estate had lately privately obsessed her. "I'm more than prepared to talk about men."

So they did, as they always had. In their thirties now, they understood when they were tipsy, when it was best to head home, order in dinner, shower, hydrate.

"You guys are all set," the bartender told them, collecting spent glasses in her long hands, a turn of phrase chosen to avoid the explicit mention of money.

Kim reached for her wallet. "Let me get the tip."

They'd not protest, normally. It wasn't a gesture of friendship, one friend treating the others. It was equity, a bit of justice in a world where that was in short supply. But thirty dollars was nothing, especially for seven seventeen-dollar martinis. Brooke stopped her. "No, let me."

Kim asked whether she was *sure* using no words, only her eyes, shorthand between people who'd known each other their entire lives. It was an insignificant moment. Kim shrugged and said thanks.

Brooke laid out the ten and then the twenty. That was enough, right?

She walked home because she could, not for fear of the Subway Pricker. An amble through the indifferent streets she thought of as hers. Brooke lingered in the vestibule to unlock the mailbox, which she checked only sporadically. As she climbed the stairs, she sorted through the gas bill, the coupon from Bed Bath & Beyond. There was an envelope that seemed to be a check, though it might have been one of those canny deceptions that turned out to be a fundraising appeal. The return address peeked out of its own cellophane window, Jaffee Holdings, an address on Third Avenue. She unlocked the door and had a passing thought about the phrase *real estate*. Hardly seemed the term for her little corner of the world. But its familiar comfort embraced her as soon as she closed the door behind her. Brooke opened the gummed closure and found a check, payable to her, for two hundred and fifty dollars, signed by an Eric Stone, a name she did not know. There was no note but there was a clarifying entry on the memo line, "Lunch reimbursement." Brooke put it onto the small bookshelf, unsure if she was guilty or insulted.

I n his 1998 memoir, Asher Jaffee alleged that the high of working around the clock meant more to him than the product of that labor, the millions. He wrote that it was *a kind of addiction*; he wrote that it was a *rush*; he wrote that it *destroyed* his marriage. This wasn't accurate (Barbara loved the money) but it had the sound of wisdom. Anyway, anyone reading a business memoir didn't see this as cautionary tale. They recognized themselves. They, too, claimed that the high was the objective. A lie! It was the money. Of course it was. No one at the foundation (not even Natalie) had read Asher Jaffee's memoir.

Asher still sought a high. But he had made concessions, like a four-day workweek (Carol loved him more than the money). Thus, almost half his time he was mostly housebound in Connecticut. Sometimes, a small *do,* as Carol called these evenings of shrimp cocktail, sparkling wine, and small talk, but mostly there were just the three hounds—Asher called them, collectively, Cerberus—for company. Weather permitting but even in the occasional, rejuvenating drizzle, in wellies and hunting jackets like English gentry, Asher and Carol would tramp the grounds with the trio of dogs manic over every deer or rabbit. The Sunday *Times* in disarray on the solarium's rattan tables, husband and wife read in the silence that could be sustained when so long married. They'd put on a spy thriller or one of the weepers to which Carol was partial and Marina would make kale chips and popcorn and seltzers with fresh-squeezed juice. They diverted themselves, poking around the bookstore, eating crumbly muffins at Starbucks, touring the museum they had helped underwrite, which hoped Asher and Carol Jaffee might someday leave them their Warhol *Liz*. Every so often, Asher would swallow a potent pill, a marvel the size of a peppercorn, give it thirty minutes, and they'd lie together, awash in the fantasy that he was young again. He enjoyed all this fucking around, he enjoyed the fucking, but privately Asher dreaded these weekends, which perennially had that noncommittal mood he associated, from his school days, with Sunday.

The office was the place where things happened, the place where he was necessary, the site of his every victory. The foundation's dingy rooms were nothing like the long-gone Jaffee Corporation's home: sixteen floors—half the place!—of a Midtown tower: smoky glass, shiny chrome, a dose of grandeur. That was the point. Where the glamour of the old HQ had affirmed that enterprise's ambition, the shabbiness of this current office suggested virtue. It smelled of shampoo with a hint of pear, perfume over sweat, the heady bouquet of women's bodies. Even that bad lighting put him in the mood to focus. His relationship to his employees in the office was quite different from whatever governed the interactions with his domestic staff. In the office, he could waylay, tell stories, ask questions. He could expect the women in his employ to divulge weekend plans, restaurant reviews, spousal news, their various wonderful adventures out in the world. Asher was cosseted and hated this about himself. Too rich, too old. He missed the friction of real life. How he treasured his ladies!

None more so than Natalie, for the care she took, arranging every day as she knew he liked: milky coffee at the ready, mysteriously always hot as though Natalie could outsmart the laws of physics, and a succession of calls, meetings, meals, dealings. He was at his most content when being told by her that he was needed. What would he do without her, more loyal than any of his three dogs? That was one of the questions of his old age best ignored. They never broached the subject of her retirement (that word, ugh). Just then, he could sense her, steps away, reassuring presence, making bearable the conference call to which he was only half paying attention. Then, another voice.

"Sorry to bother you but I wondered if I could have five minutes?"

Natalie's standard reply: "I'm so sorry, Brooke, I don't have Mr. Jaffee this morning."

Have him. Halve him, put both Ashers to work. If only. Asher was touched by how she protected him. He yelled out, disobedient. "What are you talking about? I'm right here!"

"Mr. Jaffee, you're due at the Ford Foundation in twenty minutes." Natalie could be stern when she needed to be. She hovered in the door, finger outstretched, like a witch, like a mommy. "Christopher is downstairs."

"I'm done, gentlemen." He ended the call—something to do with the parcels of real estate Jaffee Corp. still held across the country—without a farewell to the lawyers and middlemen. He paid them; he didn't have to be nice to those people. "He can wait. They can wait. Brooke, come in, come in."

Natalie moved aside. "Sit." He put his hands on the edge of the desk and rolled himself back into what he had determined was his listening position. The office wasn't much—an old table for a desk, a chair on casters, a Barcelona lounge, some bentwood chairs—but there was a massive Philip Guston oil on the wall behind him. The point was that Asher's confidence was entirely concentrated in his person. The room where he did his work had nothing to do with anything.

"If you're heading to a meeting—" Brooke was determined not to be flustered.

"Always some meeting." Asher cherished his reputation as a leader—fearless but approachable. "What can I do?"

Ramrod posture and a determined mien. "There's something I'd love to discuss, it won't take long."

"A nice thing about being me is that I'm the most essential part of the meetings I take. Unless it's the Oval Office. Been there a few times. In that room, you truly are not a very important person, or I wasn't. But the Ford Foundation? I can be late." He was bragging. He hoped to impress. The reason he was going to the Ford Foundation rather than have them send emissaries; this office would not awe that lot.

She produced an envelope from her pocket. "I was wondering whether you sent this to me." This wasn't what she'd rehearsed saying, knowing that he had sent it to her.

A grin. "Yes, of course. You see my name there." The woman was stoic!

"I wondered why my employer would have sent me a check that's not my paycheck." She had settled on this language, on this distinction. She could accept her boss's money as a wage but not a present, as from some kindly uncle.

"Your *employer* didn't send that. Your employer is the Asher and Carol Jaffee Foundation." He had this figured out. "That check is from me. Personal."

"I'm not sure I understand." This seemed a noncommittal way of forcing him to explain. What had he meant by this?

"Think of it as a debt paid, if you would." Had he insulted her? He meant it as the opposite. It was a bid for her—was the word affection? "I never took you to lunch."

"I'm not sure what to say. But you did take me to lunch." It was no longer clear to Brooke the principle for which she was making a stand.

"There's nothing to say! It's a gesture. Enjoy it. Indulge me."

"It doesn't seem—ethical." She put the envelope on his desk.

"Come on, now." Young people today seemed determined to take offense. They loved it. They cherished their own umbrage. "This is my way of saying—it's an apology, if you prefer to think of it that way."

"There's no need." These were the reflexive good manners that had been bred into her. Brooke almost felt sorry for the man. He understood money more than he did people.

"But there is." Sensing the extent of his miscalculation, he rushed to explain. "There are things to which you're entitled." A wag of the finger, the specific *you*, not the general. "There are conventions I'm bound by honor to observe. A grilled cheese instead of a steak. I felt guilty, is that the word for it? Maybe it is." He pitied her, as he pitied all young people who had yet to figure out the world.

"I don't need your money, Mr. Jaffee."

He knew that most of his petitioners exaggerated *need*. Museums wanted his art, the gay-marriage boosters wanted justice, the Korean prodigy Chae-Yeong Kim had her heart set on a three-million-dollar violin. "But the question is whether or not you *deserve* it. If your mother gave you a hundred dollars, you'd just accept it. Tuck it into a pocket." The sum had been Eric Stone's guess about the value of a lunch at Keens. The idea, though, had been Asher's. He used his money as he liked; why not spend it to make a point? "Brooke, if you don't ask for what you're owed, who can you blame when you fail to get it?"

Brooke would never think twice about a bill pressed into her hand by Maggie or Auntie Sayo or Paige or Allison on visits home from Vassar, for cab fare, for coffee, just because. With them, money was not equal to affection, it was an afterthought, it was meaningless. But this was her office and Asher Jaffee was not her family. "I'd prefer you kept this."

She was working, he thought, not to seem irritated, or disapproving, or anything at all. She was trying to seem tough. Money was his language; money was the thing he best understood. Money was the point of what they were doing, but money was, she wanted to believe, independent of her. Nonsense. "Take it. Squirrel it away. Add it to the nest egg. The future comes one step at a time." He paused again. "It's a gift." He was not accustomed to people saying no to him.

"Then I'll give it to you. To the foundation. A donation."

He laughed, and hoped it was not cruel. "A worthy gesture but

I'll respectfully decline. Listen. I have to go. Natalie's going to have my head."

That woman reappeared even as he said this. "Christopher is just downstairs, Mr. Jaffee."

He pulled on his cashmere blazer as he stood, a single motion perfected over the years. "On my way, on my way. Brooke, walk me to the car."

They filed into the hallway, out of the suite, into the wood-paneled elevator. On the ride down, Asher realized that apology was not in order, but maybe explanation was. "I remember talking to my daughter. She was a banker. People said *ah the apple and the tree* but that wasn't it. I'm a salesman. She was a magician." The doors opened and he lingered in the black-and-white lobby. Everyone knew Linda was dead. No need to explain. "Linda handled imaginary financial products. She crossed borders, time zones, reality itself. She left Lehman Brothers. She was interviewing. She told me that women never negotiated over salary. It was an issue. When the offers came— everyone wanted her—she countered. She didn't *need* the money. You know some of those banks must have thought—you brat, your daddy has more money liquid than we have to our names. That was not her point. Her point was her value. I admired it, how she knew that about herself." Linda had worked at Cantor for three weeks. Then— gone.

"You think I don't do that?" It was a lesson, maybe, but Brooke heard it as scold. There was something in her, as in most, that wanted only to please the adults in her life.

He had his hand on the glass door. How could he know? She was a stranger to him. But he had a hunch. "You know where I'm going right now? The Ford Foundation. You know what that is."

"Sure. I think."

"Henry Ford. His heirs. Billions. You know what they want from me?" Asher had established his dominion. But she needed reminding. He softened: "My money."

"I see."

Yes, it was all back to that, eventually. "They want me to hand it over to them. Once I'm dead, you know. It would increase their endowment by a third. And they're the experts, right? One of the richest foundations on the planet and they want my money. But you, you don't." He was scolding. He was imperious. He was the insulted party. Who was she, anyway?

"It just struck me as improper. I didn't know." Brooke was embarrassed, no longer so certain she held the moral advantage.

"But I know. If you're going to work here, with me, you're going to have to trust me." This was important. "And trust yourself. Demand something from the world. Demand the best. Demand it."

She recovered herself. She found her manners. "I don't think it's necessary, still. But thank you."

He softened, something paternal, maybe in conjuring Linda, his baby, little girl, big girl, pride. "The foundation will survive without your gift. It's for you. I don't want to talk about this again."

She seemed chastened. "Right."

He hoped he had not been hard on her. He meant a kindness. He pushed the door open. "We have more important things to discuss. You'll see." With the vim of a much younger man, Asher Jaffee jogged over the sidewalk toward the car door held open by his dignified driver, then turned and smiled back at the girl standing there watching them.

A ll the fashionable restaurants looked the same. White tile, cane chairs, mirrors distressed to seem antique, wan potted ferns, a vague Francophile aspiration. Rachel had chosen this place because it was written up in *New York* magazine. It was, naturally, very crowded. Never mind. Rachel had made a reservation.

Brooke arrived twenty minutes early. She liked to settle in, have a drink, read a novel or stare into her telephone or watch passersby. Some (many, maybe) were discomfited by being alone in a restaurant. Possible Brooke preferred it. There was a pleasure in hiding in a crowd of indifferent strangers, and anyway, who didn't enjoy the music of metal on porcelain, glasses set down on tabletops, muted chatter in an unfamiliar room? Brooke the anthropologist, studying the clothes other people wore, trying to guess what they were saying to one another.

"Will you be joining us for dinner?" The bartender had sculpted eyebrows and the sort of skin called olive, a metonymy locating him in a place that valued olives, the Middle East, southern Italy. He was handsome in that way bartenders tended to be.

"I'm meeting some people. I'm early." She made it sound like an accident. She wished him to know that she was comfortable sitting alone in a restaurant, but also someone who did not have to. She slouched over her paperback, the adventures of some insipid girl in the big city. Brooke's attention drifted when pedestrians outside were reflected in the mirror over the bar. She drank purple cabernet, watched the bartender as she did, appreciative of his unconscious movements, a fidget, a crack of the knuckles, a hand through the hair, all that stage business of being a boy, the strange alchemy it worked on her, dumb, animal desire.

When Rachel and Alex arrived (hand in hand, the smugness of young people who believe they have invented love), Brooke requested the check moved to their table. She left the comely bartender a tip in cash and would not discover until later, when she wrested the bill from her little brother, that he had charged her for only a single glass of wine. She knew that he had watched her and her book as she had watched him and his shaker.

"A special occasion when Brooke Orr schleps out to Brooklyn." Alex signaled for drinks, a gesture that seemed to come naturally. It was a consequence of his symmetrical handsomeness, it was his way of being in the world, the expectation that it would meet his every need.

An old joke, an apt one, about Brooke leaving the island on which she'd been born. "You'll never believe where I was this morning. Governors Island."

"I don't even know what that is." Rachel sipped from her glass like a house cat. "What's there?" Rachel's conversation was endless query, like a television host. It was meant as a kindness.

Jenna from the oyster people had implored Brooke to witness firsthand the marvel of nature. Brooke had resolved to take the oyster as something close to role model. A pilgrimage. A veneration. Plus it was nice to get out of the office. "There's this school out there, these people are farming oysters, it's a whole thing."

"Farming for food?" Rachel's grandparents had kept kosher but she believed in aphrodisiacs.

Brooke noticed how her brother couldn't stop touching Rachel: knee, wrist, shoulder, all moisturized into softness, all the color of fatty cream. "It's an ecological restoration project. I guess this part of the country used to be full of oysters and beavers?"

Rachel said this was *interesting* the way people did.

"I've learned a lot about the oyster. Maybe too much." Brooke believed, though. "These people are onto something. They talk about dolphins and whales being in the waterways in the next decade or so."

"A toast to whales, then," Rachel said. "I didn't know it was an environmental charity."

"A little bit of everything. No one objective. Every objective. Make the world a better place." The menu was a single sheet of paper and Brooke rolled this into a cylinder, as though nervous.

"Is that all?" Rachel was charmed. "Can I ask? Is this what you dreamed when you were little? I wanted to be a vet. My parents would never let me have a cat. I'm curious how people end up doing what they do."

Did everyone have such dreams, and had Brooke somehow missed some crucial part of becoming? "I don't remember what I played." She lied. As a girl, she thought she'd be a spy, like Harriet, a ballerina, as Sally Freedman hoped for herself, that she'd fend for survival on an island surrounded by blue dolphins. Brooke's Barbies commuted to imagined offices and went on lesbian dates because Maggie would never buy her a Ken. She looked toward her brother. "What about you?"

He was an architect. Alex furrowed his brow. "I guess I liked LEGOs?" Perhaps they had been brought up differently, reared to think of the self as opposed to the job. "We have to order the gougères. Did you want to be a teacher?"

"I thought I did. Now I wonder if maybe I never gave enough consideration to what I would be doing with my life, how I would be spending my time, earning my money," Brooke said.

"It's not like I dreamed about working at the UN," Rachel said. "That's life, a set of steps that seem to be leading you somewhere. Sometimes it's fine, but sometimes you get to this point and it's like—where am I, who am I, what am I doing? Isn't that what mid-life crisis is?"

The gougères were warm and pillowy. Once or twice, those last years at Endeavor, Brooke had referred to her state as *quarterlife crisis.* An embarrassment to use a term familiar from *Glamour,* but wasn't it apt then, scrolling the internet and lying about herself just enough on her résumé. That crisis was over. Thank God for Asher Jaffee.

Conversation turned to the wedding, because it would, because it had to. People in love loved their love, needed to discuss it like scholars. A wedding was, what else, expensive. "Maybe we can appeal to the Asher Jaffee Foundation? Get them to underwrite this?" Alex joked.

Brooke had a strange feeling that she was reality's observer, not a participant, barely real herself. She wanted to pinch her flesh as television characters do when they need to figure what was dream. She said something noncommittal about how expensive everything was in New York City.

"Well, what are we going to do? Drop out? Become hippies?" Alex didn't have the imagination for another kind of life. Few did.

Rachel changed the subject back to their wedding, a faraway look in her eyes as she described the process of registering for gifts. Rachel described cut-glass tumblers and gilt-edged dinner plates and the heft of the flatware.

"The Missoni blanket," Alex reminded her. "I've never touched such a blanket. Like it's made of some animal you've never even heard of. You should have seen us, two idiots running around Bloomingdale's like it was a shopping spree."

Brooke had had that kind of fantasy—who hadn't? But that was just a daydream, usually. She didn't want much more than she had. Yes, money came but money went: buy an iced coffee with a twenty and the other seventeen dollars vanished, was never accounted for. Bills came due, and she paid them. There wasn't some long-dead dad to shower her with some never-named sum, but Brooke had what she required. "Isn't that the point of a wedding? It's a capitalist enterprise."

"Speaking of capitalism, have you ever tried to save up frequent-flier miles?" Alex asked his sister. "I read somewhere that they're the most commonly used currency. Or the currency with the largest circulation, I can't remember, and actually I don't know if there's a difference."

"We're trying to get to Holbox on SkyMiles," Rachel explained.

"It's impossible! It's literally not possible. It's imaginary math. It's multiplying by zero. You just keep getting nowhere." Alex needed his drink. "This is going to radicalize me. The whole thing is a trap, and we all just participate."

But this was the system. Brooke didn't have the imagination or the temerity to challenge it. "Just put that on the registry. Let your guests pay for the honeymoon," Brooke suggested.

"I want to go to Mexico," Rachel said. "I want to have nice plates. I want to get married. It's not immoral, exactly."

"It's not moral, either, is it? I mean there are people starving outside—" Alex said.

"But we ate here. Others have need and we spend eleven dollars on gougères," Brooke said.

What she meant was that she had the means. When the check came, Brooke seized it, and Rachel put a hand on Alex's forearm, urging him to protest.

"No, let me," he said. He didn't mean it at all. They needed to get to Holbox!

Brooke brandished her debit card. "Don't be silly. Big sister."

When the waiter brought the receipt for Brooke's signature, she studied her brother and the woman he would marry. Rachel now had Alex's hand on her knee, her hand atop it, as though it were her napkin. It was the hand that would keep her safe. Brooke herself had never felt this way about a man.

Brooke saw sums, digits, prices, numbers, before her, but maybe everywhere, like Alex said. You'd feel that way no matter where you went. She left an extravagant tip.

"Thanks, sis," Alex said, something he never called her.

Brooke smiled at a private little joke. Whether moral or not, their dinner had cost so near two hundred and fifty dollars that this one was on Asher Jaffee. She'd deposited that check after all.

Eileen knocked on her door as Brooke was typing up a report on her visit to Governors Island. She was busy! But did she look busy? "Come in, please."

Eileen said she didn't *mean to interrupt*. She sat with the subdued sigh and pop of the cartilage that was the toll of being in your fifties.

"Just writing up a little something about the oysters," Brooke said.

Eileen's midlife eyes were filigreed with red, either allergy or hours staring at lit screens. "Vis-à-vis oysters. You're surely tired of them."

Brooke protested because that was the right thing to do. "Not at all," she said, playing coy. Why was her instinct to submit, to excuse the world's impositions? Oysters were boring. It had been only a few days and she was bored.

More of Eileen's signature honesty. "This work is not always glamorous."

"A good learning experience." Brooke knew that she was too old for this not-quite-starter job. Logic said it was incumbent to be humble. But perhaps there was another way. Perhaps she should demand more of the world.

Eileen had good news! "Well. No more oysters. From now on that will be Kate's responsibility."

A truth Brooke alone knew: she hadn't been so bright a student. She had simply feared her teachers. Had she been caught out, at last revealed to be average, uninteresting, replaceable? "I can schedule some time with her, catch her up on things."

"That would be helpful, thank you." Eileen could read her employee's hesitation. "This isn't punitive, Brooke, you understand? It's not my idea, either. It's direct from Asher himself."

Brooke rued having made that fuss over his two hundred and fifty dollars. She was being demoted. "Is he unhappy with my work?"

"It's the opposite. Asher would like you to spend your time with him and his conversations with the Ford Foundation." She presented this information as if it were a gift.

Knowing nothing as she did, Brooke had gone back to Wikipedia to learn about the Ford Foundation. Asher wanted her to spend time with him?

Eileen went on. "He's seeing them again and wants you to come along. The short of it is they want to continue his philanthropic work—into the future." Diplomacy! Eileen's plan was that this would be the last job she ever held. She'd retire with an appointment to Ford, having brokered this deal.

They had so many occasions to speak about Asher's inevitable death. "Of course, whatever Mr. Jaffee would like but I'm not sure—"

"He wants you *along*. He wants your point of view. You impressed Asher Jaffee, Brooke."

The tender flip of the stomach that was pride. "Well, of course I'll do whatever he asks." It was nice to be told that you were impressive.

"You can drive with Asher. Natalie will give you the details." Eileen had a question, though. "I understand he's asked you to take on another project?"

Brooke could sense that beneath Eileen's interest was annoyance. "I was telling him—he asked. About my old job. You and I discussed this when we first met."

"The charter school." It was among her responsibilities to remember such details.

"I thought Asher was—maybe *spitballing* is the term." Had she said too much to him?

"That's not Asher's style." Parents spelled what they didn't want their toddlers to hear. Certain temperaments seize upon anything.

"I was explaining the school, the arts program. Maybe he was inspired by the idea." Asher Jaffee had been more interested in her ideas than Endeavor ever had been. He was a successful man and had seen something of value in her that her old employer never had.

Eileen was not entirely pleased at surrendering her chosen helpmeet. "I don't want you to lose time because of something I've asked you to do."

"If we're moving oysters to Kate—" There was some deliberation in that *we*.

"Asher is your priority." She had more to say. "You know, Brooke. I had reservations about this job. We're essentially a start-up. Traditionally, a foundation like this—you'd have counsel, a dozen sea-soned people, a mission statement, a strategic plan. And I wasn't ab-solutely certain that I wanted to work with Asher Jaffee."

This was like hearing one parent talk frankly about the other. Brooke nodded.

She leaned forward and unburdened herself. "I've always been at established institutions. The mission was clear. The processes were in place. Everyone understood what was expected, what we were do-ing. This was a gamble. A vanity project, I thought."

Eileen was trying to impart some lesson, Brooke could see. But maybe Brooke didn't need this woman's advice. She had the ear of the big boss!

The older woman continued. "Asher is an impressive man. He's made a fortune! But that's not salient, is it, to what we're doing? I didn't know if it was going to be his name on the door or if he'd be in my office every morning. I didn't know if he'd be willing to listen to me. A younger woman, hell, a woman at all. You see. On this, what we're doing here, I'm the expert. And I didn't want to sign up for some endless battle of wills with a spoiled rich man."

Asher seemed to her to cherish Eileen, to delight in her presence, her competence, her authority. But maybe, Brooke reasoned, every-one hated their boss a little. "Sure," she said, unclear what she was agreeing with.

"Where there is money, where there is legacy, there's ego. It makes sense. It's only logical." Eileen's body language said *Don't get me wrong*. "But I've come around. He's committed to building this foundation. He wants to do great things." Did it matter whether the man's ego was involved?

Brooke gestured toward the new notebook splayed open on her desk. "I'll take notes," she offered. "I'll recap with you after."

"I'm pleased that you two have so hit it off. It's a big opportunity, a man like Asher Jaffee asking you to take on a project." She was trying to praise but also to warn.

"Absolutely." Brooke didn't care if she sounded appropriately appreciative. She could see that Eileen had nothing more to offer her. Asher Jaffee held her fate.

"Just remember the mission. Asher is a smart man and a passionate philanthropist, but he relies on you, on me, on all of us, to guide him. He can be unpredictable. If there's something you need, in handling this project for him, or generally, you should come to me, or to Jody. We're in this together, is what I'm saying." Eileen had the sense that the girl didn't know this. "I think of us as the angels sitting on his shoulder. Like in those old cartoons. The conscience. The compass. We are in service to all of our partners, but we are in service to him, mostly."

Brooke heard something in Eileen's voice, a sliver of what she thought might be fear. Not of Asher but of Brooke. She didn't like there being something between Brooke and Asher, or didn't like the idea that Brooke was there, too, perched by the man's ear, whispering advice. Why did this feel like a victory? Let Kate be an oyster. Brooke would be an angel.

The chirrup of her cellphone, like a referee's whistle signaling the end of game play. An embarrassment, but Brooke was allowed to have a real life. She glanced at the screen. It was unlike her mother to call during the workday, but why behave as a secretary might, with apology? "It's my mother," Brooke said. "I'm sorry."

Maybe this was generational. Or maybe it was rude. Eileen wasn't quite sure what to make of it. They weren't done talking, were they? "Of course. Please take it." But Eileen noted, as she stood, as she left the little room, that Brooke was no longer paying any attention to her.

Brooke knew there was a reason for this call because it would have to be cataclysm for Maggie to ring up between nine and five. So it was: Paige, dead.

It was the stupidest thing Maggie had ever heard and, as such, demanded retelling. In a state, Maggie fled to the kitchen, where she might find something like comfort. She held her shoulder in a shrug to keep the phone at her ear as she foraged. "I can't believe this." The story emerged—suburban bus stop on the highway's shoulder, one of those too-large SUVs, fog, maybe, or the slick of early-morning rain, and that was that.

Brooke understood death as much as anyone could claim to: a ninth-grade classmate with cancer, her grandparents with whatever admixture claimed the lives of the old. Death was something that had nothing to do with her, like the weather report from another country. She looked at the gold bangle on her wrist and could see Paige's face and was baffled as to why she felt nothing at all. She murmured into her phone, stock condolences, the only thing to say.

"I've known her longer than you've been alive. Knew her. God. The past tense. Like you and Kim. Like a sister."

Like any group of intimates, the aunties loved to tell their origin story. Paige was a foot taller than everyone at Barnard, so impossible not to notice: ramrod posture, a flair for dress, an omnivorous appetite for the world. Paige knew about everything (Patti Smith and Talking Heads, Fiorucci and Vivienne Westwood, Italo Calvino and Wallace Stegner, Japanese food and performance art) before anyone else. For the umpteenth time, Maggie said some version of this, wanting it entered into the record. "You knew her. But as a child knows a grown-up. Christ, she was basically another mother to you."

Not a mother, Brooke didn't say. Paige, with her stubborn insistence on being only herself, was different. Brooke understood that some of Maggie's frustration was at Paige's disappearance from their lives. Paige was ashamed that she'd had to leave the city, and everyone she'd left behind was embarrassed about it. Love felt academic, or like it had little to do with what happened, which was what happened: people died. A horrible, pregnant moment as her mother's voice broke a little, a sob allowed passage. Why did Brooke not feel like crying?

Maggie had more to say. "Paige was the most interesting. The most glamorous. The most curious. The most urbane. Well. You know death is coming, but this is so demeaning. It's so—low."

"It's too young." Brooke searched for her own reminiscences, came up empty-handed. The woman who she'd have said meant so much to her now seemed distant, a thought experiment, a notion. Was this shock or was this some lack of Brooke's own imagination or, worse, her heart?

Maggie knew this was what was said. But age had nothing to do with it! "She never should have left the city."

Brooke heard frustration, as though dying were something Paige had done to Maggie personally. "She didn't want to. She didn't have a choice."

Maggie wanted her daughter to say the right thing. Maybe that was the wrong instinct, but what was parenthood but the polishing of another into something like a mirror? Neither of the children were tied to her by biology, so why did Alex present such a flattering reflection of his mother and Brooke refuse to do so? "I know that." Needing something to do, Maggie began to fidget with ingredients.

Brooke saw what was obvious. Paige hadn't abandoned them, she had been abandoned. No amount of glamour guaranteed you wouldn't die in some undignified manner. What could keep you safe in this world? "It's terrible, obviously."

That was obvious, Maggie thought. She went on. "Allison called. We're trying to figure out what the arrangements are. Some kind of— well, who's going to pay for a burial?" Maggie was thinking out loud. She would, of course, pay for it. Or Sayo would. Peter had provided for her so generously. "I wanted you to know as soon as possible."

"You'll tell me about the service." Brooke wrote this down in her new leather notebook. *Auntie Paige*, she wrote, underlined it, meaning nothing. "While I have you."

"You have me."

"I have a work question. Something has come up. I'm in search of something, like a nonprofit, a group that does something in the arts. Something worthy." Brooke was all business.

"Okay." Maggie was distracted by the heat of the small phone. Maggie was impatient. She had begun improvising a farro salad without wholly realizing it.

Brooke went on. "I thought you might know someone. Or that someone you know might know someone. Like Auntie Allison."

"God. You know what Allison said? *Maybe she's better off.* And what's awful is that maybe she's right." The private ugly thought: Paige, taking the bus, scheduling braces fittings for the daughters of Long Island insurance adjusters, clipping coupons? Death might have been the kinder alternative.

Brooke needed to shift the topic of conversation. "Auntie Allison just seemed like she might know someone—"

"Yes, fine, call her. You have her number?"

"I do."

"You know, she's bereaved. Just so you understand." A mother, sometimes, had to scold.

"I know—" Brooke tried to avoid an adolescent sigh.

"Just call your auntie Allison. At least tell her you're sorry about your auntie Paige before you ask for your favor or whatever it is—"

"I *am* sorry." Brooke hated the facts of the universe as much as anyone. She didn't want to think about her dead aunt. She wanted to think about herself.

"I'm calling to tell you my oldest friend died and you're telling me about your job." Maggie wouldn't have said this, normally, but today felt abnormal. If Brooke was sorry, Maggie couldn't hear it. Maybe she was too young, too insulated from the brute fact of mortality. Maybe she was too preoccupied with herself.

There was that hiss of telephone silence. "I'm not telling you about my job. I'm asking you a question. I didn't mean to seem insensitive."

"It does, a little. Seem that way." Maggie collected herself as she had when the kids were toddlers. Sometimes a parent had to count to ten.

In her little room on Thirty-sixth Street, Brooke leaned back in the vinyl chair and considered the harsh overhead light. She should call Kim, she knew, some sisterly responsibility for them to mourn together. She had been on the verge of telling her mother that Asher Jaffee had blessed her with special dispensation. That the executive director had come and acknowledged that there was to be a change in Brooke's relationship to the organization. It no longer seemed pressing, or like something she wished to share. Instead, mother and daughter made stabs at apology, and hung up their phones sharing a sense of disappointment that would have surprised both of them.

The Ford Foundation had been cooked up in a fit of twentieth-century optimism. Unfair how crossword makers still had you believe that Edsel was synonymous with failure: the good work he and his dad imagined continued to this day. Their Midtown building was a museum of midcentury taste, the utopianism of high design, each chaise and doorknob imbued with a sweet belief that a better world was possible.

Asher's Bentley was as well made but, in a way, distrustful of that world, aiming to shut it out. A carapace to coddle the body, the medical smell of leather so firm and fine you could scoot across it without that flatulent squeak. Just as Asher Jaffee seemed not to touch the ground, every step a bound like the men who walked on the moon, the sedan seemed to float over Forty-third Street, untroubled by the city's ruined asphalt.

The car was so big it turned Brooke into a toddler. Her boss's feet did an impatient rat-a-tat on the floor mats to say: *So, so, so?*

He wanted her opinion, but Brooke sensed that there was a right answer and a wrong one. "That was good," she said.

Asher squinted at his phone then lost patience, tossing it onto the seat beside him. "Give me more than *good*. *Good* is a meaningless word for pointless chitchat."

The Ford Foundation had put on a show. Trying to be useful, Brooke had written in her notebook *AJ seems engaged*, as though observing a bird in the wild. "They really want your money."

A mirthless laugh. "Who doesn't?" The taxman, political candidates, what little family he and Carol had, vague acquaintances with pet causes. Like pretty girls on city streets, Asher had to tune out these constant overtures or he'd never get anywhere. "You heard them. I've been doing this for three years. They've been at it for decades. Maybe they're right. I know business and they know philanthropy, and I'm in over my head, which was what they were saying without exactly saying it."

Asher had told her that she ought to ask for more in life, so she would not ask permission to be frank. "You don't strike me as in over your head." They don't, she almost said, of that conference table of grave smilers, understand you. *In fact*, she thought, *they despised him.*

He pitied himself. "They think I'll lose interest. They think I'm a dilettante."

"Why let them assume control of your—" She was going to say *money* but instead said *operation.*

"Maybe I will. Hand it all over, tell them to find jobs for you,

Eileen, Kate. From day one, Jody's been saying there's an ethical way to spend the money. Maybe this is it."

How was the car so silent? If Christopher was breathing, you'd never have known it. Brooke was touched that her own future came into it. She hadn't even thought about herself. "You like this work. And it is work, not a dalliance. You're the one who hired Jody. You want to do this the right way."

He had said, in the *Huffington Post*, that this whole thing was about Linda. Asher meant it, but people didn't quite understand. It wasn't about setting something right. Linda had taught him that he would die. And the money was a burden. He would not enter heaven. He saw it as literal, the money in his pockets preventing him passage like Shelley Winters's hips as she fled the *Poseidon*. "Sure," he said, not quite listening.

He told her he wanted her ideas, so Brooke tried to come up with some. "Maybe you—we—need more staff. More people, doing more work."

Asher changed the subject. "You told me that sob story about your teaching job. Why haven't you come to me and said let's save that arts program. You said it was ten thousand dollars? We could do that in a minute. Write a check and let you stick it to the old boss." He had issued a challenge. He'd expected her to act fast.

"Why go back, try to convince them to let me help them?" She did not think about Ivy, Malik, Thomas, Nevaeh. This was about Brooke demanding more for herself.

"What you mean is *fuck them*." Asher was pleased. "They didn't want your good idea then, so they don't get it now." Asher went on. "They destroyed the planet, you know, the automobile." Asher had a mostly clean conscience himself. "They just feel guilty, Ford."

He hadn't perfected the assembly line, but somehow the old man beside Brooke had amassed a fortune, one fifth of the Ford Foundation's endowment. This was, to Brooke, as mind-boggling as the stars, so little understood by people that we'd turned them into constellations. She thought this should mean something. "You don't need them," she said. "The Asher and Carole Jaffee Foundation does not need them."

"You know, Brooke." Asher had been a salesman. "I see something in you. Forgive me. Maybe a protégé. Is that what I mean? There's more you can do. You're capable of something." He knew just what he meant. He caught his own reflection in the face of this girl so unlike him that most people, common people, stupid people, would strain to see it.

She turned the word over in her hands like a curio. Maybe once she'd have demurred, thanked him, but what he wanted, now, was for her to rise to this. "I'm capable of a lot."

"I see that." Asher didn't make offers lightly. His daughter's death had clarified what he already knew. You couldn't waste time or energy on people unworthy of it. "I need candor. I need to have people I trust. I need advice."

The elegant French of *protégé*. A beautiful bauble. A reward. She knew not to ask what he wanted of her, because what he wanted was someone who already knew that answer. Hardly a secretary. What had Eileen said? An angel on the shoulder. A force for good. "My advice is that you tell the Ford Foundation thank you but no thank you. Then we go back to the office tomorrow, and tomorrow, and tomorrow, and we finish what you've started."

"For a liberal arts girl, you've got a real edge. You could have been at Jaffee Corp., you know. You have what it takes. But you're thinking about souls." He tapped his temple to say that he remembered. "I am also thinking about souls."

"That is the business we're in now." Brooke was certain of it.

He turned to his right, looked out the window. "I've had a feeling about you since we met." Asher didn't say what that feeling was. Maybe he didn't need to.

So apt that Realtors had these open houses on Sundays. The Sabbath was for introspection. It was possible, Sunday, to imagine what life might be. Shopping for a home (shopping at all) was a sacrament. The Charles Street apartment was therefore their temple.

Should they genuflect before that sunken living room, should they perform the sign of the cross on seeing that view, should they fondle the bath's brass fittings as they would relics of the saints?

Kim was already beautiful. Hardly fair how these rooms showed not only themselves but her to such advantage. Was it the light or was it the proximity to heaven above? "You like it, right?" She was nervous to have them there. She had all but decided that this was to be hers.

Brooke misunderstood Kim's indifference as sincere. "I love it. It's—"

Hillary, the broker, cleric in this business, was overwhelmed by curly hair and enthusiasm. "It's so *thoughtfully updated*."

The hems of Kim's pants were so near the floor that she shuffled as she joined Matthew at the living-room window. Her window soon.

"People always talk about the view," he said. "This is a view."

Kim's mother's apartment was not dissimilar, its perspective over the Hudson. "Sometimes in winter, it makes me feel cold. Seeing all that gray sky." What she meant was that this apartment would make her feel what she'd long suspected—it was predestined that she end up just like her mother. "I'd want to do something warm. Earth tones maybe? And lots of texture. Like a velvet sofa, I love velvet." Kim had a plan.

"Christ, the city looks so far away. It's just pretty like this. No smell of pee. No schizophrenics asking for change. No Subway Pricker. Whatever. Maybe *I'll* take it." Skepticism was beyond even Matthew.

Kim giggled. Don't be silly! She was the rich one. It was good to put some levity in it. She thought it would spare them if she seemed uncertain instead of galvanized. She loved Matthew and their living arrangement; she loved Brooke and their almost sibling bond and Kim loved this apartment. She had decided already.

They had all known one another long enough to understand it as well. The future that Kim's father aimed to provide for was now at hand. They were so dear to one another as to believe that nothing would change, but this was a hope, not a pledge.

"The place won't be the same without you." This was Matthew, not Eeyore, with no prophylactic wryness. He lamented the change, the passage of years, the whole dumb thing. He had been happy with Kim.

Kim meant what she said: "I'm expecting you to be here all the time. Like every weekend. Whenever."

Curly-haired Hillary could hear this. Her heart quickened, that salesman's rush, a job well done, but she tempered the enthusiasm. "I'll wait outside. You take your time. We can talk."

Brooke knew that there was some bond between the other two, as roommates, that did not include her. Maybe they needed a second alone. Also, she distrusted the seller's agent, an unsmiling redhead whose reserve probably had something to do with the presence of three Black people in this luxury apartment. She drifted into the bedroom, once upon a time called the *master*, now called the *primary*, which had no accidental overtones of slavery. There, a large window that did not open offered a vantage toward the river.

It was a mediocre day, a typical Sunday, with its melancholy cloud cover, an atmosphere of industry suspended, people turned inward. It was a Sunday with that utter liberty that felt to her not promising but terrible. Should she propose brunch? Should she walk to the green market and ponder the vegetables but buy a flaky croissant? Should she get a coffee and look at the cheap books in carts outside of the Strand? Should she suggest a movie and shake peanut M&M's into a bucket of popcorn and eat so much of it that she felt ill before the coming attractions were over? Should she call her mother, her brother? *How*, she wondered, *did Asher Jaffee spend his Sundays?*

She saw Kim's succession of Sundays in this two-bedroom apartment. She saw coffee-stained cups upside down in the dishwasher, saw flowers bought on impulse slouching on a table, saw an orange peel, dried into brittle shells, left to molder on the marble countertop. The cleaning lady would see to that. She saw comfort and solitude and joy and it looked absolutely thrilling to her. Kim was dear, Kim was good, but Kim had done nothing to deserve any of this earthly comfort. And wasn't the universe meant to work that way, wasn't it governed by justice?

Brooke wasn't naïve. Nor was she jealous. She could never live in such an apartment, leaving aside the question of the four-thousand-dollar monthly maintenance. This fit Kim. But to have a place in the world that was yours alone, that reflected who you were and what you were worth. Not the American dream even, something deeper, more profound. Kim had never even had to ask for this, it had simply arrived by legal fiat. Kim could demand what she wanted of the world. Her money meant her entire life was assured. The only word for what Brooke did then was *prayer*. She put her forehead against the window's glass, leaned as far forward as she was able, rested the full weight of her body against it, pushed herself toward the sky, and asked the universe for more than she had because she deserved it, and if she did not ask, who would? Did she think of God or did she think of Asher Jaffee?

Their reticence did not board the elevator with the three of them. They squirmed, chattered, children again. They needed fresh air. They needed honesty.

"You're going to buy that apartment," Matthew declared. He assumed she'd demur, hem and haw and raise a fuss, pretend, throw them off the trail.

Kim looked to Brooke. She wanted her approval.

"It's perfect," she affirmed. Brooke couldn't hate Kim for her great good luck. She loved Kim. Her smile was honest, almost delirious.

"I think so, too," Kim admitted. She had long ago decided this.

Hillary wore her sunglasses though they were not necessary. She smiled at them like an encouraging coach might at the children in her charge. "Thoughts?"

Brooke and Matthew were neither needed nor wanted. This was embarrassing to them each. "We should go get a bite," he proposed.

Brooke squeezed Kim's upper arm, to remind herself of her affection for the person, not to let this business cloud it. "You'll call me later?"

Hillary did what women like her were adept at: she proffered business cards, and made the gesture seem normal. "You both should call me. If I can ever be of help."

Sunday's oppressive mood weighed on Brooke and Matthew as they walked. The clouds would eventually offer rain, hot and weak. Eventually, everything would come to pass, but for now there was that feeling of suspension, of navigating some interstitial space in which progress was not possible, in which you simply had to wait, mark time, because the future was inevitable. Brooke said they should get coffee, and though neither of them quite wanted to, they did. Sometimes it was a comfort, to do what was most obvious.

untie Allison was powdery and round, and as with an alluring baby, you had some impulse to take a bite out of her. Her fat was contented and elegant, not impediment: Allison folded herself behind the small table with grace, comfortable as a cat. She considered Brooke with an unblinking scrutiny, also feline. "Why do you look so different to me?"

Brooke couldn't have said what she looked like. A glance downward reminded her. "It's the work clothes." Not long after Eileen hired her, Maggie had slipped Brooke an eight-hundred-dollar gift card to Theory. Thence, a different Brooke, one in tapered gray trousers.

The table was set with too many things: teapot, tiered tray, civilized rectangles of bread, mismatched napkins with embroidered flowers and curlicues, and, a final bit of set dressing, the West Village masquerading as London, a polyester Union Jack leaning out of a vase. Allison held both of the younger woman's hands in her own, like a medium summoning the spirits. She did not relinquish them though the moment passed. "You look like a woman with a secret. You look pleased."

Brooke was uneasy, with nowhere to put her elbows. "Same old me."

Allison poured Earl Grey.

"How are you holding up?"

Allison's dark eyes welled. "Well, it's a stupid fucking tragedy. How are any of us *holding up?*"

Brooke was holding up, though. "It's a while since we even saw her." Paige had begun to disappear the moment she left the city. Sure, there was a difference between banishment and death. Paige would never again turn up at Maggie's Thanksgiving table, never drag them, some spring Saturday, to see what was on sale at Barneys. Brooke knew that she should feel sad and could not explain why she did not.

For her part, Allison was more angry than anything. "Paige never stopped thinking of herself as that person going to Europe for the collections, hobnobbing with royalty, staying at some friend's palazzo. I went out, you know, took the Long Island Rail Road. And she hated it. She didn't want me to see her there. She was ashamed." She reached again for Brooke's hand. "That's from her, isn't it?"

In fifteen years, the bracelet's gold had dulled, but the black of her bony wrist showed it in relief. "When I turned eighteen."

"Paige in a nutshell." Allison chewed, relished the grit of sweet in her teeth. "She loved beautiful things. That was her way through life. This is mine. I eat iced buns."

Brooke mistook this as a prompt to the empty words women were too often asked to provide. *Life's too short! You look beautiful!*

Allison didn't care for this sort of thing. "You know what I did. Out of college? I took peanut butter sandwiches to boys dying of AIDS. I'm never going to apologize for eating." She admired Paige's love of beauty but knew there was more to life. You were what you did in the world, not what you collected.

Brooke envied Allison's clarity. She wasn't that hungry herself but bit into a cucumber sandwich. Auntie Allison's appetite seemed to Brooke to represent the vigor with which the woman approached things. There was some kind of lesson in this. "I've been feeling guilty or something. Upset I'm not more upset. I loved Auntie Paige." It was, she didn't say, like the frustrating tickle of a sneeze that would not come. She could not cry for the woman.

Allison was used to thinking of Brooke as a girl, but thirty-three was not so young. She stirred her milky tea for something to do. "There's no right way to grieve." Not a mother, no, but Allison could see there was something Brooke wanted. What everyone wanted: an idea of how to live. And this was within her remit, as auntie. "Living means making your peace with dying. Maybe. Eventually. Maybe Paige's dying is making you think about yourself, living. That's natural. I feel it, too."

This provided Brooke a pivot from social call to business. Hadn't she used a car service voucher, as Jody had explained was standard practice when on the official business of the Asher and Carol Jaffee Foundation? Enough of this death stuff. "You know I wanted to pick your brain."

"Tell me everything." Elbows on table, chin in palm, Allison listened.

Finally, Brooke was able to recount the story of Asher Jaffee inviting her to lunch. There was no need for embellishment: the diner, the grilled cheese, the challenge. "We talked about the arts, about children, about his legacy. He's asked me for something, for my help."

Allison was someone who said what she felt. "I'm proud of you."

Brooke jotted nothing in particular in the leather-bound book she'd found space for on the crowded table. She did not know what to say.

Allison cleared her throat. "I'm serious. He knows you love art. He knows you taught children. And he's put you in charge of something. You haven't even been—how long has it been? I guess I didn't know that this was what you were doing now. It's amazing."

"This isn't in my job description, strictly speaking. It was something that came up when we were talking about Endeavor. He liked the idea of art, and kids, and he said I should do something about that. He told me he thinks of me as a protégé." Now she was bragging.

Allison fingered the hard gold bangle that encircled Brooke's thin brown wrist. "You impressed the boss. You are an impressive person."

Brooke could not hear how her voice matched her aunt's, in its emphases, its rests, could not see how her body, slight as it was, tried to fill the space at the table. Here was a model for how to be in the world: Auntie Allison, with her lack of apology, her private satisfaction, her presence. "The pressure is on. I want to impress him." She did not bring up the question of souls.

Allison was prepared. "You need to talk to Laurie. You need to talk to Jen." Allison brushed a dusting of sugar from her lips and went on. Christie. Heather. Karen. Allison was one of these women, women with ideas. Women who met recidivism, sexual violence, and wholly failed educations with job training, subsidized cellphones, and free books. Women who knew that you had to try something, who knew that inaction was moral failure, that exhaustion was beside the point. Life was an invitation and such women answered it. It was bracing to say this to someone she'd known since she was a baby.

"This is wonderful." It had been the right instinct to appeal to her auntie.

"You're taking notes." Allison approved. "But this isn't about making your boss happy, helping him spend his money. This is what I do, you know. Your mom, too. This is a worthy way to be in the world."

Brooke demurred. "I believe in this. It's a good job, it's an opportunity."

"It's a philosophy, isn't it?" Sated, Allison continued to pick at the food for the satisfaction of it. "At some point you have to decide what sort of person you want to be. Look at Auntie Paige. A housewife in a Chevy Suburban and you're fucking dead. Maybe it mattered that she spent her life on things, on beauty, and art, and whatever, or maybe it means something to care about something bigger."

Brooke heard in this not judgment but frank appraisal. Maybe she couldn't cry about Paige because her life, accruing things and ideas and people, came to nothing in the end. That seemed crueler, even, than to die while waiting for a bus to take you to a meaningless job. "I should ask you for some phone numbers. Some introductions. Some guidance."

Allison reached for her wallet. "That's easy."

Brooke shook her head. "This is on me. On the foundation, I guess. This is work!"

"I won't argue." Her contented smile said what she would not, because she didn't want to embarrass: look how far she had come, once a baby in her own arms, now a woman with a corporate card and a sense of mission. "You want names? Phone numbers? I'm ready. Just ask."

I t had been a week of fieldwork. A group corralled ninth graders to paint murals on brutalist housing projects. Brooke toured one, hands clasped behind her back like a connoisseur. These true believers put musical instruments into the hands of Chinatown ten-year-olds. Brooke nodded as they wheezed through Bach. A troupe of Yale Drama grads staged abbreviated, modernized Shakespeare in high schools. Brooke took in a forty-eight-minute production of *As You Like It* updated to include the word *catfishing*.

There were so many people trying so many things, people who, like her, believed that the soul mattered. Brooke was swept up in this epidemic of optimism. Her mind moved more quickly than the town car she took to and from the offices of the Asher and Carol Jaffee Foundation. According to Jody, it was about telling a *story*. You had to move someone (Asher) toward feeling. Brooke knew Asher wouldn't want Puerto Rican kids being subjected to iambic pentameter or some fourth graders who spoke Cantonese at home learning the violin. Brooke knew what was expected by every teacher, by every professor, by every boss, by every coworker, and now by Asher. He'd want the story of Black kids with Black problems.

Brooke couldn't recall who had first told her about the Throop Community School. There was a hokey, cinematic quality to the moment the car emerged into light on the bridge. Brooke looked right, toward Governors Island, wondering about the oysters beneath the river's lick, but saw mostly her own reflection. Auntie Allison was right. Brooke had changed. You could see that she was a good person. It was because of Asher's money, the thing that let her treat those kind women to coffee, the thing that might make a difference in the world.

Brooklyn was forever bragging about how many churches it had. Throop Community School operated out of a church basement, not so they could pay rent because they didn't, but so the diocesan elders could reassure themselves that they still mattered. Brooke walked past three times—it was poorly marked and she was bad with directions. In retrospect this would seem something out of biblical parable, a number invested with unknown meaning.

A laminated piece of paper with the Throop Community School logo told Brooke to descend to the basement. At the foot of the steps, a metal door stood open. The place was mysteriously cold. The whitewashed floor had been scuffed by generations of Sunday-best shoes. There were framed photographs of Black children dancing and drumming. This was more like it. There was a faint suggestion of nag champa. A woman in white, silver haired, sat at one of those hulking desks from midcentury, laminated wood and peeling metal. "Good afternoon!" It was like she'd been waiting for Brooke. "Are you Sister Robin's daughter?"

Brooke shook her head. "I'm—"

"No. You favor her, though. You're not. Did we talk last week? Because, baby, it's just too late for this session. But we can look at the summer. I have space in the toddler class." The woman was firm but apologetic.

A hand on the flat of her chest, explaining. "I'm Brooke Orr. From the Asher Jaffee—the Asher and Carol Jaffee Foundation. I left a message. Two, actually." Whichever of Auntie Allison's friends had directed Brooke here had spoken highly of the school.

The woman smiled. "Well, sister." A guilty whisper. "I never check the messages, baby." She was not one for the endless chase of modern life. She found it simpler to handle things as they arose. "I'm Sister Ghalyela. Jefferson. You can call me Sister."

The chairs had nubby orange upholstery. Brooke crossed her legs, self-conscious, suddenly worried that her shirt was immodest. Ghalyela, or Sister, was sheathed in white, impossible to tell what manner of garment it was, strips of white covering every part of her strong body, almost sacred. Before Brooke could say anything else Ghalyela asked what she could do for her. She was there to do, not be done for. "I've heard good things about the school's work."

Ghalyela was not surprised. They had a reputation. "Twenty-three years."

"We. The foundation, we're looking for partners, for investments, and I thought the school might be an organization we should consider."

Ghalyela's smile did not falter. "It's a community organization.

It's me. We aren't in the position, you see. We don't have the money. We just focus. African dance, drumming. Sliding scale. Free programs in one of the area elementary schools. It's all we can do to keep this little office."

"Maybe you've misunderstood. We would be the ones. It would be a gift."

Ghalyela made paper cups of peppermint tea. Brooke began at the beginning. "Sister." The endearment was unfamiliar on her tongue. She felt like a door-to-door itinerant slinging vacuum cleaners or vegetable peelers. "Do you know who Asher Jaffee is?"

Ghalyela didn't know what oysters and gay marriage had to do with anything (she supported both; Throop Community School was a progressive institution), and when the paper cups were empty and her bladder full, she came clean. "Sister Brooke. I'm not sure I understand."

Brooke couldn't just promise it. It wasn't hers to give. "Sister. Asher Jaffee is a rich man. He wants his money to go to people like you. To do with it—you decide. You could hire teachers. You could get an office of your own. You could pay someone to listen to the voicemail messages." She spun a fantasy. Costumes, makeup, licensed workers, an endowment.

Ghalyela gathered her white garments about her. She knew what this was. Do-gooders come knocking with big promises and mess up everything, misunderstanding those they mean to help. It was plain there was nothing to fear from this awkward, thin girl.

"It's so much money," Brooke said. It could be. Why not just admit it?

Ghalyela thought about this. "Nobody gets something for nothing," she decided.

Brooke could read the woman's indifference. One step at a time. This business was slow. Good things took time. It would be decades before the oysters, still theoretical, had cleaned New York Harbor. "I don't know if I agree," she said. Something for nothing was the principle, was the point, it was the business they were in.

S asha, redolent of shea and patchouli, worked over Brooke's head with her strong hands. She buzzed and massaged and scrutinized and Brooke tried to relax.

"Can you believe this story?" Sasha made disarming eye contact in the mirror.

It seemed the only thing to talk about. A mustachioed blond from Queens had presented himself to the authorities as the subway attacker. There was a boastful mayoral announcement though the boys in blue hadn't done a thing. The guy had come forward, then soon enough his story was discredited. He had been under medical supervision during all of the attacks, was guilty of nothing but madness. "Sick people out there."

"We're almost done." Sasha spun the chair, her face close to Brooke's, appraising as you might an object. "The cops won't do a thing. Never do. A crime against women? They don't give a shit."

Brooke still didn't believe there was anything to it, the Subway

Pricker a figment of collective imagination, a mental patient's delusion. She didn't say this because she didn't want to move her body, freezing as Sasha smoothed the contour of her hair. Brooke always wore it the same: short, an echo of the roundness of her cheeks and her chin. Simple, it nevertheless required Sasha's concentration. Brooke reckoned that a natural was like a halo from medieval painting. It softened. It rendered her closer to God. No one would ever question her expense reports. "Take your time." Brooke hadn't meant to whisper. She closed her eyes.

"There we go. Your perfect self." Sasha spun the chair toward the mirror.

Brooke knew this was the sort of thing one said, especially in Sasha's trade, but the earnestness of it embarrassed Brooke. She did look nice, though. "Great. Thank you."

Sasha's ministrations were not cheap. Brooke added a tip 10 percent higher than had been her custom, just because, why not, she could spare it, it was worth it, she was worth it. In this salon, manicured women were plied with cold champagne. With their designer handbags and complicated alliances, they were a breed apart, but there was comfort being in a Black shop, which was why the institutions persisted, even in Fort Greene, where most Black people had been supplanted by Megans pushing UPPAbaby strollers, Todds in flat-front khakis.

Brooke was snobbish about Brooklyn—a school outing to see the houses at Weeksville, maybe. The constraint of Manhattan Island was something special. You felt hemmed in as in a nursery, not a prison—comfort, plenty, security. Its grid was reliable until it petered out at the periphery, because nothing beyond mattered. Brooke didn't know the streets here, and didn't like feeling out of her element.

She was late to meet Matthew and hurried through a neighborhood so popular with location scouts that it was beginning to look unreal. Every week, some film, some catalog, some advertisement for some financial services company. You'd have to have lived there for decades to remember when these houses were sliced up into SROs, but most everyone around was an arriviste. Still, they eyed the queues at the open houses and said *There goes the neighborhood.* A sign caught her notice, the familiar logo of Hillary's real estate brokerage. The card sat in an old ashtray that Brooke kept on her dining table. She'd studied it that morning.

In concession to the heat, the French doors of the bar were propped open with a cinder block. The place was empty, everyone else in Brooklyn basking in the light like logy turtles. Matthew presided over a booth, face Vermeer-lit by the phone in his grasp.

"I get lost in Brooklyn," she explained as she sat. In the moment that Matthew went to fetch vodka tonics, Brooke, alone at the table, was overcome with a brief confusion, an actor blanking on a line. Who was she again, or who was she supposed to be? Maybe it was melancholy, maybe it was a shift in hormones, something chemical and not real, maybe it was how everyone felt all the time.

He returned with their drinks, slid in across from her. "You look different."

"Just a haircut." She patted at her hair, joking, as it looked as ever it did. But had her old friend divined something Brooke had sensed? She *was* different. New job, new you. What Sasha had done to Brooke's hair was a circumstance, not a cause. It was to do with who she thought she was, or who she was becoming. If she truly had never weighed this question—who are you?—in all her thirty-three years, Brooke forgave herself. Matthew saw that she was different, understood that she was good. It was to do with the passion she felt for her work, it was akin to the way lovers seem to exist in some private realm. It wasn't about other people, her mother, her aunties living or dead, her rich friend or her poor friend, it was to do with her and, possibly, Asher Jaffee. She was on the verge of saying more but Matthew changed the subject.

"You know she's buying that apartment." He was triumphant—told you so—but also wicked. There was much to discuss, he was implying.

Brooke had seen something in Kim's face. Brooke was not surprised. "Wouldn't you?"

"So can we talk about how much money she has?" Matthew put his drink down and leaned in over the table. He held her eyes. His voice was serious. "This *trust fund* or whatever the word is."

Brooke couldn't even hazard an educated guess about the apartment's price tag. "I don't think it's a trust fund. It's something else." She didn't know the right term, either.

"I looked at the listing. That place is a hair north of two million dollars." He wanted Brooke to revel in this feeling of being scandalized. "It's a cash deal, babe. She mentioned this yesterday, that they've got a closing scheduled already."

"That was fast," Brooke said. But money made such things possible. Kim would never have to wait for anything again.

"I remember, freshman year, I went to the bank with Kim. We were going somewhere. Anyway, she took out two hundred dollars.

I think that was the limit at that machine, you remember? I used the same bank, it was the only bank. You know. And I would take out twenty dollars at a time. Who's going to spend more than that in Poughkeepsie? So I knew she had money but—"

Brooke tried to make the numbers mean something but they eluded her. Even now, she wouldn't take two hundred dollars out of the ATM.

"My question—how much money did her dad leave her that she can spend two million of it in cash?" Matthew was flushed, this perhaps the best gossip he'd ever happened upon, something to dissect, to probe, for years.

The question's implication: Who exactly was this person they'd thought was their dearest friend? Brooke had spent plenty of her own childhood in Kim and Auntie Sayo's Riverside Drive apartment, and at some point had understood that it was much nicer than her own home. Growing up even middle class in the city exposed her to the tastes, codes, private habits of the rich. Other people's money and what they did with it was never something to covet or think too deeply about. And it had never been a secret that there was a promise of more for Kim, some blessing in the distant future. Brooke had heard her mother pore over this with the other aunties much as she and Matthew were now. Money was sleight of hand— an entertainment. She shrugged her shoulders. Two million dollars was a lot, but was it a lot for a home, and wasn't it less than that violin Asher Jaffee had bought for that Korean prodigy?

"This is what you should be working on. This is what needs doing." A pause to play with the ice in his glass. "Forget changing the world or making it a better place or whatever nonsense you tell yourselves. What the world needs is a nonprofit that says, *Oh, your parents didn't work hard enough, we'll make up the difference.* Get Asher Jaffee to think that over."

She did not mention that she had leave to. That the man had indeed asked her for her input. "Kind of a Robin Hood situation."

"No," Matthew corrected. "That's stealing from the rich, giving to the poor. This is the rich voluntarily giving their money to the people who most need it."

"Eeyore. You're not poor." The thing you said reflexively, as when someone laments their weight.

He made a face of mock dismay. "Never said that. You think poor people care about money? You think poor people don't know they're poor, aren't resigned to it, aren't happy in some way, aren't at peace? The people who are obsessed with money aren't the rich who have it or the poor who don't. They're us. They're the big middle, it's all the rest of us, because we know what money can do. We know how we'll never get our hands on it, but we know it could make us free."

"I wouldn't mind buying an apartment," Brooke said, a thrill at saying this out loud for the first time. It was less that she wanted the thing than that she wanted what she knew Kim had: an assurance, a shape to the remainder of her life, a guarantee, liberty.

"That's what the Asher Jaffee Foundation should do. Oh, you're a single Black woman trying to buy an apartment, here's two million dollars. Oh, you're a gay project manager? Here's a little something toward a Fire Island share."

"We don't have Kim's dad. But we'll be fine." She wanted this to be the truth but wasn't certain that it was.

"Will we?" Matthew had finished his drink and had nothing to fiddle with. "Is what we were taught—get a job, work hard, save, be prudent, buy a little place of your own, contribute to the goddamn economy, do the thing that makes the world go round—is that even possible for us?"

Brooke felt the ghost of Auntie Paige, no longer a person to her, now just a convenient cautionary tale. Then she thought of Asher Jaffee. Brooke would choose the living over the dead. "We do all that. We work. We are prudent. I don't know, won't the other stuff just fall into line?" Was this yet another question she had never properly dealt with before?

He sat back, point made. "Is it a pyramid scheme, is that the metaphor I want? The whole system. I think maybe it is. I guess I'm resigned to it in a way. Being in the middle of that pyramid, the rich people standing on my shoulder, and me thinking someday, maybe . . . I should just ask your boss for money. To spread it around. Maybe he'd even say yes."

It was in fun. It was funny. But Matthew didn't understand. Asher wasn't on top of some pyramid. He was the deity to whom the edifice had been erected. Asher was not rich. He was free. Hence the skip in his step. His business was God's: the answering of prayers. "You do have charm. I'll introduce you."

"What about you?" His eyes were naughty. "You could make your move on Mr. Jaffee."

"I'm just an employee. No different than the maid." False modesty. She didn't tell Matthew that she was a *protégé*.

"You hear that story about the old lady who died and left her fortune to her nurse?" Matthew had this all thought out. "Anyway, an employee—what, you think the maid never thinks about swiping the missus's Prada handbag? That little Ming vase. The hundred-dollar bill that ran through the washing machine? Who knows better than the maid just how great it is to be Asher Jaffee?"

Brooke indeed knew it was great to be Asher Jaffee. And that she was lucky to know him. Asher's money could save the oysters. It could, if she needed, save her. She would not be Auntie Paige. She would be interesting, she would be good, she would be successful, perhaps with luck she would be free. "It's great being me and you," she said. Envy or whatever this was felt unseemly or ugly or beneath them. Brooke offered to buy the next round. It seemed just.

B rooke lingered on the corner, drink or perspective blurring the WALK and DON'T WALK signals into one nonsensical message. She'd retraced her steps through that Brooklyn idyll: whizzing kids on plastic scooters, dads double-parking Volvos, lululemon moms bearing paper bags of farmers market ramps, lives she didn't want but couldn't help admire, having learned to do so from television. Every real estate sign was just that, a sign. *If you lived here*, they didn't say, *you'd be home now*, also: a different, better, happier, richer person.

She needed food, but Matthew needed something else. He'd spend an hour on his phone, coordinating an assignation with some stranger. It was a subject they had tacitly agreed would not be discussed, as between siblings. Brooke bought a pepperoni slice, slick with orange oil. She chewed and watched. The night was mild and permissive parents had let their children stay up past their bedtimes. A frozen yogurt shop was doing a steady trade. Buses shuddered past, and drivers rolled windows down, bass knocking against the brick facades.

There was a Mexican restaurant across the street, abutted by a garden, bound by chain link bedecked with canvas banners bearing Obama slogans. There were tables painted citrus green, string lights overhead, and an atmosphere of festivity that felt more communal than at most restaurants. Couples in a defensive first-date position. Young parents harried by a toddler in no mood to sit. Friends laughing at some old story.

Brooke the spy, Brooke the thief, Brooke the all-powerful, the fearsome, the merciless. She observed, she noted. That utopian ideal of urban life: faces of every color. She saw joy. She felt it herself.

There was a pinkish girl in a black jersey dress, a little sweaty, brown hair frizzy. Brooke noticed that the girl carried herself with the ease of drink. She looked competent, she looked eager, she looked normal. She looked, if you squinted right, like Brooke's mother, or what someone having met Maggie might imagine when she mentioned her daughter. Brooke wondered if she'd seen the Black girl standing on the sidewalk opposite, appraising and eating so quickly her stomach would hurt.

There was something familiar about this moment, of cheap food to steady a hesitant tipsiness. Nights out with Matthew and Kim and forgotten friends from first jobs. Well drinks on starter salaries, flirting with boys and cadging their Marlboros, running a tab too high then stumbling into a bodega in a shrieking scrum to buy Takis and seltzer. Brooke always left those evenings early. Drunkenness made some want salt; it made her want solitude. Brooke, breaking free, would weave a little down the sidewalk. She wanted to be asked to stay but she also wanted to simply be home.

Such days—youth itself—were behind her. Kim moving out signaled the end of something Brooke hadn't realized she'd held dear. The future was nearer at hand than she'd guessed. But life was still unpredictable, and so much was possible. Brooke might have crossed the street, entered the Mexican restaurant. She might have pantomimed some business: she was meeting friends, she had dashed out to the ATM, she belonged. The music inside would be too loud so Brooke would walk out to the garden where the pink girl sat at a long picnic table slightly apart from the other three people there.

Brooke began the way things began: "How's it going?"

The girl's eyes were bleary with dream and drink. "Can't complain!" A bright voice, maybe abashed about its own enthusiasm.

Can't complain was a whole philosophy. "I hear you."

The girl wanted to know if Brooke was there for Patrick's birthday. "I'm Melanie. Did we meet? I'm sorry! I've had four margaritas."

"Maybe we should get you some water." Brooke fetched cups from a self-service station in the corner. Melanie might proclaim her a *lifesaver.* The girl would glug like an animal. Brooke outwitted her. "How do you know Patrick?"

Melanie's drunk mind crept unsteady as feet seeking purchase on wet stones. "My roommate's friend from college. Lindsey."

If Brooke repeated the name as Melanie was saying it, simultaneity would suggest knowledge. It wasn't even hard. "It's such a nice night."

Melanie's humid hand on Brooke's was childish and poignant. "You're so pretty. You must hear that all the time."

Brooke thought people complimented her looks to establish something about themselves. They had noticed her; they appreciated a woman with short hair, with dark skin, with big eyes. Years ago, a boy had told Brooke that she looked like someone from a fresco in Pompeii, too specific a compliment to be insincere. She did, she thought, look a bit like some doomed soul on an ash-covered wall. "You're pretty," she returned. It wasn't a lie but it wasn't accurate. Brooke really did see in this girl's face a shadow of her own mother's.

"I'm ready for cake. There better be cake." Melanie was unembarrassed by her own desire.

Brooke envied her. That was it. "There has to be cake!" She laughed. Then more seriously: "It's a bit of sweetness. You deserve it on a birthday. The passage of time. The inevitable. It's a distraction. Where are we going? What are we doing? Never mind. Have some cake."

Even drunk, Melanie had a handle on the feminine business of comforting a stranger. "But we're not old." She thought that the worst thing that could happen to a person.

"I'm not afraid of aging. But is it time? Do I need a plan for my life?" Brooke tried to work out what this girl did for a living even though she knew that counted for nothing. "I bet you have one. A nice guy. A good job. A house in Montclair. A kid. Two."

"I've thought about that stuff." A nervous laugh, more sober now.

"I don't want much. I want freedom." Brooke took the girl's wrist in hers. "You have that, don't you? You have it. I want it. I don't want what I have. I'm nothing. I'm no one." She wanted safety in a mad world. She wanted what people most wanted and was the thing that rich people hoarded: not money, but the grace of God and the universe, a way to be in the world and enjoy it. She wanted selfhood. "You're not no one."

"What do you mean?" Melanie turned more serious.

"I want to be you. I want to look like you, I want to want what you want, and know that sooner or later I'll get some version of it. I bet your mom calls you every weekend and tells you she's so proud. I bet nothing bad has ever happened to you and that you know on some level nothing bad ever will."

Was Melanie offended? She was too baffled to mind, or the alcohol mitigated whatever response she was having.

"Trade with me. Be me." Brooke was serious. She allowed it with this person who did not, would not, could not know her. "I can't change. I don't know what else to do." The restaurant was loud with festive Latin music. Brooke heard nothing but her own words. So often, she thought herself strange, or different, or apart. She was too young to understand that how she felt was simply how most people felt, at least on occasion, when they were being most honest with themselves.

Did the apartment look different in that morning's hazy light or was she hungover? Was it time for a plan for her life? She had that now. This was the plan. She was enacting it. Brooke dressed with a sense of purpose, disregarding the heat that had settled on the city like fog does in Northern California, too early for this sort of thickness, but that was the direction in which the world was moving, wasn't it? Worse.

Brooke, one of the 6 train's dozens, head at acute angle, was vulnerable not to some hallucinated man with a syringe but the more commonplace pain in the neck. She thumbed an invitation to Kate, *Let's have lunch*, affecting chumminess, intending to take the girl to the very diner where Asher had once taken her. There, Brooke ordered the same grilled cheese sandwich, which she barely ate. She was not hungry, was sustained by something else now, an exhilaration. She brought up the subject of oysters.

"One million. A million." Gummed with black, Kate's eyelashes were blinking for emphasis.

It's not appropriate, her makeup, Brooke thought. *Someone should tell her what her mother hasn't.* "A million dollars!" An encouraging tone, as to a pet. "Aren't you pleased? Happy? Proud?"

Kate was scandalized or surprised. This was reality? She fiddled with her own sandwich. "For oysters?"

Brooke had overheard what she was not meant to know. Asher's money was thriving. It was growing. It was itself a bed of oysters. Each one with a pearl. A diamond. A thousand dollars. The metaphor didn't matter. "You read the presentation. You know what it's for. It's for the future, the environment, the harbor." Poor, silly Kate. What did she think they were doing? This was the job!

"It just seems like so much money for—" Kate thought of her mother, when her little brothers refused their chicken casserole: starving children in Africa, in Bangladesh, hell, just down the road in Detroit!

Brooke summoned a patience she would not have guessed she had. "Beavers, then dolphins, then whales. Someday, Kate, when you're a grandmother, you'll be pushing the stroller by the river and you'll point to the water and you'll say, 'I helped do that, I helped change the world.'"

Kate was too young to imagine across time. "I just wondered. What if I went to Asher—we could feed starving children in Africa, Bangladesh, Detroit!" Kate was still young enough to want to please her mother. She would show how well she'd listened.

"You understand the oyster money is less than one percent of our endowment." It was, Brooke did not add, an even smaller percentage of Asher and Carol Jaffee's worth. It was nothing. And it could do so much.

"Maybe." Kate's voice trailed off.

Brooke could see Kate's skepticism. It wasn't Brooke's job to prose-
lytize, not to her colleague. Let Kate not understand, let her be the
secretary in this equation, from whom nothing more was required.
"I'm working on a bigger gift. That's my goal. To show Asher just
what his money might accomplish, in the right hands."

Kate said *Wow* with her face and they picked at their sandwiches
and drifted into talk of the weather, the headlines, the idiosyncra-
sies of the women they shared their office with, the usual conspiratorial chat between colleagues.

Brooke handed her corporate card to the waitress with a sense of
satisfaction. Maybe she should let Kate in on the secret that Asher
had divulged; life was what you demanded it be. "If you want to take
Asher a proposal regarding hunger in the city." But Kate was not a
protégé! Still, Brooke could be magnanimous. "Or any city. Let me
know. I can help you with that."

They walked into the heat, a tangible thing, a wet mass. It was
quiet, everything muted in the face of this weather. Optimistic Orthodox wholesalers leaned in doorways, checking their watches. Some
West Africans were picking up the cardboard they had spread on the
sidewalk, an improvised place to pray. A panhandler taking a break
with a cigarette stepped into the sun, not exactly barring their way.
"Hey, sister." A honeyed voice, comfortable, the ease of a doo-wop
singer.

But young women found no comfort being waylaid on city streets.
Sidestep was literal: Brooke and Kate moved in Rockette unison. Neither acknowledged him because you mustn't.

"I said *hello*, sister."

Brooke was streetwise and he lied: *hey* was not *hello*. A grimace
with a trace of a smile in it, the same steady pace that asserted her

ownership over the street, the city, the day, the moment. "Have a good one." You had to say something, firm but gentle, conclusive— no, declarative.

Kate had never learned what you did in this situation, didn't know that you kept talking, dissembling, pretending. You tested the eyes in the back of the head.

Behind her, Brooke somehow saw the man stub out his cigarette, no particular hurry. His lope was healthy. He was nearly upon them. "Miss, miss." Something musical, a little refrain. "I need to speak with you."

Brooke had the instinct to take Kate by the hand, tender a big sister's reassurance, but that would have been overreaction, and anyway, this man had not seemed to even see Kate. She traveled into a future that Kate could not summon. The air-conditioned relief of the badly lit office, its promise of safety.

He fell into step behind Brooke, as though they were on the same errand, as though they were father and daughter (and what if they were?), as though they were husband and wife. The proximity of paternal pride or uxorious love was easily breached, it was the length of one arm gripping a syringe, it was close enough to be threat. She had appraised: his clothes were worn but not filthy, his face was creased but not hard, his body well proportioned if not well fed. He could have been thirty, forty, fifty. "Sister, I just need to speak with you."

Enough was enough. "I don't have time." She could see he held a much-folded coffee cup full of pennies and nickels.

Sometimes he got tired of it. This game always went the same way. He could be forgiven impatience. "You've got time. You don't want to hear."

He wanted money. He had chosen well. Their job was to give

money to people, and did he need it more than New York needed oysters? This happened every day between strangers the world over, the one breaking some unspoken agreement and asking the other for their money, their time, their attention, so minor a violation you couldn't feel it unjust. It was merely something that happened.

"Please, miss. I need to speak with you." There was no pledge not to hurt her. Maybe he thought that obvious. Maybe one dollar, five dollars, ten, would make a difference in his life.

Would a passerby know Brooke needed a savior, or would they see two Black people and assume they belonged together, not pause to reconcile her Club Monaco trousers with his cup of change. They might have seemed intimately bound together, locked in the silence of some private disagreement: dinner plans or an office conflict or a household matter. The block seemed so long, distance, like time, flattening or stretching, depending on what you most wanted. "Get away from me." This with a quiet fervor belied by those Club Monaco trousers.

"I only want to speak to you."

Brooke didn't care what this man wanted. Maybe a better person would. They had reached the corner and Brooke's stance declared it her territory. There was a window into a Starbucks, a modern Hopper: a clutch of people in their private reveries. She would, if it came to it, demand from the world what was hers: the peace of walking the street. "I don't care what you want!" She heard the quaver in her throat, her inability to express conviction. She was not a serious person, she was no one to fear.

"Okay, baby." A shrug in it, a resignation, but also an indictment. He lobbed her insincerity back in her direction.

A metallic taste in her mouth, sweat on her back. She began to understand or put words to it. "Nothing gives you the right. Don't you dare." Brooke took Kate's hand like she was her child and they rounded the corner toward the office.

Though the man did not shout, somehow his words reached around the bend as they pushed on toward the office: "You're too good." An observation, a fact, a condemnation.

She did not scream back that in fact she was, or that she wanted to be.

Kate was spooked. There was nothing more to say but she went on. "This is what I mean. There are people. Right here. Who need."

There was still that high, a mix of fear and triumph. Brooke calmed herself. "You think Asher Jaffee's money can make it so that bums don't accost people?" She liked the weight of that old-fashioned epithet.

Kate had a genuine feeling. "What I'm saying is that we could try. It's as important as oysters at least."

They stood side by side in the little elevator. "You should talk to Asher." No, this was not right. Brooke had dispensation, but this was special. "You could talk to Jody. You can talk to Eileen."

Kate's plain face said plainly that she was intimidated. A good suburban girl who respected rank. Brooke saw that she herself was included in this. The girl looked up to her. Why not? Wasn't *protégé* a kind of promotion? "The poor will always be with us." She mangled the Gospels, what did she know? "But if anyone can help, it's Asher Jaffee." Amen, she didn't say. Wasn't that Matthew's joke: the foundation as some kind of solution to every problem everyone had? It contained, as any good gag does, a kernel of truth. Asher Jaffee could solve every trouble she had, and there was nothing wrong with admitting that.

T he week ended in tabulating and collating. It was a way of taking stock, of accounting for not only dollars but your efficacy. Summarizing the expenses and expenditures of five days of official business was like the personal inventory of bedtime prayers. Brooke made neat piles of receipts. Starbucks and vouchers from the car service; she could tot up the sums in her head, carrying the digits as some long-forgotten teacher had shown her. She paper-clipped the paper slips, printed the requisite form, walked these to the tray outside Eileen's office. Such a cute, old-fashioned ritual, like raising the flag on a mailbox when a stamped letter waited within.

Almost five, but Brooke knew Natalie would be at her desk. Fridays, the woman might not have bothered. Easy enough to man her phone from the comfort of her one-bedroom in Flatbush. She would never! Just because Asher was away didn't give her the right. Natalie was their metronome. Natalie was their beating heart. Come quitting time, Natalie's *good evening* was like the whistle at a factory. Natalie was dependable as the moon.

"My dear." There was some contradiction between her kind words and her inscrutable eyes.

"Happy Friday." Why did it feel like the older woman had some advantage, why did a mundane interaction have anything to do with power? "I'm sorry to bother you, Natalie—"

She said that this was *never a bother.* That was the sort of thing Natalie did. She reworked a person's words and handed them right back.

"I just need some more vouchers for the car service."

"You've been busy." Natalie saw all. Natalie noticed. She stood, unlocked the desk drawer, counted out three of these slips, tendered the papers to her younger colleague.

She *had* been busy! There was a quick visit downtown to the oyster people's offices, hand-holding Kate, though Brooke didn't resent this, indeed had relished being the senior person in the room. Brooke had gone back out to Brooklyn to see the wizened woman at the Throop Community School. But despite the fact that they'd made arrangements, Sister Ghalyela had failed to appear. Brooke found only the locked door in the church basement and a telephone that no one answered. She remained undaunted. "I've been busy." She was proud.

"Well, you must remember to get out this weekend. Lovely forecast, finally a little less of this awful humidity."

Adulthood: so much time spent discussing the weather. "There's something to look forward to." She didn't want to ask, but how would Natalie spend her weekend? "Anyway, it's been another good week doing good. That's something."

Natalie was grave. This was important. "What you do matters, Brooke. Not many people could say the same." She returned to her perch, smug.

Brooke thought it dangerous to be too self-congratulatory. But she didn't want to seem a cynic. "I agree."

"Asher Jaffee is a great man." It was said as though she were correcting someone who had alleged otherwise. That she believed this was evident to all.

Sure, he was doing good things. Maybe *great* was the apt word. But some instinct made Brooke challenge Natalie: "You think so?"

Not a shred of doubt. "I know so."

Brooke was conciliatory. "It does sometimes hit me. What we're doing here—"

Scrupulous Natalie's interruption communicated how keenly she felt this. "I've been with Mr. Jaffee since before you were born." This said something! She went on. "I've always admired him, but I'm not sure I would have predicted this." She gestured at the office around them. "But it makes complete sense. It's the sort of man he is."

Brooke heard something that could never be challenged. Natalie wanted to share. "It is noble, absolutely. To devote yourself to caring about people." Natalie knew there were skeptics. She knew his accountants and executives rolled their eyes. She wondered whether Mrs. Jaffee didn't entirely understand. "It's not for attention. It's not guilt. It's a sense of responsibility. Do you know—well, no, you wouldn't know, no one does." She had told this story many times. "A long time ago now, my mother was ill. She'd had a stroke, you know, and a bladder problem. There's no one to help but your family. Greatest country on earth." Her people weren't connected to a temple. There was no sense of community.

A failure of Brooke's imagination, unable to come up with Natalie's mother, a creature of diaspora, a relic of history, a vanishing species.

Natalie went on: "This was when Mr. Jaffee was selling the business. A busy time. No. A high-stakes time. Constant phone calls, meetings. My part in all this, it's small, but it's important, keeping all these schedules straight, coordinating all these discussions. And my mother, at her absolute worst. I failed. I just couldn't do it."

Brooke made a supportive sound. Only a secretary, but maybe the secretaries of the world mattered, too.

Natalie held up a hand: *let me finish.* "I'm an only child, Brooke. I was the one my mother had. So I did what I had to do. I wrote a letter of resignation. I called a headhunter and said send the best people. I wasn't going to leave Mr. Jaffee in the lurch. When I tell you I felt guilty. A bad daughter, a bad employee."

This old-fashioned fealty to your employer. So few people thought this way anymore.

"I couldn't tell him. I put it in the letter. Left it with the papers for him to review in the car. That's what we did in those days before email. And that night. He called me, from home, and Mr. Jaffee said, 'What's all this, Natalie?'" She talked to the man every day for years but it was difficult to explain why this conversation, pacing her small living room in the small circuit that the phone's cord would permit, was so different. "I was ashamed. I was disappointed. I had failed to be the help he needed. I was failing my mother. Do you know what he said?"

Natalie took a deep breath. "'Why didn't you come to me about this?' Mr. Jaffee refused to accept my resignation. When I tell you I cried that night, Brooke. Was barely even able to eat."

This was as fascinating as hearing a story about your parents in their youth, before you existed, before you'd been thought of. Asher Jaffee's disapproval could move a woman to tears!

"I tiptoed into the office that next morning, just terrified. But we had to finish this, you see. Mr. Jaffee said that I was being *ridiculous*. He said I did not understand." What he had said, what she would paraphrase to keep it sacred: *You've given me your whole life. I owe you something.* "You won't believe it. It wasn't me. It wasn't some other assistant. It was Mr. Jaffee who called around. Who found a place for my mother." The man himself. "To this day, I'm—it was more like a resort than anything. He sent me there in his car to see it with my own eyes and I said, 'No it's too much, it's not possible. What could it possibly cost?'"

"That's very generous." Brooke could not help but be moved.

"You don't understand." Natalie had a tiny tear in the corner of her left eye. "My mother lived seventeen years. Seventeen years in absolute comfort, doted on by nurses. She was so happy there, Brooke. 'It's nicer than home,' she used to say. By the end, bless her, her mind was gone, mostly, but she smiled every time I saw her, smiling like a girl. He gave that to her. I never saw a bill. I could never even get them to tell me what it cost. I asked, I needed to know, and Mr. Jaffee said to me, 'Natalie, you're hurting my feelings. You don't understand how to accept a gesture.'"

Natalie had more to say: "He scolded me: 'Don't ever ask me how much this costs again.' But you see, what he said was, 'It's selfish. It's because I need you. It's worth it. Every cent.' But that's not true. He pretended not to be who he is. He's kind. That's the man we work for."

Brooke wondered, and then wondered whether Natalie wondered:

Would Asher Jaffee send Natalie to the same old-age home? Natalie had no Natalie of her own. There was a risk to being alone in the world. You needed an Asher Jaffee to care for you. There weren't many of him around but Brooke had been right. He answered prayers. "That's an incredible story."

Her act was finished. "He should put that in his book, I told him. I told him, 'Mr. Jaffee, you should have told people.' And he laughed. He's too proud. He spent all that time in business, he didn't want anyone to know what he's like, deep down."

What was generosity and what was selfishness? Money didn't matter to someone so rich. There was nothing to be gained by any further inquiry. Natalie's image of Asher Jaffee was one of her most prized possessions. "I guess you know. We know. What he's like."

Natalie scoffed. "Who can say. Ever. I just wanted you to know. If you doubt that. What we're up to here, what you're doing." She had said enough. She had said that good things were possible.

Brooke, too, believed this. Good things were possible for the world, and most importantly, good things were possible for herself. What had Asher Jaffee told her? Ask for what you want. The secret of life.

A public school: metal front doors inset with chicken-wire glass, a confusion of lines in the grid of ceiling overhead and the grid of tile beneath your feet. Strange color schemes of blue and purple and yellow, and the smells: the powdery scent of pages fresh from the copy machine, fried food, and a trace of Bounce because the school kept a washer and dryer, laundering the clothes of students who spent evenings in the city's shelter system. This bouquet cast Brooke back to the previous decade at the Endeavor Charter School. She barely thought of that place anymore, as if it had been an unserious love affair and not what she once thought her whole life might be.

The safety officers in the lobby demanded every adult visitor's driver's license. What became of those sign-in sheets, where they dutifully recorded addresses and signatures? The uniformed guard handed back Brooke's ID. Brooke asked for directions to the auditorium. The woman pointed Brooke down a hot, bright hallway.

The silver handle gave easily under her weight. There was that woosh of entering a vast room, then the din of youth: soprano squeals and fidgeting limbs, and above this the proclamations of Ghalyela, in holy white. There must have been thirty of them, younger than Brooke's kids at Endeavor, bare brown feet smacking the shellacked stage floor. Ghalyela floated above the children like a cloud. Even these kids, cellphone kids, video-game kids, designer-sneaker kids, paid obeisance. Something in Brooke, call it her heart, filled up. There it was: feeling.

There were rows of wooden seats designed for the small bodies of children. The floor sloped to the stage. Brooke's shoes squeaked on the linoleum. She sat and she watched. It wasn't the Swiss precision of ballet—they were children—but there was some improvisatory beauty in it. Bodies coming together, moving apart, knees bending, forms launching into the air. Ghalyela carried a drum, kept time almost absentmindedly. *What would Asher make of her?* Brooke wondered, with her pilgrim's raiment, her powerful voice, her conviction. He would, Brooke guessed, consider it a job well done. Ghalyela was the person he would expect Brooke to come up with; she was the person he would want to help.

A creak beside her. A guarded smile from a young woman. "Good morning."

Brooke tried a warmer expression than was her custom. A nod instead of words.

"I'm Michaela." Then, explaining: "Ghalyela's daughter."

Something had taken hold of her lately. Brooke minded her posture, spoke with more authority. A kind of romantic feeling, the sort that makes you stand up straighter, present the most flattering vantage, when a certain someone was near, eager not to disappoint. "I'm Brooke Orr." She added that it was *nice to meet*. She should have known. The younger woman looked just like the older.

On her first visit to the Throop School, Brooke had pleaded her case:

"Sister, I think we should talk about what we might do together," Brooke tried.

"Sister, you understand I want to help," Brooke tried.

A second visit, Brooke went further:

"Sister, I've talked to Asher Jaffee about your school," Brooke lied.

"Sister, there is money at stake," Brooke tried.

Ghalyela had said only that her interest was the needs of the *scholars*. Not *students*. Brooke found this charming. Auntie Allison's many friends had told Brooke that she should simply refuse to hear *no*. Those women had defeated logic time and again. You had to, to do good. But they meant from the institutions and the gray people who ran them, not the very people they were attempting to help. Brooke was determined to win over Ghalyela. It mattered.

Michaela was intervening. Perhaps she had been dispatched to do what her mother could not: get rid of Brooke Orr. "Remind me where you're here from?"

"The Asher and Carol Jaffee Foundation. A small organization giving away a huge fortune." Brooke held the woman's eyes. "Your mother does not want to hear my pitch." Ghalyela had apologized for standing Brooke up but there was a message in it.

Michaela's smile was bemused. "She's like that. What are you selling exactly?"

"That's the thing. I'm not selling. I'm giving." Brooke wasn't sure if the endearment could be used on this younger woman but she tried it all the same. "Sister, this is an opportunity."

Michaela shrugged to say that this was her mother's affair. "She pretends not to listen, but she heard you. She doesn't want it." She gestured at the stage, the room. "You know, she made this. Out of nothing. Volunteers. Stubbornness. She thinks it's going to ruin twenty-three years of work."

Brooke could see that Michaela was herself twenty-three or so. There was no ABOUT US on the school's website. These were all her children. "I don't want to ruin anything." She loved this. She wanted to save it.

Michaela went on. "This was just something to do, at first. This was before mommy-and-me yoga or whatever. It was a different neighborhood then." She was proprietary, but of course she was—this school was her whole life.

Brooke did not understand how these people could not want Asher's money. "I see what she's done. I respect what she's done. This isn't about undoing that. Let's imagine. Salaries. Health insurance. Full-time employees. Costumes. Instruments."

Michaela laughed. "We've always just made things up as we go along."

Brooke wanted her to do as Asher had advised and demand more. To save souls she would have to sell dreams. "Imagine college scholarships. Do you understand how much money we're talking about?"

"There's more to life. That's what she'll say." Michaela's pause said that maybe her mother was right.

Onstage a little girl had started to weep. One of childhood's many insults, or a low blood sugar, or a sensitive soul who had missed a step and hated herself for it. Acorn colored, baby hair smooth, pulled away from an angular face overtaken by emotion. Then, almost as quickly, mollified. Ghalyela offered not a hug but a private word of encouragement, deploying the girl's name firmly, the only word that carried in the big room: Sistine. Incongruous but unmistakable. Actually, maybe it was fitting. Something divine in this child's common beauty.

Brooke needed to give this money away, because she needed to satisfy Asher Jaffee. Brooke had not anticipated meeting any resistance. This was a test. If she could not give, she would never receive. Asher's grace depended upon her success. "I'm not trying to put a price on anything. Your mother's work. I'm trying—"

Michaela could be honest where her mother could not. "She doesn't want to be saved. She doesn't see it's needed." Michaela understood this perspective. She was her mother, as most of us are. "Is she so wrong? We don't need someone to save us. We are fine. We're happy."

What would Brooke's own mother say? Maggie knew how to get things done. But the government, ignorance, and the patriarchy were her antagonists. It was harder by far to go up against an old woman in Brooklyn who just wanted to teach some children to dance.

Brooke didn't know how to phrase it. Would the money not make them happier? Wasn't that how money worked?

The action stopped and Michaela began to clap. Brooke joined her, and there was scattered applause from behind her. She swiveled and saw mothers, fathers, big brothers, leaning against walls, perching on seats, catching up on gossip. After some final word of instruction from Ghalyela, the children swarmed and skipped toward their adults with that fervor that children bring to most every task.

The no-longer-weeping Sistine brushed Brooke's arm as she trotted up the sloping aisle. Her beauty was intact but seemed different, more subdued, more quotidian, now that she'd left the stage, now that the tears had been forgotten. But Brooke was taken by the child, that collapse into emotion familiar to all who remembered being young. A beaming woman, the girl's older double, wrapped her in a hug, whispered a private word. A parent was uniquely able to console.

The woman could have been Brooke's age. *Unfathomable,* she thought, *to have a child at thirty-three, even if it's within the average.* Brooke had never felt a pull toward maternity herself, but there was something in this scene. She could never ask: Why Sistine? Was it because the mother had taken a trip to the Vatican at a formative time in her own youth? Was it the sound of the word, which Brooke knew from art history merely designated something as related to the handful of popes called Sixtus? Or was it because the mother found the daughter otherworldly, holy, even if she was only an eight-year-old in Velcro sneakers and rose beige tights, a girl like millions of others.

The racket in the big room had grown louder than Brooke might have thought possible for so few people. There was jubilance in their voices. Maybe it was ecstasy. *Asher Jaffee,* she thought, getting up out of the creaky wooden chair, *would love this.*

T he cellphone earned Asher's reproach. He thought younger people addicted. In some ways he was just another old man dreaming of the way things once were.

Brooke, beside him on the leather seat, nodded at the news from Natalie: Tessa, gray-suited woman of the Ford Foundation, had been struck by a car. Bad luck at a notorious Queens intersection. An anecdote about how life could change in a moment. Tessa wasn't indispensable, but it was unseemly not to cancel. Brooke gasped at the gross coincidence of two car crashes affecting her life. "Asher, our meeting has been postponed."

The pedestrians on Forty-second were moving more quickly than they were. He hated disruption. "They insisted we come when there's nothing to—"

"Should I ask Christopher to go back?" As though he weren't right there, as though he were unable to hear. These jaunts to various Midtown conference rooms, Brooke had felt the driver watching. One day he spoke to her, the kinship of another Black face or some paternal feeling. He had, he told her, three daughters. One was a nurse. One was in college. The youngest had tested into a Riverdale private school. He had thought Brooke would want to know this, thought she would recognize something, that she was some version of his girls, all grown up. Brooke was cool to him. She had little desire to be his child or his ally. He would be, to her, only what he was to Asher. Brooke read the boss's frown and explained the postponement.

A general announcement to everyone involved: "We're getting out at the corner." A suddenly surplus hour!

Natalie would want him returned to the office. In her new proximity to the boss, Brooke was often deputized by Natalie. But it did not do to question Asher's caprice. The fundamental task was to make him happy. The car stopped and Asher was gone like a liberated pet. Brooke clambered after him.

A summer day with a prevailing delirium, the liberation of a promised holiday, everyone a schoolkid once more. "There's something I need to do anyway."

It remained unclear what she might demand. Could a protégé insist upon an explanation or did she obey without question?

"Ask Natalie to send flowers." Asher crossed the street and continued uptown. When Brooke did, that afternoon, she would find that Natalie had already placed the order.

Tourists took photos of nothing in particular. Midtown's cacophony of traffic and construction. Brooke admired how Asher seemed not to notice—not the slobs from the provinces or a glum woman with a fistful of leaflets, not the deliverymen wielding trollies or the bus driver exercising his vehicle's horn. Asher lived in some other, better place, some improved reality. "Should we get a coffee?" He could hold forth and she could take notes.

It was Asher's habit to say nothing when his answer was no. He turned onto Forty-ninth Street. "There's something I need your help with."

The air in the lobby of Christie's was beyond conditioned; arctic, cryogenic. Maybe it had to do with the preservation of the master-pieces therein. There wasn't much to the place, white expanses of floor and wall as you'd find in museums. Brooke kept a modest wife's dis-tance as Asher beckoned the receptionist. "Can you tell Sara I'm here? Asher Jaffee."

Some strategy in how he wielded these names. Asher knew that even the girl at the desk would know who he was and be able to de-duce which Sara he had come in search of.

It didn't pay to dawdle when Asher Jaffee beckoned. Sara's body was not hampered by the taut pencil skirt or the lethal heels. This was a woman who knew what time meant to men like Asher Jaffee, the men (it was always men) she spent her career dealing with. She approached with outstretched hands and campaign smile. "Mr. Jaffee." She lingered in the handshake for longer than most would have. She said that it was *wonderful* to see him.

"I hope it's okay." Asher tucked his hands into his pockets. "Drop-ping by."

"It's always a pleasure. Don't be silly." She had her arm in his.

"This is my colleague, Brooke Orr." This moment of introduc-tion had become a part of their show. Asher saw it as significant, and Brooke had come to rely on it. She was practicing eye contact, firm grip.

Sara glanced back at Brooke and said that meeting her was, too, a pleasure. "Come, come, one and all!" Sara did not need to know whether this girl was mistress or money manager. She led them down a tiled hall and through a large set of swinging doors. There was more hallway, a turn, and another turn to a smaller set of double doors. These were opened to reveal a room, a chamber, high ceilinged but windowless. The hush of a library, a sense of purpose so intent that silence seemed warranted. There was some generically handsome Greg or Craig in a black blazer, and there were two armchairs, and there was a painting larger than a person, upright, braced by steel. No, not a library, it was like a chapel. Sistine, wasn't it?

Sara lingered behind them. She knew how to do this. "Mr. Jaffee. Welcome back. And Ms. Orr. Welcome. Here we are. *Sea Level*. Helen Frankenthaler. 1976. It's acrylic on canvas. The current owner acquired this directly from André Emmerich. It's been in that collection since."

Asher did not want to seem old but he wanted to sit. He took one of the leather armchairs. "Here we are." His repetition was to buy himself time. The facts—yes, 1976, yes, Frankenthaler, yes, acrylic on canvas. But what was he supposed to feel? "It's big."

Brooke was unsure if she could, or should, then sat. Her mother owned a Frankenthaler lithograph, a small thing, a modest thing, but something of which Maggie was quite proud. What to do with that strange coincidence? Nothing. Brooke could see her boss trying to make sense of the painting, misunderstanding how this worked.

Sara was talking about scale. "To me the word is *vast. Geologic*. It makes you feel small, in this case, both literally and psychically."

Brooke watched Asher frown. She turned to see Sara, hands clasped behind her back. An absurd attraction to the woman, as though they were sisters and Asher the distant father each was eager to please.

Sara could sense her prey had less attention today than usual. She communicated with few words to the young man to adjust the lights. "The piece is signed and dated on the back, if you'd like to see." An apprentice salesman, he sounded nervous.

Asher pushed himself out of the chair. "Well, let's see then." No point coming all this way not to.

Brooke followed him. The two circled the big canvas. They lingered behind, sheltered from something in a private sanctuary. It felt wrong to see it from this angle, the thing so vulnerable, so nude. On a curl of the canvas, pencil scrawl, name, date, the title. She recoiled to see him touching the painting. But precious was for museums. This was simply something to buy.

"It's Mrs. Jaffee's birthday next month." Asher thought ahead. Asher had always been generous. He was a man who availed himself of the pleasures of a great fortune. "So. What do we think?" A woman would know, and women loved to be asked about this kind of thing.

It was a pleasure to feel dwarfed by the painting. It might fall on them. It might swallow them. There was an oceanic blue and the suggestion of mud and sunset. What did she think, what a question, it was self-evident, it was impossible to articulate. Fine, there was a word. "Beautiful."

"This is not a piece that has traveled much or even been widely seen." Sara loved that the painting was shy. The painting was a recluse. The painting was a mystery. "If you ask me. And what do I know. Frankenthaler is undervalued right now. It's the male abstract expressionists most people want. I would be betting on Helen."

He wouldn't brook this. "It's a gift. Not an investment." Everyone always talked at him about money as though this were the only thing he understood or cared about.

The word for it was *exhilarated*. Like she'd run a race: the damp awareness, the heart in her ears where it did not belong. She didn't envy Asher the long European holiday, the stately car, the chauffeur, the rest of the stuff she couldn't quite imagine: fine bed linens, custom shoes, food more delicious than what she got to eat. Maybe his towels were softer, his soap more fragrant, his coffee more potent. But that transcendence could be bought, it could be sold, and most people knew nothing about these transactions. Brooke simply marveled. This was what money got you. This. Christ.

Sara knew not to say more. "It's a special piece."

Brooke wanted to say that her mother had a Frankenthaler. That it was funny that Asher Jaffee brought her to this anonymous Midtown room and showed her a Frankenthaler. That life sometimes organized itself around these motifs (not one car crash but two!) and you felt some responsibility to figure out what they meant.

Asher stroked the canvas, index finger dipping into that pool of blue. "Give me views. Rooms. An object. Something I recognize. The abstract stuff always feels like a test."

She didn't wait for permission or invitation. This was her purpose. Brooke's education in art history had well prepared her, as though some long-gone version of herself had foreseen this very moment. "That's the point. A mystery. A feeling." Brooke wasn't chiding him but wanted to. An abstract painting was the shadow of the painter's body in motion. An old man should understand that. "It's like everything. Cave painting. *Kilroy was here.* It's all human activity. It's meager, it's nothing. A shout into outer space." She pointed.

There it was. The painting still endured. That was the miracle of it. That was the profundity of it, an idea Helen Frankenthaler had decades ago and here it was. Asher alone, of the people in that room, could possess it. There was no justice there. It was a fact. "Immortality."

He liked this girl. He liked how she talked to him as he imagined he talked to others. Something about her almost reminded him of his mother, though what Ilona Jaffee would have made of that, who could say. "Who's doing the selling here? You work for Christie's now?"

Brooke knew that he wanted her to go on and so she did. "I don't know Mrs. Jaffee. But how could anyone look at this and not feel?"

Asher was exasperated. "That's my point. A litmus. If I don't get it, I'm at fault, I'm the one who's wrong."

"You are wrong." She was there to tell him the truth. "You like Monet." She knew he'd once owned that Monet. "You like Cézanne." She knew he still owned a still life. "You don't see how it's the same thing? She's finishing what they started. She's beating them. You don't see how Monet would have loved this? If he were here, what would he say? He'd say, *Yes, the sea, of course.*"

Asher sat back down. "They're motivated to sell?"

So this was what it was back to. Brooke couldn't hear this business about whether the number was competitive. She didn't even want to look at the painting. It felt strange to.

"There's of course so much more." Sara knew how to do this. "We have the whole world. If you'd like me to take some time—"

"No, this is it." There was no question anymore, was there? Immortality, as Brooke had told it. He liked that. "I need it out in

Connecticut. Before the twenty-first of July." Asher turned to his protégé. "You just cost me eight hundred and fifty thousand dollars."

Brooke had witnessed something that she barely understood. Eight hundred and fifty thousand dollars seemed both deranged and simply what it was worth. What that affectless room must have seen. Rich people come to acquire the thing they alone could; time itself. Asher asked her to call Christopher to fetch them.

T he city—her city, always had been—was revealed anew from the low back seat of Asher Jaffee's car. That one tower loomed taller, other buildings she'd never noticed presented themselves, and so much stuff: postboxes, telephone kiosks, dented trash cans, streetlights, wooden police barricades forgotten somehow, a great mess. She loved the place still. Strange how even her home now looked different: the kitchen drawer slipping out of place, the feces of some never-seen mouse peppering the cheap white stove, the condensation on the toilet tank dripping and pooling on the cracked tile. Brooke loved that place, too, still, maybe.

Brooke emerged from the shower as the coffee machine finished exhaling. Because National Public Radio had nothing positive to say (war underway somewhere far off, an M train rider *certain* she'd been pricked on her morning commute), Brooke put on optimistic, summery clothes. That distortion of time, not yet left but already thinking about returning home, slipping off dirty canvas sneakers and stepping into a cool shower. Keys in fist, Brooke switched off lights, rattled the door to test its lock, and descended into the world as a fire truck, not in emergency mode, glided past, pollen and dust in its wake.

She had learned to mix industry with distraction on her girlhood Sundays—mother and children itinerant: the diner, the playground, the homes of friends, the museum, the market. That was city life. Brooke wished that Matthew hadn't been busy, she wished that Kim had answered her texts, but was company enough for herself. She bought a bagel and more coffee. As the sidewalk tables were occupied by couples squinting with hangovers and friends dewy from spin class, Brooke settled inside, her stool facing the window, and did not pretend to read or be busy with her phone. She chewed and stared, a contented and pointless moment.

That vibration of someone standing too close. That prickle on the back, holdover instinct from when people were prey. Brooke barely had to swivel to see a redhead in a plaid shirt. Brooke prepared a gracious expression, but no apology was forthcoming. The other woman's attention was fixed on a too-big dog who did not want to sit. A mutt of indeterminate color with a tapered snout, the animal stretched against the green canvas lead. In her other hand, the woman held a drink, ice cubes clacking against the plastic. "Isaac, sit." She said it without affect, without conviction, with an air of resignation, and the dog, naturally, ignored this.

Had they been there, Brooke would have mouthed or whispered *Well, excuse me* to Matthew or Kim. But Brooke was alone. She turned her attention back to the street beyond the window, tried to find something fascinating there. She sat up straighter, made some kind of noise with the paper-wrapped bagel, cleared her throat a little. How had she gone unnoticed?

"Isaac, you're going to make me spill. Settle." The woman spoke as though dogs obeyed words instead of tone. The animal continued to stretch and fidget.

The stranger was too near. Some charge was between their bodies, an unwelcome intimacy. Since when could you bring dogs into restaurants? Now something knocked Brooke's head: the familiar bump of a cotton bag bearing too much stuff, the sort of thing you ignored on the subway but not inside a café. Brooke turned more fully toward the woman.

"Excuse me." She was no longer attempting apology, but employing the disappointed scold she had wielded, once upon a time, on a classroom of adolescents.

The redhead, straw in mouth, was rapt at the sight of her own phone.

"Excuse me."

"No, you're fine." The stranger was offering Brooke forgiveness.

But that was all wrong! "Your bag is bumping into me. Do you think you could—"

"I'm waiting for my order." Not the affectionate brusqueness one expected of city dwellers, but laconic, flat, rude.

"Maybe you could give me a little space—"

The dog paced and snorted like a thoroughbred before the Preakness. He barked, once, a sudden sound inside the small room.

A bearded barista approached with tentative hands. Conversation dimmed as everyone in the room eavesdropped. "Miss, maybe it would be better if you waited outside."

132

The woman was energized, spoiling for a set-to. "He is a service animal. I have a letter—"

"It's a little crowded—" He wasn't, he said with his voice, his posture, his being, paid enough for this.

"Well, he's a service animal and we have a right." The unhelpful Isaac chose this moment to lunge at the man, play indistinguishable from parry. The woman's bag smacked into Brooke again, this time harder, as she was pulled by the strong dog.

The room had that air of strangers united in common purpose. A subtle sound of disapproval as in a sitcom audience.

"He's fine." She meant the dog. "Settle, Isaac."

"Excuse me, I'm sitting right here. You just banged into me—"

"You see my dog is a little agitated. I'm waiting to be served."

There was a disapproving cluck of the tongue from somewhere. The spectators were alert and they had taken Brooke's side.

Something welled in Brooke. People couldn't be this way. Once, she'd have stood, left, a shake of the head to assert that she knew she had the high ground. Now it seemed that more was required. This stranger had a piece of paper attesting to her dog's rights. Brooke did not need a certificate to sit, to eat, to exist. "Excuse me."

The woman did not acknowledge her. She tapped her right foot but otherwise did not move.

That surge of adrenaline in the veins, that whirr of the overheating mind, a sense of possibility, of opportunity.

Maybe.

An arm outreached, a tentative touch on the shoulder as reminder of their shared humanity. Insincere apologies, rolled eyes, a heavy sigh; the illusion of tender peace.

No.

The yoga-toned arm has velocity, and the touch is a shove. Plastic and ice clatter across tile, and patrons frown, complain, and want to applaud as the underpaid barista shows two women and one dog to the door.

Or.

Instead of raised arm, a raised voice. Excuse yourself, how dare you, *fuck you*. Who said what and how? The woman's exit was pure theater, a huff, an adolescent tantrum.

But.

The same words, only now Brooke, sour metal of fury on her tongue, was following woman and dog onto the summer street.

There was violence in the air. It was on the subways, or so everyone kept claiming, but it was also inside Brooke, inside everyone, like microplastics. This was how the world was now and Brooke didn't even fear the dog's intercession—a nip, a bark, a bite—her mind a hot void. The woman at spitting distance, as they said, at pricking distance, you might also say. It began as touch then was something else as the woman stumbled forward. Brooke could not see the abraded skin, the woman's pinkness dappled with scarlet, nor could she see the blood around her loosened tooth.

All this, no, maybe, but, perhaps, all these possibilities, all these selves. Did she feel good? She did. Brooke knew the choreography, slipped into a purposeful pace, breathed deep on this dazzling day. Her phone was in her hand, maybe it had been there all this time, only now it reminded her, in the way it usually did, that she was alive. She looked at the time and was reassured that she was not late, though some minutes had been lost, hadn't they, slipped away from her, disobedient. She could not say, and would never have to, what she had done, what she had not done, where she had been, who she was.

Hillary waited, as they'd arranged, on the corner of Twenty-ninth Street. The breeze of passing traffic lifted her hair. "Brooke! Good to see you again." A salesman never forgot a face.

"What a morning." One of those days like a gift, optimistic boys stripping off their shirts in the park, sidewalks all couples hand in hand.

"We're going to start right here." Hillary pointed at the white brick building behind her. "Then three more stops. I'm here with any questions. What a day, huh? What a great day to find your own little slice of the city. Your new home."

They called it a white lie. No, Brooke didn't have the money, not then, not exactly, not for the down payment and the closing costs. Still, she had called Hillary, thinking the temporary problem would be easily solved. Her future was still assured, or it could be if she began now. "I'm ready," she said. A cloud moved past, freeing the sun from its bondage, and Brooke felt the warmth on her face, knowing that everything looked like a sign if you were in need of one.

The building was big but gave the impression of being small. Yes, the hallway carpets were frayed, the elevator poky, the doormen indifferent. There was that smell of airless interior space. It didn't put you off, but it didn't welcome you. Maybe that was why this apartment had sat unwanted so long. Brooke enjoyed the rite of greeting the seller's agent, pulling soft mesh sacks over your shoes, conferring in hushed tones as though there were a sleeping baby somewhere close by. There was a television on the wall like a painting. There was nothing in the kitchen because they wanted it to seem bigger and because they were selling a fantasy: a clean, efficient self, easy to contain within these walls. Brooke shuffled around, luxuriating in the unvarnished parquet beneath her soles while standing in the sky.

"Very nice." Hillary liked to reassure not the seller's agent and not her client but the apartment itself.

Brooke lingered in the living room and took in the vista. There was not that sweep down an avenue or toward the water, there was not some tantalizing glimpse of landmark. The view was a jumble of geometry, a Cubist thing implying the shape of the whole city beyond the reach of the eye. It reminded her of the street glimpsed from her mother's kitchen. It reminded her that this city was hers.

Brooke might never have seen this apartment. It was all chance, everything in life. Now, having stood here, she wanted it. She had arrived at herself.

The bathroom was too small. Its door opened the wrong way, out instead of in. There weren't enough cabinets in the kitchen. There was the sound of plumbing from someone else's apartment. But all the data—square footage, estimated taxes, board fees—could not communicate the thing most meaningful. Might as well list your beloved's height, weight, and eye color. Love was a synaptic flash, it was a chemical response, it was a hunch, it was a leap into the void. She could live anywhere, but this apartment would make Brooke the person she meant to be. The matter of money was a problem for later. Brooke had never had a problem that had gone unsolved.

Brooke didn't need Matthew or Kim along after all. She didn't need their perspective. She didn't hesitate. As the elevator closed them in: "I want it."

Hillary took her hand. The elevator's descent was so slow. "That's wonderful!" She meant it. Each and every time, Hillary was moved. She had brokered love.

Brooke thought it straightforward. "It felt right." There was something necessary about a home. If that was assured, you could face what the future held.

There seemed to be no one else on the street. There was birdsong, so the silence was less unsettling than surreal. The city fell away. Was someone, then, watching from some apartment overhead, seeing the tall white woman and the less-tall Black woman in conversation by the yellow fire hydrant? "It's important to listen to your instincts." But Hillary urged caution. "I usually give my clients twenty-four hours to think something over. It's prudent."

Brooke felt exhilarated, like an athlete victorious in some contest. She wanted to strip her own shirt off, feel the air on her body. It didn't matter at all, somehow, that she didn't have the money, the letter from the bank, the plan. That would come in time. Brooke knew that if she could intervene for Ghalyela and the Throop Community School, someone in turn would intervene for her. It was karmic. "There's not much for me to think over."

Hillary reminded her: shabby lobby, poorly maintained elevators, the fact that the place had not sold after weeks on the market. Brooke barely heard, and when Hillary broached the question of whether Brooke was, like Kim, a cash buyer, she demurred, changed the subject, drifted away, because their business was done for the day.

The evening air congealed into cloud but she hardly noticed. She didn't feel the asphalt beneath her shoes but the apartment's floorboards. She didn't hear the traffic or conversations of strangers but the sealed quiet of the place on the eleventh floor of that building on Twenty-ninth Street. There was such satisfaction in existing only within yourself. What she loved about urban life, to be among others but apart from them. An apartment, that apartment, would be that feeling, made concrete, made permanent, a self transubstantiated into walls and floors. She wouldn't even be a person anymore, but a place, much as a snail or a turtle manages the trick of being both. She needed something, an act of God if you like, but she would get it. Math didn't matter. Something was set in motion. Brooke did not care. She was in love and fairly danced into the lobby of her mother's building as there was a percussion of fat drops on the awning overhead.

The rain was falling heavily as Brooke entered the apartment, summer storm with multiple thunderclaps not quite in sync. But the windowless foyer felt as ever it did, a snug little enclosure, subtly lit. You wouldn't knock on the door you considered your own, so Brooke's entrance startled Rachel, who had one hand on the knob of the door to the powder room.

"Brooke!" Not yet quite family, Rachel was on her best behavior.

Brooke's hello was less enthusiastic than it ought to have been. A kind of madness and it took a moment to remember who this lovely curly-haired girl was. "Rachel."

"You look so—beautiful, Brooke. So alive. You had a good day?"

She had had a good day, she thought. She had seen the future for maybe the first time. It was right there. "It was a nice day. What about you?"

Rachel covered her face with her hands as though her smile were something she needed to physically restrain. "I have had—we have had. A day."

"Good one, I hope." Brooke leaned against the wall to release first one then another foot from her shoes. "I walked. Just beat the rain, I think."

"How are you with a secret?" Rachel's face made it plain that no matter what answer Brooke gave, she'd disclose this. It was too urgent not to.

"Good as most, I think." Brooke knew, as she said it. It was in the satisfaction of pretty Rachel's pretty face. "Let me guess. No wine with dinner."

"You can't tell your mom." Rachel looked abashed. "I can't believe it. We were not planning on this for a couple of years at least."

"It's great news, though." Brooke put a steady hand on Rachel's fine shoulder. "You'll get it out of the way. Be the youngest, hottest mom at the playground."

Rachel laughed, forgetting her own conspiratorial whisper. Then, quietly, "I'm happy. We're both. Of course. But we're going to keep it under wraps. Not a secret from you, though. Alex said you would get it. He said you could be trusted, not like the grown-ups. Your aunties. My folks. I hope he's not mad I told you without him!"

"He won't be." She knew her brother would have seen this secret as the opportunity to kindle sororal affection between the two women in his life. Brooke thought it mostly that Rachel was bursting with that urge to share something that had happened to her. Something that would make her special. It would show that she was progressing through life properly. She was to be admired. Brooke had felt the same way, still did, clomping into her mother's apartment with the intention of telling her family about the apartment she'd just seen, about her intention to remake her own life. Her little brother and his future bride were doing so; why shouldn't she?

W hen Rachel complimented the snacks, Maggie forced another on her. For Maggie, food was an index of love. Brooke watched this interaction and wondered whether she should have made a fuss. Someday she'd be unable to compliment her mother's cooking. Auntie Paige was dead. Kim's dad was dead. It happened to everyone, there was no justice, no escaping it.

The subject brought Rachel to their caterer. "The passed course, before the dinner. It's all vegan! You'd never notice unless I pointed it out."

Maggie was rapt. "Are you expecting a lot of vegan guests?" Kids today!

"We just felt it was responsible." Rachel put a possessive hand on Alex's bicep to underscore that *we*. "We'll have chicken and fish. But incremental choices can make a difference."

People's charming delusions. The idea of stuffed mushrooms staving off the planet's death. Brooke had learned how you really make a difference.

"Have you settled on bridesmaid dresses?" If Maggie felt the contradiction between the life she'd lived and this enthusiasm over her son's wedding plans, she was at peace.

Rachel showed off her phone. "They're grapefruit pink, but it's very subtle, hard to photograph. Brooke, you would look amazing in this color."

That matter was settled. Brooke would be her brother's best man. Brooke had gone to the formal-wear place down the hall from the foundation and been fitted for a suit meant for promgoing teens. "But I look incredible in my tux, if I do say so myself."

Maggie thought this irreverence but parents never understood. Brooke was so *lovely*—slight, finely wrought, with elegant hands, perfect posture, skin that was both dark and luminous, which did not seem possible. This deserved to be shown off! Yes, it was wrong to want her to be conventional, feminine, adorned, and adored, Maggie knew. She kept it to herself. "These two were absolutely obsessed with each other when they were small," she explained. "Even as teens. Never a fight I can remember." A favorite memory, a story often told, the day Maggie found toddler Brooke with baby brother's foot in her mouth. She loved him so much she wanted to consume him.

"Brooke's the best dude I know." Alex knew he'd done his beloved sister a favor, saving her from his bride. "It's the only possible solution."

"They say the wedding planning is the first test," Maggie said. "You're both so calm. This bodes well for the future."

"Speaking of the future." Brooke didn't want to talk about grape-fruit pink dresses. "I'm moving."

"What do you mean?" Maggie, collecting spent napkins, hadn't quite heard.

"I've been looking at places. And I think I found it. The one. I mean. Hillary, the broker, she's the one Kim used, she wants me to think it over. Give it a night. But I can just tell." She was talking more quickly than she'd meant to.

"I love your place," Alex said. "And it's kind of a deal."

"It's time to move on. It's time to move forward, I think." He was getting married, she wanted to say. And having a baby. Wasn't she allowed to grow up as well?

Maggie knew her daughter's salary, her expenses, her savings. "Your brother's right. Your place is a steal. Maybe it's prudent to sit tight there another year or two. Concentrate on saving."

"I have confidence it'll work out. The market is just climbing every day. Why wait? Why not get in on—well, not the ground floor, but the eleventh." It was as obvious to her as the munificence of the oyster or the genius of Helen Frankenthaler. But Brooke was gentle. They hadn't seen for themselves what she had.

Maggie tried not to lecture. "The bank is going to want you to have been in this new job a bit longer. It shows that you're a steady person. Reliable. True, you were at your old job for a while but that didn't work out—"

Brooke knew this was how people, including herself, until recently, thought: that money, like grace, would be accrued. "I'm a steady person. With a good job. I'm not that worried about what the bank is going to say. I can sense that this is the right next step." She didn't want to say *I'm serious* because it would sound like a ten-year-old stomping a foot.

"It's not a feeling. It's a transaction." Her child was a dreamer. Her child was unlike her.

Brooke knew about transactions. On her say-so, Asher Jaffee had spent almost a million dollars on a gift for his wife. Transactions were her business. "I know what it is. I know what I'm doing."

Rachel had rightly gone quiet, as this was not her affair. Alex, ambassadorial, tried to change the subject. "I think it's exciting. It's a big year for us. We're getting married, you're moving—"

"I hate to see you get in over your head. That's all I'm saying. There are always unforeseen things. Complications." At eight, Brooke had become fixated on a Barbie Dreamhouse. Scissored it out of an unwanted Sears catalog, pasted it into a spiral notebook. Child of New York, what was more exotic to her than a house: cutaway ceiling so you could manipulate those plastic avatars, the double front doors, the louvered windows, the skylights. A mother could only see most of what a daughter did as childish whim.

"If that's how you feel, maybe you can help out. As I assume you're helping with the aforementioned wedding." Brooke leaned back into the downy sofa. Her point had been made. Some barrier had been crossed. They were so keen for Rachel to be a part of the family, then let her hear.

"Look," began Alex, peacemaker, the easygoing one.

"I don't think that's fair at all," Maggie said. She hated how often things came down to money.

Rachel busied herself with the cheese straws. She felt hot in her cheeks.

"I'm helping out," Maggie continued. That was normal. That was what parents did. "It's not very much."

"I don't need very much," Brooke said. She wanted only something small. An apartment. A modest one. One bedroom. A place to be truly herself, apart from the world and the systems that governed it. "I don't see how it's different from Alex and Rachel. It's about what's fair."

"Don't turn it into some—thing," said Maggie. "Don't make it all about money."

But everything was about money, already, and that was not by Brooke's design. "I'm not trying to—"

A mother knew her children. This was Brooke, but this was not her. Maggie felt responsible. That there was some sour feeling she had not noticed, envy put simply, to do with Alex and Rachel. "We'll discuss this. But this isn't the time."

It was the time, Brooke did not say, because her mother's frustration and her brother's embarrassment were the answer she needed. She might yet count on Maggie for a guilty contribution equal to whatever subsidy she was providing for Alex's wedding. But Brooke didn't want to come by her future that way, pleading and arguing for her right to some happiness. She would, instead, demand something. That was how you got things done, that was how you lived. "Now," she said, "is the time." She was mostly talking to herself, or she was the only one listening to what she had to say.

B rooke had been granted access to all the Asher and Carol Jaffee Foundation had at its disposal, and was shrewd enough to understand that one of its greatest assets was Jody. They huddled in the office's empty corners, so many of those, conspiring.

Brooke said that she couldn't imagine anyone turning their nose up at a blank check.

"It's sacred, to her," Jody said. "If she invites you and Asher into the school that she has built, she risks losing control."

"We don't want to take over. We want to help." Aunt Allison's simple phrase—*How can I help?*—was that woman's entire philosophy. Asher Jaffee's, too. Now Brooke's.

Jody had palms on the round table cluttered with paper. "What is the story of Throop Community School, and how do we tell that story, to Asher Jaffee, to the rest of the world?" She was narrating something, she was beginning the tale. "How can the Jaffee Foundation support this work? How can we replicate this success in other organizations? Asher is looking to make a big impact. We need the learnings from this one case to have a broader impact."

Brooke knew just how to reach Asher. Souls. Black souls. Her own. "But the problem now seems to be how to explain the story of the foundation, of Asher, to Ghalyela." How would you persuade a woman to love money?

"That's the easy part, Brooke. Trust me. Why don't I go with you. Schedule something. We can put on a show." Jody liked her younger colleague, was happy to help, and also Jody was a little bored. There was not much for her to do, though no one looked askance at her invoices.

The appointed day, Ghalyela was thirty minutes late. Brooke and Jody sat on those folding metal chairs in the little anteroom that smelled of wet umbrella. Brooke felt abashed, like a child she'd never been, sent to be disciplined, waiting for a tribunal. It was Jody's habit to have no emotional response to anything in her work. Being a consultant required this psychic armor. When mother and daughter arrived, their tardiness gave the encounter the well-meaning antagonism of surprise party or intervention. Ghalyela, in white as ever, didn't shake hands but offered an aristocratic nod.

Michaela was apologetic and a dynamic was established—good cop, bad cop, or perhaps friendly cop, reticent cop. Four women in an almost-empty room in an often-empty church, asking searching questions. It was like Bible study or an AA meeting.

"I understand what you do," said Jody. "Tell me what you need."

"Sister. That is it. We don't need anything." Ghalyela thought this was the crux of it.

Michaela gave a little click of tongue against teeth. She had more latitude than these strangers. She had a more modern attitude. "Mama."

"We are not in need." This was plain. Some were, some were not. It was not a question of shame. Luck and God's grace and a million other factors were at play. She had entertained these overtures from well-meaning people more than once over the years. But she had made a life, for herself, her family, her community. "If your boss wants to give away money, that's his right. It is a blessing. You don't have to look very hard to find someone in need."

Brooke had failed to tell it properly. The gift of money was not a story of shame but triumph; it wasn't a story of being humbled but being blessed. She needed to explain to the older woman how to live. To demand more than you had. To think like those people who were victors over life. "It's not a handout. It's an investment. Maybe that is a better way to think about it."

"You come here and tell me that I must need something." Ghalyela was resolute. "But, sister, I did not ask you here. And I did not tell you that we were in need."

Brooke's pride had never mattered that much, because she'd always been assured of it. It was different for a woman Ghalyela's age. "What about. Want. Ambition? Hope. What do you hope?" She was cribbing from Obama without realizing it.

Michaela tried to soften her mother, some mix of embarrassment and intrigue. She had done her googling. She understood that real money was at stake. "That's an idea."

Ghalyela had an articulate body, a dancer's body, and didn't have to bother with words. Her posture said that Brooke hadn't truly asked before. No one had ever asked her what she wanted. That was life, she figured. If you're not given everything, you find it for yourself. No, she didn't need anything. But she hoped for plenty.

"We're talking about dreams." Jody understood. "Everyone has those. I'm sure you've had such ideas—what a stable budget might allow you to do."

"I have dreams." Ghalyela could access those. She was less certain if she could share them. You didn't simply chat about such things. They were important.

Brooke could see that the woman was considering it. Like a child facing off against the flickering birthday candles, she was wondering what to ask of the universe. Brooke should have spoken to Ghalyela as Asher had spoken to her. This was a seduction, and like any, it had reached the moment for candor. "We have an opportunity. You have an opportunity. We don't know. We can't tell you what to do. But we can hear what you want, we can work to make that happen."

"You understand that this is my school. I've heard this so many times over the years. Grants, gifts, whatever. My scholars' parents have ideas about how I can improve things, get more money, because that's what they mean, they don't mean improvement, they mean money. But in my experience it comes at a cost."

"Asher Jaffee was a CEO. That's over now. These gifts, there are no strings attached." Brooke was fairly certain this was true.

The old woman knew what she most wanted. "A home." Ghalyela said it many times to people who were willing to truly listen to her. "A place to be. Where my scholars will be safe, and loved. A place they know they can count on." That was what was missing in their city, in their neighborhood; a place of safety, an anchorage. You needed a home to be a person, and the world had conspired to make some believe that this was, perhaps, too much to ask.

Michaela was watching this intently. She thought it, herself: that was too much to ask. But Asher Jaffee had a lot of money to get rid of.

"Real estate." All that time spent helping Eileen sort out her paperwork meant that Brooke was privy to a secret. "It just so happens that the foundation is engaged in a big gift, at the moment, of real estate."

Jody cleared her throat and hoped it communicated caution. "The real estate gift is a complicated one. A separate matter." She cared about her work. She cared about doing good. But she cared, mostly, about satisfying her boss. This was all dreams and chitchat. This was a junior employee getting carried away.

Brooke interrupted. "You're on that project, right, Jody? As you say, this would be so much simpler, in the scheme of things. So easy!"

Ghalyela had thought it a bluff at first, but now it seemed the correct answer, the thing to demand. "You understand what's happening in this zip code? All over the city. They called it blight. The city left our parents here with nothing. Now it's what everyone wants. A million dollars, two million dollars, for what used to be a rooming house. For what they liked to call a crack house. There always was value here. But now you can put a dollar amount on it. Seven figures. Where is that money going?"

"We can invest in Throop Community School. Make a physical space in the community a reality." Brooke could see it as she said it. No more damp church basement. No depending upon the goodwill of the local school principal.

There were limits to Jody's sway here—a consultant was not really a conscience. She did not even sigh. "There are steps. A feasibility study. We don't have to go too into the weeds at this stage. But what we need is a proposal. What we need is an ask." She didn't say what she truly believed: that she could never bother one of America's most prominent businessmen with the sob story of a woman in a church basement who hoped to teach children how to dance.

"You came to us." Michaela was as shrewd as her mother. "We don't have the time, or the interest, to jump through hoops for a favor we didn't ask for in the first place."

"Nothing like that." Brooke was resolute. "This is part of the gift. My work, our work, our time. We need you to be partners but there's a lot at stake."

"We cannot measure everything in terms of money." Ghalyela knew this was important. "I told you before. No one gets something for nothing. I need to understand the cost. I have a responsibility to my scholars, to my school, and I cannot spend my time on day-dreams."

Brooke let it pass. So much could, in fact, be measured in terms of money. "I wouldn't be here if I didn't think we had the chance to do something significant. That the Asher and Carol Jaffee Founda-tion could do something lasting and real for your school, for this neighborhood."

Jody was the one who had told Brooke to tell a story and now Jody found herself persuaded by it. "We do have a lot of experience in making these gifts. In helping organizations like yours plan for the future."

Ghalyela was a philosopher. She didn't know how secure the fu-ture ever was. Money was a hedge against that, just like faith, or superstition, or the thousand other strategies people used to survive a day. She was the only person in the room old enough to comprehend this. "A home. You asked and that is what I want. If you can provide that, then we have something to discuss. If you cannot, I have other responsibilities."

"I'll work on it, Mama." Michaela thought that she knew something her mother did not. She thought this was generational. "I can be your point person. I can be the one you bother."

"There is rather a lot we need to get through." Jody spoke of due diligence, of budgets, operating costs, enrollments, nonprofit status, legal protections.

"There's always that. The work." Brooke believed. She wanted to luxuriate in this success. "Let's take a minute to acknowledge a new partnership. A step toward a new future." But they were not holding champagne flutes. They were four women in the basement of a church in Brooklyn, the vague hiss of summer rain in the distance. Nothing much had been accomplished, but Brooke thought the occasion momentous all the same.

This was their place, or they were proprietary about it, but so was everyone who crowded around them. You could only be fond of this funny bar where the Central American staff wore cheap old-fashioned blazers and ruled by caprice, inflating the cost of a cocktail by two bucks if they had a certain feeling about you, sending free bread and olives if they had another. They'd once been too young to understand that the simple food was in fact not very good, that the untidy bathroom was not charming but gross, that the ceiling was too low so it always felt stuffy in there. Now they were tethered to the place by an affection for the kids they'd been together.

Someone had played ABBA on the jukebox, and this made it still harder to hear. "How's the move going?" Brooke cupped an ear with a palm as if that might help her understand Kim's answer.

"I decided to do some work. Eeyore is generously letting me extend my stay."

"Long as the rent check clears." Matthew, who had won the favor of the bartender, pulled apart a loaf of free bread.

Brooke couldn't imagine how that apartment might be improved. "You're renovating?"

"Nothing major. Two or three months max. I just didn't want to sublet. Or move back to Mom's place. You know, I'm kind of getting into it. I hired this decorator my mom knows, and it's been so fun— no, interesting, actually, working with her. I'm thinking that maybe that's something I could do."

One of the things Matthew liked about Kim was that she was game. He'd come home from work and persuade her to bake one of those cylinders of prepared cookie dough in a giant skillet, rewatching *Sex and the City*, shaking drinks into chilled glasses right on the summer stoop. It might have chafed to watch her flit from one not-quite job to another, but that was her life. "I could see that for you. Color schemes. Choosing fabrics."

Kim allowed herself to be excited. "It's not that far from fashion, I don't know. I'm thinking of asking her, when we're done with my place, if I can, like—learn the ropes."

She did not intend to, but Brooke laughed.

"You don't think I could?" Kim's pretty face, expressive as a toddler's, hardened a little.

"It's not that." Brooke was distracted by the men beside her. Their voices seemed put on, still a hint of squeak beneath that studied, masculine basso. They were discussing either a band or a woman or a television show. "I didn't mean to laugh. I was just. We're thirty-three. It's time to decide who you're going to be."

Kim lifted her glass to her lips but did not drink. She may have looked otherwise but she would defend herself. "I hear that. But you know. To be fair, I recall you spitballing about careers six months ago. Maybe I'm a late bloomer. But I don't remember laughing when you were like *Maybe I should go to law school,* or whatever."

Matthew understood the situation. He sighed like a put-upon father and played referee. "First, you're being rude. Second, Kim's right. You took this job because it was the only one. The only good interview. The only actual offer. We remember. We were there. I'm glad you like it, but you're talking like it was your lifelong mission to work for Asher Jaffee when we all know otherwise. Because we were there listening to you complain about your old job and how you couldn't find a new one for the past five years."

"Why are you attacking me?" Then, horribly, Brooke began to laugh again. It was outside her control, like hiccups. She held up hands in surrender. "Forget I said anything."

"But you did say something." Matthew was calm. "You think we're too old to decide who we are, so who are you? All this change-the-world stuff, you're on fire with it. Fine, good. But Kim can't be an interior designer? There's a contradiction."

The place was crowded, bodies at her back. These people were variations on a theme, alternate selves. Maybe your demographic was your destiny. Maybe they, maybe she, was the same as everyone else in the place—thirtysomething, world-weary, prepared to spend fourteen dollars on a cocktail. Brooke wanted to be a different person. It came with such clarity that it was frightening. Change her. Save her. "Sorry. Kim. Be a decorator. You'd be amazing at that. You have beautiful taste. And you don't need the money anyway."

Kim frowned down into the bar. *This is too far,* she thought, *or a place we've never gone.*

"Another low blow, Brooke. But if I may." Matthew saw the opportunity. Something had shifted and they were being honest. "You don't believe all this razzmatazz. All this song and dance. All this *heal the world, make it a better place* like you're Michael Jackson."

The men beside them were onto a new subject, Obama, Cuomo, someone. Why did their chat sound so familiar? Comic timing, a roll of an eye, an exaggeration with the pronunciation of certain words. This was how people talked now, as though the pleasure in their conversation was in their performance, their interpretation of a script provided for them. She hated it. What had happened to everyone? A real moment, that was what was warranted, that was what eluded her. A sincere experience. Something honest. "My boss asked me. Well, you wouldn't understand. I'm not his employee. I'm his protégé. He's challenged me to bring him an arts organization deserving of his money. Just find someone. Give them money. It's harder than it sounds but I did it. So, yes, I believe in what I'm doing."

"We're happy for you." Matthew's *we* revealed that he and Kim had discussed this. "I remain skeptical that some old white guy is up to only good stuff. Madoff redux, right? Maybe that's my problem. I won't try to talk you down, but then maybe you can return the favor and not talk to Kim like that."

This again, the tight bond between Kim and Matthew, from which she was excluded. It had something to do with their having lived together, she was sure of it. She'd known Kim all her life! "Kim. You have money. It's not a secret. Why can't I say that?" Brooke thought of the apartment on Twenty-ninth Street. No sunken living room, no Hudson view, but the place would be the thing to which she could tether her life. It would be her spouse, hold close her secrets, promise a steadfastness that people could not. People failed. The real estate market did not.

Kim spoke at last. "I never said it was a secret. My dad's money has nothing to do with who I am, it has nothing to do with us."

Brooke laughed again. "You wouldn't be considering a career as an interior designer right now if not for that money. Let's not pretend."

"Maybe honesty isn't always the best policy." There was the threat of tears so Kim's eyes darted this way and that, as if they could be outmaneuvered.

Matthew ran his hands over his head. "Brooke, I don't see what you think is gained by talking about this right now."

"It's the only thing to talk about," Brooke said. "It's the whole world. Kim's money means that her every need, her every want—a new career, maybe—is hers. We all have things we need. I'm trying to succeed at work. And I'm trying to buy an apartment myself, just so you know. I've got a lot going on."

Matthew finished his drink. At work, at the agency, daily, they invoked a hypothetical customer's *wants* and *needs*. The gospel of advertising, the gospel of America. He collected himself. "It's not the only thing to talk about," he said. "It's not the whole world." He hoped that was what he believed but was not quite certain.

Brooke looked at her two oldest friends and felt, strangely, nothing.

He'd have guessed that old age would be the same as any. You were just yourself, the body's changes immaterial. Not exactly. The body told some truth about the self. The low-sodium diet and you couldn't conjure the taste of salt. The teetotal life and you forgot about wine. Salt and wine! You believed they were elemental but then you just never thought about them. You woke before five, before the damn birds, an abrupt fall into awareness, and knew precisely why. There were only so many hours left. Don't squander them on sleep! Carol's breath was a reliable cadence, and Asher Jaffee put on a shirt and went downstairs.

Mornings he could be alone. There were so many people, so much of the time. There was Agatha, the Polish house cleaner, who lived in, and the two women in her employ, who did not. He could never remember their names, these silent figures in hospital scrubs, intent on something, scurrying out of any room he wandered into. There was Grey, catchall helper, whom Asher knew was de facto man of the house: the lifting of heavy objects, the technological problems of the television, the instructions to the Spanish-speaking gardeners. There was his driver, Christopher, and Carol's driver, Shimon, who, when not piloting or washing the cars, lingered in the kitchen, sipping coffee and talking about the cars. There was Mark, the personal trainer, a homosexual with dyed hair and Olympian physique. Come to think of it, he might have competed in the Olympics at some point. There was Stephanie, Carol's personal assistant, and there was Marina, the chef, who preached veganism but would roast a chicken, grind beef into a tartare, stun raw fish with lime, whatever Asher's heart desired. There was the party planner, the shopper who also handled alterations, the once-a-month doctor and nurse. There were yet others about, whom Asher did not even see, names he'd never learned, faces he'd never recognize, the people who put soap in the guest bath, made sure there was food in the cabinets, watered the houseplants, picked errant leaves from the beds of white gravel, ensured the bicycle tires were always plump with air, cleaned the mud from the soles of the boots they wore to tour the grounds, whisked out-of-date magazines out of sight, left the mail in neat piles on his or Carol's desk.

So, this early-morning solitude was a blessing. Even a man who loved people needed the occasional respite from them. The last thing Marina did, nights, was fill the coffee maker. It was rigged to a timer. There, waiting for him, was the mug he liked, a teaspoon on a linen napkin. Silly that in the quiet of the day's start, Asher felt connected to some past self, that he was once more a competent participant in real life. He opened the refrigerator, perused the labeled jars of oats and quinoa and berries softened overnight into mush studded with slivers of almond. There were bowls of cool, sweet pineapple and chubby hothouse strawberries, hulled by Marina, who steeped the cuttings in water that she used to prepare refreshing juices. She deplored waste. Asher had requested pastries and Marina baked fist-size muffins of grated carrot, coconut, sunflower seed, date.

Grey would bring the paper in when he arrived but that was hours away yet. Someone—who?—had plugged in the sleek little computer in the breakfast room, just for him. Asher sat with coffee and muffin, flicking at the screen, turning virtual pages. He was inattentive to the crumbs, having unlearned the decorum his mother had instilled in her children. Still, though, he could hear her Brooklyn voice, her one-liners: "You want a maid, check into the Waldorf Astoria." His mother had made him, and she had made him want a maid. Asher had employed dozens over the course of his life. As a joke so private that it was for him alone, when he was divorcing Barbara, Asher had stayed at the Waldorf for months.

That sudden bleed from night to morning—day was inevitable, so why was it always a surprise? The pink crowded out the shadows. The grass was hysterical with dew. The birds were common but their optimism was a balm. Living in the country—they called it the country though it was the suburbs—was Carol's idea. She liked a bite at La Goulue, a movie at the Paris, a Vesper at Bemelmans, but she *loved* tromping through the underbrush, tossing a stick into a pond and watching the setters lose their minds. She had grown up in St. Paul. Asher had come to understand that this was pleasure: simple, quotidian, the body in the world, no matter how much age had changed it.

His trade was the search for information: bombs, elections, a Malaysian airplane vanished beneath the sea. Only God could say what it *meant*. You had to infer or, failing that, ask the right questions. What would that plane do to the price of Boeing, the behavior of the Chinese economy, the politics in the area. That was his work, interpretation, men like Asher no different from critics or philosophers: guesswork, hunches, ideas. Instead of virtue or sin, there was gain or loss. It was all attended by risk, the quality that made it thrilling, as salt made a margarita delicious, as death made life worth living.

There was still money, yes, ever in flux, like the unobserved multiplication and death of cells. Asher said he intended to ignore it. He was giving it away. That was the business he was in now. But old habits! Obama had pulled off the trick of righting a panicked economy and Asher hadn't been able to resist getting in the game again. It felt good just to play, better yet to realize he still had a genius for this. He knew that his advisers thought Asher's office on Thirty-sixth Street nothing more than simulacrum, like those old-age homes that comfort dementia-addled seniors with decor reminiscent of Eisenhower and sock hops. There was soothing Natalie, there was that big Philip Guston, a present from the Japanese, who really knew how to give a present, there was even a staff. The advisers indulged the big boss.

Then the advisers began calling, realizing that he'd made a windfall. Carol got involved. This was just so much money! It seemed a matter apart from his promises of charity made in the *Huffington Post*. This was money he had only just made! Asher held off his advisers but could hardly ignore his wife, so it all became his early-morning thoughts. He'd pledged to give away a fortune and then made another. It was a rhetorical matter more than an ethical one.

For so long, Asher had said that his life changed on 9/11. The veracity of words repeated so often did not matter, the same principle as prayer. After Linda died, Asher thought it was a bill come due, karma. But what had he done that was so bad? Had he not tried to be good? Should he not continue, now, to try? Those first months, sleep eluded him: a dryness in the mouth, a trouble with swallowing, the unpredictable movements of his mind.

He consulted a psychiatrist called Simpson, a fat brunette with a pained look in her eyes. He wanted a pill, he told her.

How Dr. Simpson had laughed at this. "You think there's some solution."

He said there were solutions to every problem he'd ever had. Look at him. King of the world. Luckiest man alive. How did she think he'd got where he had? By finding the answers that eluded other people, lazier people, stupider people.

"You'll never get over this, Asher. This is who you are now. Bereavement mellows. It never vanishes. It's not an absence or a lack even. It's more present than that. It's a change. That's life's nature. It changes."

He liked who he had been. He didn't want to change, certainly not against his will. More laughter from Dr. Simpson.

Asher had eventually broken off their sessions. The woman irritated him. The raw feeling was not to do with Linda's death. Dr. Simpson saw what was ridiculous about him. She was the first person he'd spoken to in years who was honest with him. He was not a king in a castle. He was a spoiled little prince. He had lost touch with reality, no matter how many newspapers he read. His facility with money was a pointless skill, like juggling, a diversion for a child. That was what he was, in his ninth decade. Funny, what he found irksome in the shrink was what he liked in Brooke. She was candid with him in a way no one else dared be. Headstrong and handsome, like someone Katharine Hepburn would play in a film, alluring because she refused to try to win him over. Sunday morning thinking of Brooke. Would she also be thinking of him?

Some shredded carrot fell to the table. It would go unnoticed for hours, faint vegetal color leaching into the white marble. Someone would clean it. What would his father say about the oversize table, hell, about the whole ersatz English manor with its creaky wood floors and hand-painted wallpaper, set amid topiaries and gardens. What would his mother say about the existence of a vegan muffin? *Vegan? What is this? Some new fruit?* There it was. He was just an old man sitting at a table and thinking about his mommy. Asher prided himself on being able to laugh at himself, and so he did. Perhaps now he was ready for Dr. Simpson, equal to the task of picking his own psyche apart. But why bother? He understood! He woke at four because he was almost out of time. He was as resigned to his own death as one could be.

He saw the problem with the latter two thirds of his life. You had to want something. If you had everything, life held no point. That old saw. That old moral from fairy tales that every human society had ever come up with: gratified wishes turn out to be a curse. He had purpose now, because there was something he wanted—to give it all away, to feel good, no, to be good. Maybe to think about Brooke was the same; a goal to keep him alive.

A Friday morning like every other. Carol emerged from her night, dropped a kiss on his forehead. The personal trainer guided Asher through stretches and movements. A hot shower, a plate of warm barley and shaved asparagus. Carol was eager to talk about Michelle, the most especially beloved of her nieces. They were paying her tuition at Stanford, so the girl felt bound by honor to call often. They walked the grounds and Carol extolled Michelle's academic rigor, her ineffable charms, her beauty.

Carol's feeling about Michelle seemed not unlike his about Brooke. He didn't say that. He only listened to his wife. But he thought about Brooke, whom he considered a mystery. This relationship to her niece, Asher could see, gratified some part of Carol, maybe the ego. To know this girl, to be tied to her by blood, however tenuously, to be the one responsible for her education, satisfied Carol. He let her enjoy this without mentioning Brooke. Not because it was secret or unspoken, nothing was, but because he didn't want to lay claim to his wife's happiness. But he understood because he felt something similar. Maybe this was among the things he now wanted, those wants that were keeping Asher Jaffee alive. He couldn't say what it was he wanted of Brooke because that did not matter, to know it. He loved Carol. Her happiness mattered more to him than his own did. In fact, Asher was learning, at the end of his life, that he did not matter at all.

Brooke wanted something. No: she deserved it. She had called in sick, a white lie though she was feeling worn down, so why not order in? A bacon, egg, and cheese sandwich, a side of Tater Tots, a hot concoction closer to chocolate milkshake than cup of coffee. No one would ever know besides her and Hanif, the Somali who delivered the stapled bag to her door. She didn't have to excuse indulgences that no one else could observe. Or at all.

She opened the sack, humid with steam, and turned on the television. The warmth of the food on her lap dissipated into her body, and the palliative television dulled her mind. She ate. She watched. She sipped the chocolate coffee. The morning passed, and she didn't feign concern about it. This was something Brooke had learned from observing Ghalyela. The word for the business the foundation was in was *charity*, but Ghalyela didn't want that. She took care of herself because she figured the world never would. Instructive. Brooke could give herself joy, small and private. She wanted nothing more, in this moment, than what was at hand. How often was that true?

Hours moved as ever they did, the dull palaver of reality television, the business of putting rubbish away, unpacking laundry, arranging the various objects you owned where you wanted them to be. Hunger came upon her again and she was ashamed until she realized she'd spent several hours doing nothing at all. Still, to want more, after such a big breakfast. She could thus far rely on yoga, youth, and luck, but the last would be poor bulwark against time's passage. She would thicken, soften, sag, age; we all did. There was generally, for Brooke, little interest in the question of her parentage. *True* wasn't even the fair word for it. Maggie was her mother, biology something else. Anyway, there were few questions unresolved about herself, and what could a total stranger have to tell her? But Brooke knew that our mothers were a glimpse of our future. Was her skin luminous, was her waist narrow, were her eyes wide, were her hands soft? As there was no sense of what awaited her, she used lotion and the gym.

Hillary called as Brooke was coming back inside from taking out the garbage. Brooke picked up and began to pace, which was how she handled such conversations.

"I'm calling about Twenty-ninth Street." There was a steadiness to Hillary's voice. Her business was emotional and so she tried to remain cool. "I heard back from the agent and the sellers have accepted your offer. Congratulations!"

Yes, a formal offer. Who cared? Brooke wanted it and said so. Hillary was talking about the timeline—one week, two weeks— but Brooke did not listen. The when and the how would come. There was happiness with an edge of nausea. Mostly Brooke felt relief. She didn't want anyone else to step on those beautiful floors, be annoyed by that weird bathroom door. That apartment was hers, or would be. She just needed the money. It was not so big a deal.

Her heart filled too much. She needed to do something with this feeling in her body. Get out into the city berserk with that summer energy. Out there among the college kids walking in too-large packs, the old people muttering to themselves, the harried parents pushing strollers, the girls swilling Frappuccinos, the girls leaving the gym, the girls walking to the grocery with reusable totes on their shoulders, the girls who, like her, had no real aim. There were deliverymen on bikes and people smoking cigarettes and, as ever, dogs shitting. There was music trickling onto the street from somewhere. No one was looking at her. No one knew anything about her and there was nothing to fear in that. Indeed, that was the point; that was the city.

Brooke didn't think about down payments, mortgage rates, closing costs, math. You could not solve an equation with too many unknowns; she remembered that from high school algebra. No, she didn't think about lawyers or banks or inspections. You couldn't worry about such things, or worry would always be waiting for you when you were prepared to face it. Sure, Brooke had lied, sure, she was lying even now. Sure, you might call it fraud but you could as well call it bluff. Much as she had solved problems Ghalyela didn't know that she had, Brooke would turn to her own soon. X would equal something. She'd written a fairy tale, herself its heroine, something to do with the apartment that fit like Cinderella's slipper, something to do with destiny, and it was as yet not clear to her if Asher Jaffee was the prince or the fairy godmother, all her problems dispatched either by a kiss or a wave of the wand.

This feeling was all that Brooke wanted in life. To merge into the traffic of life; to withdraw from it when she wished. That was the whole point of the apartment, wasn't it? It would provide her a place from which to observe all this. It would be her refuge from all this. It would answer who she was or would be; she was the woman who lived on Twenty-ninth Street.

She walked uptown from her apartment. The buildings grew taller. The blocks were coated with afternoon's shadows. There were tourists craning necks to take in the Empire State Building, buying toy taxis from a sidewalk vendor, hopping onto or off of buses with upper decks open to the air. People had claimed patches of Bryant Park with old blankets. There was a busker with a few dollar bills in his guitar case. Men in business casual swarmed, common as pigeons.

Somehow so fitting that the store was beside a cathedral. She chose the profane over the sacred. The air was perfumed. Too-groomed women posed at glass counters teeming with bounty: creams, fragrances, scarves, wallets. In little naves off the main floor, men in slim-cut suits handled handbags as though they were newborns. People milled, examined, considered, fretted. Brooke waded past this to the elevators, rode to the fourth floor: diaphanous things on heavy hangers, shoes with the perverse smell of uncorrupted leather, belts coiled like snakes on wooden tables.

She could regret the twenty-one dollars wasted on breakfast or she could spend still more. Perhaps what she needed was to get rid of it all; perhaps then the salvation she believed in would arrive. It was American. If she couldn't be rich, she could at least possess some of what rich people did. To participate in this would get her nearer to that apartment. Or it was patriotic.

Sequestered in a fitting room, with its powerful air-conditioning, its revelatory light, its honest mirrors. The door closed, there was no sense of other people, she was alone in the world, safe with these lovely things. There were jeans of stiff denim that had never yielded to another body, a thick plastic security tag piercing the waist. She turned. She evaluated. She posed. She took these off, folded them up, put them onto the upholstered chair provided. Brooke put on a navy dress, austere, modest, a brass zip up its back that she couldn't quite reach. It didn't matter. The dress left the impression of a beautiful body, concealed. It revealed her, didn't it: young, elegant, powerful. Impossible not to hold yourself higher. It was a glimpse of the future, a foretelling but also a hope. This jacket, cotton and collarless, didn't it make her look as she ought to? A V-neck, cashmere so thin you could see right through it, didn't it feel made only for her body?

She moved with utter control, garments slung over a forearm. A salesgirl relieved her of these things. Brooke sat on an Ultrasuede sofa and stepped into shoes, something architectural and leather, something sensible and low to the ground, something sweet and barely there. The sounds of the place—the music playing, the muted conversations of other shoppers—fell away.

She thought of Rachel and Alex, loose on the uppermost floors of Bloomingdale's, zapping at whatever caught their fancy, the things they decided other people owed them. Rachel had said it was silly, childhood dream of a shopping spree, but you had to say that kind of thing. If Rachel could see her now! Or Kim, with her command of fashion. Would she approve of the dress, the jacket, the jeans, the sweater? Would she flinch at what it all cost, wonder how Brooke was going to get away with this? But didn't Brooke deserve something, too?

"That's everything?" The salesgirl was delighted.

It was everything. The dress, zipped into a vinyl bag. Those jeans. A little leather belt. The sweater thin as a spiderweb. These were layered in tissue, precious, fragile. The black shoes, spindly and dangerous, and red shoes, small, nothing to them at all. Each fragrant and potent, each in its own heavy box with embossed lid. Then more, why not, still more, a lipstick, something between red and brown; a crème that promised to do something to the skin beneath your eyes; a balm for the hands that smelled of clouds. All of this in a bag, two, so sturdy, so lovely, so solid; the softness of the bag's rope handles in her palm made Brooke feel alive. She put down the mint-green corporate card with a satisfying little snap of plastic on wood. What difference was there between Brooke the person and the Asher and Carol Jaffee Foundation, really? The tiny sound of the card on the table was Brooke's contribution to the symphony of American commerce, a whisper that said she was there, she was alive, she was this person, she was worthy of these things, and deserved so much more than she had.

Brooke thought this was a strategy session, the usual Monday-afternoon business, a private consultation, even a stab at détente. So Brooke came armed with papers in their folders, imagined facts and figures, alluring hypotheticals. Michaela had mentioned, meaningfully, that her mother would not be in attendance. But she was not, as Brooke expected, alone: she shared a table with a stranger with perfect posture and braids down her back. Introductions were made. Alissa McDonald, old friend from the neighborhood, daughter of a Montessori teacher and lifer in the Manhattan branch of the Internal Revenue, raised in a brownstone not two blocks over, was now a candidate for city council.

The glass-and-chrome place was bright and clean as an operating theater. The steamy shriek of the espresso maker; they might have been anywhere. "Nice to meet you."

"I've been after Michaela for this meeting." Alissa had the cozy tone of someone who believed they were born to politics.

Michaela looked guiltily at Brooke's file folders. "I hope that's okay. Not exactly official business. We've known each other a long time." Michaela's hand on Alissa's hand. "Basically, anything that happens, I talk to Alissa. I call her a one-woman think tank."

Brooke almost said that Kim and Matthew provided the same for her, but it seemed, just then, not quite accurate. She nodded to say *go on.*

Alissa fancied herself someone who spoke plainly. "I'm a Black woman, running for office. You're a Black woman, proximate to power and money. We ought to know each other." That *proximate* was a gem retrieved from the thesaurus to flatter.

Michaela's laugh was nervous. "Alissa was telling me—well, it was her idea, but it's not a bad one. I thought we couldn't discuss this in front of my mother."

Brooke understood that some things you had to leave mothers out of. "She's not here."

"What if. I was wondering if we could make one of the conditions of the Jaffee Foundation's gift a job for me."

Alissa chimed in. "Michaela said, 'Oh, Brooke, she thinks big. She has ideas.' I told her that she needed to do the same thing, right?"

Brooke was pleased that the gospel of Asher Jaffee was spreading. "I'm listening."

Michaela hesitated. "If we could have the foundation underwrite a master's degree in education—"

"Then she could command a higher salary," Alissa pointed out. "It expands, you see, the impact of the gift. It changes the fortunes of the students, but also the school's leadership. It helps ensure the institution's future. So ten years from now they don't need to cobble together a succession plan."

Alissa, Brooke saw, had mastered the art of storytelling. "All good points."

"My mother thinks this is a labor of love," Michaela said. "But I could leave my day job. I could prepare for my own future."

"I can make it seem like my idea and not yours." Brooke thought Asher might be as taken with Michaela as he would be with Ghalyela.

Alissa crowed. "You see how simple? So maybe we can chat a little about me and my campaign."

"The Asher and Carol Jaffee Foundation doesn't make political contributions."

Alissa took this in stride. "You're a Black woman, I'm a Black woman. There's a common endeavor."

Brooke had heard this all before. The power of tribe. Even if they looked one way, they were nothing alike—a church girl from Brooklyn, with a vast network of cousins and vague relations, and a private-school kid from Manhattan with a white mother, a white brother, many white aunties. Brooke spent most of her time with white people, who never discussed the allegiance of race, because they did not need to. Somehow to hear it thus seemed demeaning. Brooke didn't want to be used. "Sure. The common endeavor of— existence."

There was a silence that only Brooke found awkward. "Why don't you tell me how you came to work for Asher Jaffee?"

"I wondered, too." Michaela and her mother had told Brooke so much about themselves and their lives' work. Brooke had shared nothing of her own.

Brooke knew that her answer would not satisfy. A click on Linked-In. A lucky meeting. A chance encounter. A Vassar education. The happenstance of launching into adulthood during an economic contraction. A failed attempt at teaching. She demurred. She said nothing of substance. She mumbled some words.

"I was under the impression that you had a passion for this. For what we are doing at my mother's school." Michaela sounded disappointed.

But Brooke was most passionate about Black art, Black lives, Black matters, when her boss asked her to be. "Asher Jaffee is a generous man and I feel lucky to be a part of what he's doing." She shrugged. "But you and your mother are the ones who are doing the good work."

Alissa did not give up. "I'd love to introduce you to some people. There's a group of us, some from the nonprofit world, some in the government, and then a handful of people from finance and tech, trying to think through some of the systemic problems in this city. Ensuring that Black communities enjoy some of the benefits of the larger boom."

This woman wanted to draft her into sisterhood. "I don't know if I bring anything to that particular table." Alissa had imagined her to be some other kind of person. It was a case of mistaken identity. She was her own woman.

"You're Black. You're connected. You're young." Alissa paused. "We're trying to capitalize on what the Obama moment has shown the structures of power. That we are here, that organizing on the ground level is the way to get to the top. And you're someone who's damn near close to the top in philanthropy so I thought you might be interested."

"I'm not a joiner, maybe. It's just my nature." That was it. She wanted to be left alone.

"It can be scary to risk what you've got. What you lucked into."
Alissa didn't like having a door closed in her face. "You get that
money for the Throop School. I respect that."

Brooke didn't care to defend the fact that she felt more loyalty to
an old white man than to a Black woman her age. He was her men-
tor. Just as Brooke didn't owe Alissa something because they both
happened to be Black, Asher owed her nothing because he happened
to employ her. There was genuine mutual feeling. A sincere connec-
tion that she didn't need to excuse. "Yes," she said, simply, "I work
for Asher Jaffee." Let them misunderstand. Brooke knew precisely
what it meant.

D inner, I think." Asher declared more often than he invited.

Brooke looked at her seat-belted lap to remind herself what she was wearing and be certain it was, a word her mother would have used, *appropriate*. It was the sweater she'd just bought at Saks, and it would more than suffice. "Dinner," she agreed, "would be lovely."

There had been a reception for something to do with microfinance. Despite the remarks by a woman involved in the enterprise, Brooke had no idea quite what the organization did or the purpose of the party. Just another Midtown room with strong lights where disinterested servers clad in black poured sour sauvignon blanc.

There was always a table for Asher Jaffee at Jean-Georges. He lived upstairs, and had a long-standing arrangement. They were shown to a spot in the center of the dining room. Brooke wondered whether she felt eyes on her and whether they were curious or judgmental. Maybe indifferent. Old men and younger women? The city was lousy with them. Look around. Two tables over sampling the Côtes du Rhône. In an empty gallery, discussing Adrian Piper. At Barneys, testing the heft of a Lanvin satchel, salesman attentive as a croupier, waiting to whisk away the credit card. Asher and Brooke, in the Bentley's back seat, or striding into the Thirty-sixth Street vestibule, paper coffee cups in hand, or fidgeting at a conference table, or at some joyless fete for microfinance, whatever that might be. This was just the way of the world; how had she never noticed before?

The chat between Asher and the sommelier might have been conducted in a foreign tongue. The room had a sustained, steady hum. It was bright and it was clean, it was elegant but not silly. You wanted to be worthy of the place.

"Patrick. Give her a taste, too." Asher meant this to be an education.

The man spun a glass so its mouthful of red washed up the sides.

She tasted it and paused, knowing you were supposed to. "It's nice."

"Mum's the word, Patrick. Mrs. Jaffee doesn't need to know."

Am I the secret? her face asked.

"We are going to drink two bottles of wine at dinner. Carol would not approve." Asher trusted his protégé. "You'll understand, someday. How it is in a marriage. The necessity of honesty but also the utility of discretion."

"I'll take your word on that." More talk of marriage. The subject bored her.

"You think it'll be different. I was the same way." The longer he looked at her, the younger she seemed. Not a line on her face. Not a worry on her shoulders. Not a flaw on her hands.

"I'm not planning on marrying." Brooke had said this before. People thought it a provocation. Or perhaps it was only her mother who did. Brooke knew there was a lot of future yet ahead of her, and none of her daydreams or plans seemed to include a man. She generally said that it must have something to do with her wiring. This phrase was the equivalent of a shrug. Sometimes, privately, she worried it was something lacking. Mostly, she gave the matter little thought. She would not allow that there was something unnatural in being her own first priority.

She really was young. "No?" Asher found this funny. "I've done it twice. I'm a big proponent, personally."

Hadn't her mother and the aunties insisted otherwise? "I was always told—like a fish needs a bicycle." Strange how her mother and the aunties now reliably asked whether there was some man (a few times, in her undergraduate days, a *woman*) who Brooke never mentioned. "I was taught to take care of myself."

"You're formidable. That's the word exactly." Asher's parents had never told him that he was special. They had raised him to be part of a collective. He had shown them. He had shocked them. "But I wouldn't discount the importance of other people. The thing that makes life interesting is that it ends. The thing that makes love worthwhile is that it's all we've got."

This was a corporate titan, a man of legend. She was more willing to listen to him than she might to her mother or Auntie Sayo. But there was something in her that was not comfortable with romance. She didn't like to linger on it because she had to then wonder whether it was a deficit, a disorder, a problem never to be solved. "I expected to talk philanthropy, not philosophy."

"No one wants to indulge an old man." He chewed on some

green. There were all these lettuces now that no one had eaten in the past. That even food itself could change! The world was so funny.

"I'm listening!" Brooke put her heavy fork onto the white plate. She liked the philosophy. Brooke felt her mind whir and click like the perfect machine that it was. It had lain dormant too long.

Everyone wanted his money. A museum, the University of Minnesota library, his nieces telephoning with an awkward question. This girl wanted his company. He could tell the difference. This dinner was work, and if it also brought him private pleasure, all the better. "I sent you on a mission. I gave you a challenge."

She needed more time. She hedged. "I have found the perfect place. It's a school in Brooklyn. A one-woman operation, but it's thrived for decades. Dance. Music. I'm very excited to share the whole proposal with you. It's everything I think you're hoping for."

"One woman? It sounds modest. I'm interested in the world being a better place." He softened. "But I trust your instincts."

"This isn't your name on a room full of Impressionist paintings." Brooke knew that when he saw it, he would understand. "It's human. It's what we talked about." The matter of souls.

"When you're ready. I'm sure you'll wow me."

Dirty plates were removed, steaks delivered. The sommelier brought a new bottle, and this time Brooke was able to taste an unfamiliar something. Maybe the wine was good. Maybe the food brought it to life, or maybe she was hungry or maybe she was drunk or maybe she felt, after half an hour with him, like Asher Jaffee himself, entitled to a four-hundred-dollar bottle of wine. She would wow him. Brooke was certain of it. "How is Mrs. Jaffee's painting?"

Asher looked up. "I'll have to ask Natalie where it is. When it's arriving. You're interested in paintings, aren't you? I have some upstairs. We should go see after dinner. What does it do for you, I wonder. Looking at a painting?" She'd lectured him about the one he'd bought for Carol. There had been a fervor that cowed him, delighted him, attracted him. The fever of a youthful, perfect mind.

"I don't know." Brooke stopped eating. "It makes you feel. That's what art does. It reminds you that you feel, or asks you what it is you feel. The answer doesn't even matter. It's the question."

"This is what I meant about getting married," Asher said. "You need a feeling, for a person, for your work, for yourself. The way to get through this life." He looked at her. "You feel it, though, for this work. That it matters to you."

She nodded.

"Good girl." Like his pet, like his child. "It matters to you. Only you. How you spend your time. You're young, but you'll see."

There might be a lot of life left, as Asher promised, but maybe Brooke was not prepared enough. She'd go into those years without plates and sheets from Bloomingdale's, without a long-dead father's surprisingly large fortune. What was she doing with herself, what was she doing at this nice restaurant with this rich man?

Asher ordered them hazelnut cakes and espressos. Not since she was a child had Brooke had someone else order for her in a restaurant. It seemed to give him a thrill, and she allowed this. She had agreed to be his guest. She had agreed to be his protégé. She had agreed to him at all. She thanked him for dinner politely.

Asher did not say *You're welcome* because he rarely did. He gave and gave; people thanked and thanked. That was the way of the world. "It's dark now. Let's go up. Up, up, up."

T he numbers aren't right." There was a large bright antechamber with no windows. There was a round table with nothing on it in the room's center. "It says the forty-seventh floor but I think it's actually the fortieth." This amused him. Numbers were objective but could not always be relied upon; you could use them as you wished.

Brooke noticed he didn't even have a set of keys to toss onto the table. The door had simply been open. She expected baronial splendor: ornate carved furniture, Asian rugs of knotted silk, paintings in gilt frames, the sort with their own light source affixed over the top. Instead the place was vast, empty, modern—bleached-wood floors, low furniture, and the glass wall facing the expanse of Central Park. They were drawn toward this first, immediately.

"Actually the view is better than any painting I've ever seen." Asher had paid dearly for these windows and the silence. He knew the former would impress but fretted the latter might betray him. His body: some impertinent squeak, some gastric burble, some reminder that he was old, breaking apart. He offered her a drink, because he wanted one. This was like some night from a time long past; a long dinner, the satisfaction of wine and conversation. There was a woman, Marguerite, in some bedroom behind the kitchen he'd never even been inside. He would not call out for her to serve them.

The two lingered by the window. Brooke put a hand to it even though it was impolite to leave fingerprints. It was like visiting an aquarium: some instinct to commune with the strange form of life on the other side. Only, instead of cephalopod or idle shark, there was Olmsted's triumph, vanished into shadow. Brooke couldn't see the Gilded Age confections on Fifth Avenue, the up-lit modern buildings, including the one where she'd grown up, just there, in that general direction, but hiding. "I'll have one if you are." Brooke didn't have to turn away from the view because she could see Asher's reflection.

This was Asher Jaffee's vantage on reality. It was out there, somewhere, distant, something to look down on with amusement. She knew that she was not there for him to fuck her, though she knew it would seem so to most. Those people had no imagination, or didn't understand that something more profound might be happening.

Asher was beside her, held her glass improperly, fingers on the rim from which she would drink.

She raised the whiskey in salute. "To Frederick Law Olmsted."

He sipped his cold drink. "'Look on my works, ye Mighty, and despair!'" He didn't mean the park but this slice of sky from which he might observe it. The joke was just right. Asher understood that someday someone else would stand at this window, proprietary. He would be forgotten.

Brooke saw the Monet above the sofa reflected over her shoulder. The huge orange muddle she'd once glimpsed behind Barbara Jaffee in *Architectural Digest*. She walked toward it.

"You know who I hear from, two, three times a year?" He addressed her back, pleased by how intently she was studying the thing. "Our friend Sara Fried, from Christie's. She's got a Chinese billionaire who has his heart set on that thing. Full circle. I bought that from a Japanese guy. They're wild about the Impressionists, the Asians. The acme of Western art. Do you like it?"

It was too sentimental, too lovely. Art for old people, foreign industrialists, greeting cards. But why did the received opinions crowd her out; why could she not answer whether she liked it? Who was she not to like Monet? "I thought this was Mrs. Jaffee's."

Asher sat on the sofa. After a certain age, you did that with a small, unconscious sigh. He didn't ask how she'd have known such a thing. "The painting was mine. Barbara never had any feeling about it! But she has good lawyers. She put up a fuss but we knew the truth. Anyway, she got her way, was photographed by the magazines. Then, a few years later, I get a call, *Asher, you always loved the Monet, why don't you take it?* Why don't I buy it, she meant." So he'd paid twice over; the Chinese billionaire would pay him more, if he ever decided to sell. "I won. I always win."

Brooke wondered if he cared, even, about the painting itself. It didn't matter; he owned it. Something they used to say, kids on the playground squabbling over some toy: *possession is nine tenths of the law.* Why that strange fraction, and what had they meant as kids anyway? The temperature in the quiet room was perfect. Brooke sat, slipped off her shoes to feel the thick pile beneath her soles. The sofa was velvet. Asher had his glass on the table without a coaster, and would leave it there all night, because someone else would clean it up. "I don't know what to look at. The Monet or the view."

Asher knew that this girl, sensitive on matters of the soul, would be conflicted by all this sublimity. He could not stop himself showing off. "Look at both. I can tell you, later, which one cost more. But yes, I know, value can't be measured in dollars."

This was something only rich people would say, that money didn't matter. Brooke said so. That was what she was there for. To tease him, to confront him, to remind him that he was still alive.

Asher relented. "Fine. Money matters. Lots of things matter." This was what he knew now, and had not before. Everything mattered, everything in the world. It was so much to bear that sometimes you couldn't. That's why it was so easy now for tears to well in his old damn eyes. "That's why I think you're wrong to say you'll never marry. Even if you end up divorcing and fighting over a goddamn Monet. It matters."

Brooke said nothing to this. Good God, this apartment. Rooms in every direction, a sense of space all around them; beyond those, the unending sky. Somewhere out there was everyone else in the world, and none of them could see Brooke. What a life! Did Asher know how special it was? He did. She knew it. And he was telling her that such a life was hers, too. "I love it here."

"Carol hates it. She wants to open a window. Feel the breeze. But you can't, this high up. She feels trapped. She says it's *airless*." Carol was not wrong. When they had parties there, the rooms smelled of fried appetizers and the bodies of strangers. After, Carol would light candles. Asher was defensive because he loved the place. He stroked the sofa as if it were a house cat.

"I'm buying an apartment, myself," Brooke lied. Was it a lie, though? Was it a wish? Was it a leading statement? "I want that same feeling. Possession." Would he know how it felt to covet but not possess something?

"New York real estate, real estate at all, it's a sound investment." He felt paternal pride.

"It's like the Frankenthaler. Not an investment. It mattered to you because it matters. It was worth it to you because it's worth it. It's remarkable, Mrs. Jaffee is going to love it. My apartment is the same way. It's special, it's magic, because it'll be mine." Brooke was certain he would see this.

And he did. "A person needs that. A place where they can be." He knew not to say that a woman needed that, that a Black person needed that. It was a human need.

A thrill to be understood. A relief to speak the same language. "I told my mother to think about it this way. Me, marrying an apartment. She did not like that one bit."

"Parents want their children to be happy."

"I am happy. My brother's getting married. That's what he wants. That's what he needs. Not me. I want this."

"I never thought I'd remarry." He had hated Barbara for a time. It mellowed over the years, as things did. Linda's death meant a rapprochement. What was the point in hating each other when the best thing they had managed together was vanished into history? "The world is mostly good people. And the future is impossible to predict."

"The whole point of the foundation, though. There are so many problems out there." Brooke thought of the people sleeping in front of the Duane Reade across from her apartment. Five of them, ten of them, the lot of them could live in Asher Jaffee's penthouse the four nights a week he was elsewhere. Impossible but also not illogical. This was the world. It made no sense.

"That's work." Asher knew that a couple of billion dollars wasn't enough to change the world. But the intention counted for something. So what difference did it make if he didn't ultimately give away the whole lot? It was the thought that counted. "You're buying an apartment. You said yourself it wasn't an investment but something—what's the word? *Sacred*?" His pride was misplaced. It belonged to Linda. Surely she had known how he treasured her, how she impressed him, the depth, breadth, extent of his pride, his love. If she hadn't, he could not correct the record now. It was too late. He was in some kind of muddle. He felt a tear in his eye. Why was he moved, why wasn't he done with all this feeling, or why could it come for him with no warning?

Brooke did not envy him, could not hate him. She could ask Asher Jaffee to buy her the apartment on Twenty-ninth Street. Maybe, if she got to her knees, as some part of him must have hoped she would, he would grant her that favor. There was right and wrong and there was what you did, and no one but you was keeping score or no one cared. No one with a billion dollars, never mind two, three, four, had done only good. But it got Asher Jaffee this astonishing place and the Monet painting that his ex-wife claimed to love deeply and everything else he had ever wanted. "Yes. It is exciting." It was a lot of things, a delusion, a fantasy, an error, a lie, but all of those things did excite.

"I'm very happy." He tried to communicate something to her. Words were not adequate. He put a hand on her shoulder, so thin and firm beneath the fine fabric of her clothes. He put another hand on top of her head, so noble and handsomely sculpted. He had to turn a little, into the sofa, to lay hands upon her. He tried to make it seem like a blessing, but maybe it was only an excuse to touch her, to bring them closer. He was, he could admit, curious about how her clothes might feel; he was, he could admit, curious about how her lustrous skin might feel; he was, he could admit, curious about how her shorn hair would feel. He thought it would be kinky and coarse like the pubis, but it was soft and fine as the hair of some special animal, the sort you pluck to make a paintbrush, the sort you use to paint a masterpiece. He rested his hands there in bene-diction, the elegant arc of her skull, the softness of her. He said he was happy, and he was.

ndrea at Chase knew everything about her life. Brooke had never even laid eyes on the woman. But Brooke had emailed her bank statements and tax returns. Andrea had run Brooke's credit report and checked in at every address she'd ever called her own. The name of the bank turned out to be apt, Andrea the functionary chasing down everything about Brooke Orr. But all this was mere data. Brooke didn't think it told the story. What was needed was someone like Brooke to observe herself, determine whether she was deserving.

"You haven't filed a federal return since you've been in your current job?" Andrea at Chase was all business.

Some quality in the woman's voice—no more was necessary—and Brooke knew that she was Black. Just as Alissa McDonald would, Brooke could press that advantage. An appeal under the guise of *sisterhood*. This was business, and how things were done. "I started in April of this year," Brooke said. "I'm there now." She rapped on her desk with her knuckles for emphasis.

"Yes, I called you there." Andrea at Chase was no-nonsense.

"It's good you caught me. I'm often out. The work sends me all over the city."

"What I'm going to need is some documentation of your salary. Because you haven't been in the job very long." Belief didn't figure into it, for Andrea at Chase. There were simply things to be seen to.

"That's not a problem. I'll ask them to send you a letter. I'll do that right now." Brooke hung up the telephone and looked around the little room with satisfaction. There was a private feeling. Fundamentally human but never discussed; the sort of thing you catch a toddler in and avert your eyes. Kids are too young to be ashamed of what makes them human and this was embarrassing to witness. That was the thing that separated people from animals. Hence clothes, soap, politesse, all of society. Brooke was pulled away from these things, into something nebulous, indefensible. She was in a state that either no one else could see or everyone else turned away from as though she were again a two-year-old with her hand down her pants. She needed; she wanted; she coveted. She felt itchy and on fire.

Someday soon, God willing, if Brooke did her job, Ghalyela would receive a windfall. Michaela would get her subsidized master's degree and a commensurate raise in salary. There was nothing in either woman's data, the figures that trailed them, as all of us, year after year, that indicated this. Strange things happened and there was no way to persuade an underwriter of this.

Brooke opened a new file on the computer and began to type. The power of numbers! Multiply by a humble two, three, four, and they quickly transformed into something. Brooke wrote, *To whom it may concern.* She tried two but the resulting salary was still modest. This was the Asher and Carol Jaffee Foundation, not Jaffee Corp.

Asher had told her that she would have thrived there! Three, then. Why not four? She typed Eileen's name. Brooke could scribble an approximation of her signature.

Asher said she had acumen, an instinct, and maybe she hadn't been imaginative enough. She could turn a profit listing her place on Airbnb—the management company would surely never notice. She couldn't sleep at her mother's home (the spare rooms the province of women in crisis), or Matthew and Kim's (too many questions). But all around her was the underoccupied expanse of the Asher and Carol Jaffee Foundation. Brooke could stretch out for the night on Asher's Barcelona lounge. She could set the alarm for five, she could shower at her gym. She could keep the lights down low, steal around on stockinged feet. It would be a game, Anne Frank in her garret, only with a happy ending: *In spite of everything I still believe that people are really good at heart.*

Sure, Brooke understood it was all algorithmic, but everyone knew computers weren't impartial. Who, after all, had designed the computers? Who, in the end, did the underwriters truly believe in? Not single Black women! Brooke could imagine an *amen* from unseen Andrea at Chase.

Perhaps this was not thinking big enough. She could persuade Ghalyela that there was a finder's fee owing, some gesture of thanks, some concession from the check that the Asher and Carol Jaffee Foundation would eventually deliver. Money was everywhere, and it was a failure of Brooke's imagination not to understand this.

The shared printer was down the hall, in a nook beside the copier and the never-used fax machine. Brooke's steps on the industrial carpeting were silent. In the moment, she was still inside the fantasy, she was living in the office, moneymaking scheme but also a measure of her commitment to the cause. She was evading discovery. Were there mice at night, darting around these rooms, these long empty halls, in search of the scant crumbs humans always left in their wake, and would they frighten Brooke or would they be her companions? In her mind, she was alone, it was late, the only sounds were the chorus of city noises, distant sirens, passing vehicles, car alarms, the occasional shout. She started as she entered the copy room, Natalie's bent frame holding a piece of paper.

"I'm sorry," Brooke said. "You surprised me."

"Then I'm the one who's sorry, my dear." The anthracite of Natalie's irises beneath her glasses.

"Oh, don't apologize." Brooke crossed her arms across her chest for need of something to do with her hands. "How are you today, Natalie?"

"This is yours, dear." Natalie handed her the paper, still warm from the machine's work.

Brooke thanked her. She folded the paper into thirds. The warmth had already left it. "Are you ready for the long weekend?"

Natalie busied herself with something. But she came to her point. "That looks like an official letter."

"That it is." So the woman had read it. No matter. If anyone there was a secretary, it was Natalie. Was a secretary to be feared, or weren't they outranked by a protégé? "I'm buying an apartment. I shouldn't use the day to catch up on personal matters maybe—"

"I don't mean to pry." Natalie did not believe this. Everything that happened in this office was within her purview. She was Mr. Jaffee's eyes.

"Not at all." Brooke improvised. "It's a full-time job. The paperwork, I mean. The bank wants this and that."

"On top of everything you're doing for Mr. Jaffee," Natalie said. She had seen girls like this one before. Maybe most of them were like this. People didn't take things seriously anymore, hadn't for a long time, and it had only gotten worse. They thought a job a lark, an opportunity to take advantage.

"I consider this work a privilege." Brooke figured that these words would go directly to Asher. "It's demanding but understand—it makes me feel good. There's this other value to it."

"In addition to the salary, you mean." Natalie tidied her stack of copies. "The work isn't just its own reward. We're paid to be here. We are fortunate twice over."

Brooke was not stupid. "We are blessed."

Natalie had long harbored a suspicion she could not articulate. She intuited that people would have said it was racist. But she was simply clear-eyed. Natalie was too old to fool. "You saw the news, I'm sure. I hope you're being careful out there."

Brooke seized upon the change of subject. "I'm not sure what you mean."

"The Subway Pricker!" Natalie was scolding. What else, she asked, were people in New York talking about? "The madman with the needle! The lunatic at large!"

This again, Brooke didn't say. "Do you think that's happening? Aren't people overreacting?"

"My dear, you ought to listen to the radio. There was another attack just hours ago. A young woman on the four train downtown. She had some kind of fit. Maybe it was poison this time. Maybe it was stress. Maybe it was the effect of a crazed lunatic shoving a needle into her. She collapsed on the platform, screaming that she'd been assaulted. They stopped the train two stations away, but the police came up with nothing."

Brooke was surprised. "I guess I thought it was some kind of—collective hysteria event? Like one of those stories where a bunch of high schoolers break out in hives or can't stop coughing and it turns out to be all in their heads."

"I don't know about that." Natalie thought the girl was delirious. "There were two more women besides. Union Square, on the platform. Then another one at Seventy-seventh Street, on the six train." Natalie counted them off on her fingers. "I hardly think these strangers got together and made up this implausible story. What can he be trying to do, do you think? Pricking strange women. It must be—it's perverse."

Girls with dutiful mothers were inculcated from birth with the knowledge that the world was unsafe, for women anyway, while also being told they should venture out into it. "Perverse." She nodded gravely. *Prick* was only another word for *penis*. She could hardly say as much to Natalie but—prick, prick, she got it, she'd be ever on guard for a malevolent penis. "We can't be afraid, I guess. Life goes on."

Natalie held her own papers against her chest. "I would be careful, Brooke," she said, the last word on every matter. It was a warning with many meanings. "I would be careful if I were you."

T hat hour: the people rushed and the trains slowed. Maybe life elsewhere indulged you in the illusion of control. You were at the city's mercy and you had to make your peace. She had a native's grasp of how to jockey for space, watch for psychos, tune out fervent declamations of Jesus, sway the hips to adjust the body's movement as the train pulled to a stop. Brooke knew just how tall she was (not very) so politely pushed into the car's center where the bar ran floor to ceiling. Beside her, an impassive Chinese woman had a paper towel in hand as not to touch the germy metal.

Brooke could slow the breath and stop her hearing. She could be like one of those dumbstruck monks in lotus position, living for fifteen decades without ever eating. Satori. The uptown train— Matthew often chose restaurants in Hell's Kitchen; *Where the boys are*—slowed, stopped, and an express train passed on the parallel track, an impression of light, the thwack of displaced air. Brooke looked ahead. Eyes at rest, she saw but did not see her own reflection, the backs of the heads of the passengers seated before her, the tableau of bodies behind her.

Then her eyes did focus, awake and aware. Behind her a cloud, a mass, a suggestion, a color. The bar in her palm was warm. There it was. It was a prick. He got her! Triumph more than fear. Satisfaction more than panic. She'd dismissed this as hysteria. Now she had been chosen. He got her! A sliver, so slight, the width of a hair, a pencil's lead, a blade of grass, but hard, unyielding, entering her. Through the clothes, through the skin, into that soft spot between the vertebrae. The center of the body, the center of the self, even; you imagine the soul located there, now violated, pierced. Something entered her. Who knew what it was? The doors closed and the train began to move and Brooke looked at the window and was not afraid. The tangle of heads, shoulders, arms, bodies, everyone in New York City, everyone in the world. He must have been right behind her! All she could see was the Chinese woman with her paper towel. Was she the pricker? Brooke didn't want to scream. She just wanted to know.

Then again. The pleasant pressure of cold metal piercing the skin, delivering whatever it was into her bloodstream. No. At her neck. In her bicep. Behind the ear. At the elbow. Pricks all over her. *Oh, he's real*, she wanted to say, *he's real, and he got me.* Natalie, with her witchy glasses, had known! She had seen the future in which he, if the pricker was a he, thought Brooke worthy. A cure or a poison, it did not matter. It was in her.

Brooke pushed out of the car at Fifty-ninth Street. She stopped on the platform and put hand to her neck, her wrist, her back. How could you know if you'd been pricked? It was a fleeting delusion or it was a flight of fancy or it was a waking nightmare. These urbane

folks with their headphones, their private struggles, their appoint-
ments to keep, ignored her.

But, no, she was fine. Nothing had been done to her. Her trick-
ster brain up to its old—but if he was real, he was out there, and he
could get her whenever he wanted. That was being alive. How could
a person stand it? How could a person live knowing that anything
could happen to them, or how could a person assure that nothing
ever would?

The city in summer's grip. The green of the leaves brought hope
to the soul. The spume of pollen brought tears to the eyes. The restaurant was between a Starbucks and a bank. She was there first,
was shown to a small table. There were more people out because tomorrow was a holiday; here, mostly Midtown salarymen in khakis,
masculine voices bouncing off the low ceiling. A waiter ferried her a
glass of pink wine beaded with condensation.

Matthew arrived, loosening his tie without seeming to notice.
Brooke saw him with a sister's eyes. Those had somehow lost focus
of her actual brother, but Matthew, dear Matthew, he was still hers.
Was she his, though? She would have to defuse whatever was between them. She had to joke. "Hot enough for you?"

He liked people's animal instinct to revel in the sun, knowing
that winter would, as ever, return. It was hard, on a perfect day, to
feel dissatisfied. "Tomorrow's the Fourth, it's supposed to be hot."

Brooke finished her wine and told him he needed to catch up.

"You're celebrating." He ordered a glass of the same and examined his phone by habit before putting it away and looking at Brooke
across the unlit candle and salt and pepper shakers.

"I'm buying an apartment, I told you." Another sip of the tart
wine.

"You told me, but you didn't explain." He didn't add that she had been too busy attacking Kim. It wouldn't do to go back to settled business, but he was on guard. She seemed different, distracted, strange, maybe even angry. "I can only assume this has something to do with the big boss. My theory is you fucked him and he was so grateful that this apartment is a little token."

He didn't understand, but she didn't fault him for it. Would she fuck Asher Jaffee? The truth was she had come to love the man. "I think I remind him of his daughter. I think I remind him of his youth. I think I remind him of himself. But he didn't buy me an apartment." She had faith. Asher Jaffee had taken care of Natalie's mother. Maybe there would be some consideration for her in his will. There was a way. This was what she did: she got money for people who deserved it. "It'll all work out."

There was conviction in her eyes. Maybe, if you looked long enough, it would seem like madness. Perhaps there were ways to do the impossible, a secret to life that he alone had not yet found. "You're doing that New Age thing. You're visualizing."

Maybe it was that simple. "I'm asking the world for more. It's the only way I know. I'm ready for life to begin, I'm ready for more. But you have to ask, Eeyore. You have to ask, or it will never come."

"Who am I asking?"

Brooke didn't bring God into it. "Do you know how Asher Jaffee lives? We think this is reality." Her left arm indicated the vague restaurant around them. She meant not just this establishment but the street, the neighborhood, the city, the country. "We're being deceived. There's another place, adjacent to this one, so much better I don't know how to explain it."

"That's through the looking glass. That's Narnia." Matthew meant that this didn't excite him. "Lifestyles-of-the-rich-and-famous stuff. It has nothing to do with us."

Brooke shook her head, scolding, stern. "Once you know it, once you see it, you feel like—why don't I want more? Why shouldn't I? And there's no answer. If someone can be allowed to have all that, why can't we be allowed to have something so much smaller?"

The answer was simple. "Because he has the money. And I don't."

Matthew didn't have the imagination. He hadn't learned what she had. The money was such a small part of it. Everyone deserved something. "I'm going to show you."

It sounded, he thought, like a threat. "I believe you. I'm sure you will."

That wasn't what she meant. She didn't mean prove it, have the last laugh, triumph over Matthew's persistent skepticism. She put her mind to the logistics of it. It seemed imperative that Matthew see the world from the beautiful nest Asher Jaffee had made. She would show him the world that was possible for Asher Jaffee and it would change Matthew's idea of what was possible for himself. They would hold hands, plunge from that vast window into the dark night like Peter and Wendy, bound for a better place. "I'm going to show you something incredible."

She remembered his face. Brooke always took note of the Black people, as they always took note of her. It was something you did because you'd always done it, like picking pennies off the sidewalk, smiling when you saw a baby. It was a survival strategy, it was a tool.

There was a marble desk, the sort you'd find in those churchy banks, with copper domes gone green, with ballpoint pens chained to blotters, with deposit slips and envelopes laid out like playing cards. He wore an old-school uniform. He could have been their father. Maybe that was the game; she and Matthew, junior and sister, come to say hello.

"Excuse me." There was no guile on her face because this was not a mission of deception but salvation. She put into her words a note of apology and need.

He said good evening and "How can I help?" and was so good at his job, you almost believed he meant it.

"I don't know if you remember me." She paused to give him the chance to do so. She had a feeling he would summon her face. She hadn't liked it when Michaela and Alissa had asserted sisterhood to Brooke. But Brooke could do it in turn, to Andrea from Chase Bank, to this silver-mustachioed man. You had to take whatever advantage circumstance offered.

"Don't tell me." This salt-and-pepper fellow did not smile with his mouth but his voice. He had it: "Mr. Jaffee."

"Bingo." She was pleased. "I'm Brooke. We didn't get the chance to meet."

He took her outstretched hand. "Peter."

"Peter. I'm in a bind." She looked at her watch to say that time was of the essence.

He served people. There was always something. The dry-cleaning had gone missing. The maid had locked them out. The dog had messed the floor of the elevator vestibule. "Well, I don't like to hear that."

There were important papers to be retrieved from the Jaffee residence. Mr. and Mrs. Jaffee were in the country. Marguerite only lived in Sunday night through Thursday morning and no one seemed to know her telephone number. The Jaffees would not be back for days and she needed someone to admit her to the penthouse! It was as close as you could get to emergency in her line of work. The lie came to her so easily, unplanned, though maybe this was just the story-telling Jody had said was so potent.

Peter understood what was being asked. He had, in his years, fielded more outlandish requests. "You're in a jam."

"The thing is." Her lowered voice invited him into conspiracy. "I could call Mr. Jaffee." She did not use his first name because she knew Peter would never. "But I would as soon . . . not."

Matthew watched this exchange, not recognizing Brooke at all. It was a seduction. He didn't know that she was capable of being this person.

Peter nodded. Men that age were moved by some mixture of paternal and sexual feeling, the whole thing tumbled together.

Brooke looked guilty. "His bark is worse than his bite." She wondered whether Peter was thinking of his generous holiday gift. She was certain Asher Jaffee tipped well.

But there were limits to what a doorman could do! "It's not the way—"

She said it like it was so reasonable, barely a favor, nothing worth worrying over. "Ten minutes. I'll have to. Well, I need to find these papers. Mr. Jaffee isn't exactly the most responsible when it comes to things like this. But then it's not his job to be."

"It's yours." He trying to impart some wisdom. He was teasing but scolding. But it was a father's job to grant the mercy the world would not.

Brooke's contrite face was to conjure for him a daughter, a niece, a sister, a wife. And one of the great mysteries of her life was that this man, though he looked nothing like her, might well have been her father. "I'm out of ideas. I thought I'd just plead my case."

This was not the way things were done, but it was. Life's rules were suggestion. Peter had already made up his mind though he kept this from her. He was human. He was kind. He believed more people were good than bad. "What you're asking—"

"I need the keys. I need to go upstairs. Ten minutes. Fifteen. I need to find these papers. My friend Matthew. He'll be with me. We'll leave the keys with you fifteen minutes from now. Twenty, absolutely, at the most." She did not say that he could trust her because that would be too obvious a lie. He could not trust her! And he could not accompany her, though she knew that he wouldn't. He was needed at his outpost.

"Brooke?" He was testing out her name. It was a code word of sorts. It had been given as a token. "You're asking a lot."

Another bluff. "Collateral. Good faith. I could leave my phone with you. But—"

He shook his head, no, that was ridiculous. She was trustworthy. He unlocked a drawer in his desk. He removed a key ring and slid it toward her. "The small key is for the elevator. The big one is for the door, but that's probably open. I'll be right here at this desk. You put this key back into my hand in fifteen minutes."

In the speeding elevator, their stomachs lurched in near unison, registering the progress skyward. "What are we doing?" Matthew asked. She did not answer him. The apartment was silent, though Brooke could not know whether the never-seen Marguerite was within. What would Marguerite make of someone breaking and entering in order to steal not a thing but a moment? Brooke would deal with that, too, if she had to. Marguerite, too, must be Black. She imagined a thickset woman with a singsong patois. The interior door was unlocked as Peter had promised. The lights in the foyer came on because some hidden sensor understood that they were there.

"Jesus." What else could you say? A room this vast and pointless, nothing but an empty table, excess space in a city where that was the most precious commodity. Matthew had seen such things on screen but never in life.

"Wait," she said. There was so much more!

They crossed spotless floors to the living room, its glass wall.

They both stopped there, cowed by the same old New York, a different thing when seen from there. Matthew whistled in appreciation, a masculine response that surprised even him. "Not bad."

Was it bad or good, all those buildings, all those people? It was a matter of perspective. She felt something in her veins. A desire to keep humanity at this great distance, to look down upon it, be reassured that society continued, but that she was safe from it. It was a feeling of pure ego. There was something monstrous in her. She could, if it came to that, be a person who did bad things. She would do what was required to protect herself, her solitude, her happiness. "This is how Asher Jaffee sees the world that the rest of us inhabit." He was like God, she meant. What those people down there were up to had nothing to do with him. If only they knew! That wasn't even what she wanted him to see. "Look at that." Brooke pointed at the painting.

"Monet?" Matthew appreciated it, sure. He knew it was special, he knew that it was expensive, but why did it matter, if it did at all?

"Asher and his ex-wife bought that painting in 1984 for seventeen million dollars. When they divorced, there was a dispute over two assets—the town house on Eighty-first Street and that painting." She was authoritative as Wikipedia. "Asher got the house. He sold it years later, to Madonna. Barbara got the painting. A few years ago, Barbara approached him and offered the painting back to him. She wanted the money. I couldn't find out how much he paid her but let's say it was the original sale price. Say he paid thirty-four million dollars for the painting."

That sum meant nothing to him. It did not compute. No one could make sense of it. "We should not be here."

"But look at it. See it." She had let her eyes' focus slacken, the thing just a wash of color. Then she'd adjust them and it would come into relief, show her what the artist wanted her to see.

He couldn't understand what she saw. He couldn't understand how Brooke wanted him to feel, because he couldn't understand how she felt in that moment. A rich man owned an expensive piece of art. "I see it. I'm looking. This isn't art appreciation with Miss Orr. What are you asking me?" It seemed to represent something else to Brooke, though what Matthew couldn't quite grasp.

"I'm not the one asking. Claude Monet is asking. The question and answer are between you and him." Her smile was like the Virgin Mary's, subdued and private. "This is what is happening. This is what people are doing. There are men with this much money and it's not that they control the world. They've defeated it. They've left it. They live somewhere above the rest of us and we spend our days not knowing this because if we did we would all lose our minds." She thought this was very clear. She was mad at the immortal fools and philanderers and egomaniacs atop Olympus. The rest of us go about the stupid business of life and why?

The losing of minds? What else were they doing, two Black people in a stranger's home, talking about the world as though it were something they, too, might conquer? They had lost their minds, or one of them had.

Brooke was not hysterical. She was resolved. "Do you see?"

He saw the painting, so he nodded. But Matthew did not see. "I think we should go."

She was not making herself understood, but epiphany wasn't something you could force on someone no matter how much you loved them. "I want, too. I want. It's just the fact. What I want is modest. And it's what everyone is entitled to. I want my place in the world,

I want my guarantee. I want to have something in this world that is mine. A place where I can be. It is so small, Matthew, what I want. And it's so close. I wanted you to see this. Because it's beautiful. Because it's amazing. This is how Asher lives, a few days a week anyway. This is not fair but everyone knows that already, right, the nature of the world, its unfairness. But I think it's good to look right at it. To see that, to stare at it, to force ourselves to acknowledge it. To say fuck that. To say we will do what we have to do. Because we will do what we must."

He was too conscious of the ticking away of the minutes to pay attention to this speech. "We have to get out of here."

Brooke breathed it in first, the astonishing silence of those thousands of square feet carved out of the heavens, and agreed that they needed to return to earth and whatever awaited them there.

T hey met, that Monday morning, in the elevator. It seemed if not fraught then charged. It seemed providential. Brooke smiled at his reflection in the dull silver doors. "Nice weekend?"

All of Asher's weekends were three days long, more than enough. Independence Day? He was already free. Forced jollity, hamburgers at a neighbor's, a phalanx of other people's towheaded grandchildren, introductions to strangers. An old man, he was granted a seat at a table, pushed warm potato salad around a plate. At one point his heavy fork fell to the brick underfoot and Asher was furious and embarrassed. "Fine, fine. You had a good holiday?"

What did she care about fireworks or the nation? Brooke was supposed to go to Auntie Sayo's for a terrace cookout, but had feigned a summer cold because she preferred, that day, to be alone. "Lovely. Did you and Mrs. Jaffee celebrate?"

Imagine if he'd turned up at Skip Huniford's with this Black girl in tow. He'd lost his head for her! The most expensive woman in his life since Barbara Jaffee. She had advised him and he'd spent almost a million dollars. A madness, but one long weekend and he—well, he missed her. "You remembered about tonight?" He wore a linen jacket. He wondered if his hair was kempt.

She remembered. Before the long weekend, Natalie had summoned her to Asher's office. There was a concert. He would like her to join him. It was a professional obligation, he had intimated. "Naturally!"

At day's end, Christopher drove them to Lincoln Center. Brooke and Asher lingered by the fountain in the center of the square, because something about the sound of water falling made you want to stop. Brooke took in the columned portico, like something from de Chirico, or the night just felt surreal. Old men in rumpled blazers and women in cheap shawls swarmed. Did anyone notice the two of them?

"What a town." He knew how old-fashioned a thing it was to say. "You know, tonight Mozart's Masonic funeral music is on the program. A favorite." This was the whole reason they were there. No one else on the board expected him to attend a summer performance. Asher had wanted an excuse to hear this, and a pretext to see her outside of the office.

"I'm excited to hear it." She didn't know anything about classical music.

His imagination had come up with a boyfriend: square jawed, blue shirt with sleeves rolled up over the forearms, a kid from the trenches at Goldman Sachs. He knew this type, and what they most wanted was to take the place Asher held. It was Oedipal. Asher had outlasted them. Now he fretted that one might be in bed beside Brooke, nights, chuckling about him. "Let's go inside."

We use the stuff of kings—deep purples, marble, velvet, gilt—to venerate art. You could only feel enriched. The aisle sloped toward their seats. The expectations of the audience rose to the ceiling miles overhead. Sweating palms rolled programs into cylinders. The crinkle of cellophane resounded, the dutiful elderly hoping to keep coughs at bay. They were both quiet, some instinct toward reverence that came upon you beneath a ceiling so high. It was religious feeling. This was a cathedral. The acoustics carried to them the footfalls of musicians onstage, the scrape of their chairs, their hushed conferences. Asher leaned in and said something she didn't quite hear.

Asher's posture was erect. He was attentive when in an audience. The musicians trod into Beethoven first. Notes cobbled together out of nothing centuries ago; it didn't make any sense. It was impossible to think about.

At intermission, they stood in the lobby with plastic stemware. "What did you make of it?"

Brooke had felt her mind wander into strange, uninteresting territory. She'd thought of a long-ago Christmas outing to see the Rockettes, an old boyfriend of Kim's, a trip she and her mother had once taken to Amherst, some story Auntie Paige had told her about Hong Kong. "I feel like I should be paying closer attention."

Asher felt that was right. "That's the trick of it. You want to think about the music, but what you're hearing turns you inward. Or it puts you to sleep." He winked instead of laughing. He put his empty glass on top of one of the garbage cans.

Back in their familiar seats, Asher crossed a leg over the other, knee bouncing the seat back in front of him. Brooke forgot Asher's presence, though there he was, warm and eager, limbs sometimes brushing each other's on the velvet armrest. Music like this was one of the hallmarks of civilization, or maybe it was civilization's point. Listening to it in 2014 tethered you to the millions (was that the number?) who had heard it the previous centuries. You felt small and big at the same time. This wasn't something that could only belong to Asher, though these tickets would have cost a lot of money. It could also belong to the souls above them in the cheap seats, the hundreds near the spectral chandeliers, closer to God.

A hand on her knee. Gentle pressure, a reminder. The first note was somber. Yes, funeral music, mourning music. Brooke focused not on the faces of strangers or the memories that bubbled up but on the sounds. There was a beauty in unison; all those strings after the same thing. Sometimes, a lone instrument emerged from the thicket and she was chastened to realize she couldn't identify it. It didn't seem like a clarinet or a piccolo, it sounded like some message from elsewhere. The notes strained higher. They were not plaintive. They were furious. There was some terrible knowledge in the sound.

Asher had pulled one knee onto the other. It was familiar, this music, and he leaned forward, as though there were something to see besides the faces of the players. What would she make of it, the girl at his side? Mozart seemed to be asking a question. The notes called out into what felt like night and the only thing that returned was an echo of the music itself. He thought about everyone he had ever known, his parents, his daughter, Carol, even Barbara. They all seemed to be in the room, maybe everyone in the world was. Could one man have committed to paper this dialogue with eternity? It did not seem possible. He knew it would happen and it did. He began to cry. His eyes were open. The music grew quieter, and he stared up at the stage, and tears fell onto his cheeks.

Brooke noticed. Of course she noticed. The music drew down into itself. It was quieter in some way that was unbearable, and Asher's tears were also quiet. They were steady, they were mournful. It was not awe at beauty, or simply that, but the knowledge of his own mortality. The music was about death and death came for us all. He cried. He cried, and continued to cry as he clapped his hands together. Brooke wished she was the sort of woman to have tissues in her bag. Some of the crowd were moved to stand as they applauded. Asher stopped clapping, covered his face with his hands, not ashamed. Let her see. He trusted her. It might have looked like he was crying for someone else. This was not it, and he sensed that Brooke knew it, and forgave him. He wept for himself, the life that he had loved and was now almost over. She put her hand on his shoulder. He continued to weep for what seemed a long time, but it was only ninety seconds or so.

T he other night, the girl who cooks for us, she made these bars. Like from a midwestern potluck. Downright Lutheran. She knows I have a sweet tooth. She does them with fruit and chickpeas or some stupid thing, it's basically a vitamin. So it's late, we're in the kitchen, prowling around, peckish, whatever, and I say to Carol, 'Hand me that,' and I stop. Because the word isn't there. I can see the thing in the crock on the counter and I don't have the word." He looked at her from across the table. A votive flickered in its séance way.

Brooke wasn't sure what word he meant. They were drinking a fine, sweet whiskey.

Asher's eyes were so clear. Not even red from the tears. Disembodied, you'd not have taken them for decades old. He was vain about them. His mother's had marbled with cataract. "*Spatula*. But I stood there—*Hand me that*—and Carol is looking at me because she sees what the problem is."

He went on. "Like I said, you hear music like that, your mind wanders. But there's that risk that it'll wander right off a cliff." He was excusing his tears. He had been unbearably moved. No human was a match for Mozart. "We say all that stuff is about God. Mozart, Bach, Notre Dame."

"The Sistine Chapel," Brooke added. God was other people, was that something that was said? Or was that hell?

"All man's greatest achievements. They're for God. Maybe there's something to that." Once a month, a doctor came to his house, accompanied by a nurse so sexy she was like a gag, pillowy tits and Bratislava accent. Asher sat on the edge of his own bed and had his blood pressure taken, his eyes illuminated, was interrogated to test his body and mind. He was healthy, occasional forgotten word be damned. Why was he afraid of God? "What do you want from me?"

It was simple. She wanted him to change her life. She wanted him to take care of her, as easily as he'd taken care of the humble oyster. As easily as he would take care of Ghalyela. *Buy me this apartment*, she could say. *Make me your daughter. Care for me. Protect me. Love me.* She had ordered fries, and was impatient for them to be delivered. "What do you want from me?"

"Aren't we friends?" Asher finished his drink. "Of course, people will say we're in love." He had pretended pique, but it had privately thrilled to see himself and Carol in the *National Enquirer.* "But maybe I do want something from you. I can't quite pinpoint what it is."

"I want you to show me how to make a life." She was hedging.

The waiter set down a bowl of fries. Asher picked one up and studied it. "That's easy. You have to marry, Brooke. Find a Carol. Someone to take you to hear the Philharmonic and cry when they get to the Mozart. You'll think of me, maybe." He saw her phantom boyfriend again: a firm handshake, a cleft chin, beach-colored hair.

This again. She worried what was deficient in her, why she was so different. "I don't want love. I want myself. I know this makes people crazy when I say it." She knew Kim and Matthew discussed this about her just as Brooke and Matthew discussed Kim's fortune. "Maybe there's—maybe something's wrong with me," she ventured.

Asher thought he had the answer. "You think it's convention. Something to *disrupt*. Your generation is so keen on that. What you can't comprehend is that it's human nature. That's where social convention *comes from*. Love is what people want, it's what you want, in some part of you that you pretend doesn't exist. Who is going to take care of you?"

She had a theory. She never spoke it aloud. Perhaps she could not offer love because she had been denied it. Her own mother, not her true mother but what they called her first mother, had not wanted her. Who then ever would? "Can't I take care of myself?" *Can't you,* she almost added. "I don't know how to be another kind of person. This is who I am. I don't want love and romance. I want a promise for my future."

"No such thing, I think." Asher sipped his sweet, cold drink. "Is that what you want from me? Some guarantee that everything will be okay? You know everything about my life. You of all people should know I cannot make such an assurance to you. Life does not work that way."

"How does it work?" She would accept this from him: some explanation for the world. She spooned out mayonnaise, suddenly so hungry.

"Mine's almost over and I don't know. I was thinking. Mozart made that music. Just some guy. Two centuries ago. And we still hear it. That is a legacy. That is a life. What's next? Nothing?"

As protégé she had no insight on the question of the afterlife. "You will leave an extraordinary legacy. The violinist. The library. The oysters."

He had forgotten about the oysters. He didn't know what she meant. "You know what? I feel guilty. About dying and leaving Carol behind. About wasting decades on making a business. Not money, a business." Brooke reminded him of his old shrink, Dr. Simpson, so he talked to her as though she were his confessor, bound by discretion. "Long time ago. Just starting out, my uncle Iz, he gave me a break when he let me take over the company. Left his money in it." Asher had used that as operating capital. He'd made a shrewd deal, and quick. It paid off, and he simply paid the sum back to his uncle. "He owned the thing. He didn't understand. Thought he was doing his nephew a favor."

"So maybe he was." Brooke didn't see the moral failing here because she didn't want to. "It was a long time ago."

"I was wrong. It was not ethical. He was my uncle, for heaven's sake. A good man, would have given me anything. It was decades ago. He's dead. I still think about it. But my God, I wanted that first thousand. On and on. I wanted that first ten thousand, the first hundred thousand, the million. You know how long it takes to get from a million to a billion? It was all I wanted in my life." What a thing to do with your time on this planet. Mozart would scoff. Mozart would laugh.

He was a saint, but he didn't see it. "Life is long. It's complicated. You're not writing music but you're doing something." He could, she wanted to say, help her. That might assuage his conscience. "You'll leave the world a better place."

"You don't know anything." He was so good at understanding people but struggled to understand this Brooke. "You have a whole half century, more, ahead of you. You can't be so cautious. You must love. It's all there is. There's nothing else."

"I'm going to take care of myself." She was working on it even then.

He should take care of her. He should put her in the will. He should cut her a check. That's what she was getting at, surely. But she hadn't even wanted the amount he'd tried to give her for lunch. "It's a tall order, taking care of yourself." The way they were talking! On some level he was shocked by it. Maybe this was bad, a kind of infidelity.

"I understand the world better than you think I do." She had learned that it was a game, fixed. You got good grades and ended up with nothing to show for it. "I'm thinking about myself, because I understand that no one else will."

He was exasperated. "That's *why* you get married."

"Is that why Carol married you? To take care of her?"

Asher ate one of the fries. "We love each other." Carol had known about the four billion dollars before she'd ever shaken his hand in a San Francisco conference room. And Carol had understood why he had to give it away. But Carol had also pointed out that he need not give it *all* away. Carol had consulted with the managers. Carol knew that Asher was toying around in the market again. Carol understood that he had done well. Like riding a bike, as they said. Only last week, Carol had come to him, and asked that he leave a bit more for her than originally planned. Well, why not? He loved her. He would provide.

"You're one of the few people who can actually take care of the people you love." He was the only one she was likely to ever know. "You could take care of me."

He said what people with money were obliged to say. "It's about more than money."

"I don't need someone to talk to about what we heard on NPR. To sit next to me at dinner parties." She wanted what Natalie's dead mother had: a place to be.

This was important. He had already wept, there was nothing left. "I don't want you to have regrets. The worst thing." He waited. "So take this. Be my heir. Continue my work." There were no tears this time. "I want to save the whales. Ban the bomb. Every good thing we ever talked about. I want to do that. I want it. Carol's too young. It's not urgent for her, and it's not the money she made. You under-stand me, you believe in our work. And it is ours. Take it from me."

Brooke was quiet. She was drunk and too many things had happened. He was offering her something, but it was not what she wanted. She hadn't asked for a sanctified responsibility. She wanted something smaller, more base, more selfish. She thought she knew who she was, that most fundamental of things, but proximity to Asher Jaffee had somehow obscured her sense of herself. Strangely, it didn't make her want to get away from him; rather, it made her want never to be without him.

S he lived alone and didn't need to make excuses for herself. Brooke privately thanked Rachel, without whom she'd never have tried this restaurant, then fretted, briefly, that her brother and his bride-to-be might show up. How would she explain herself? Brooke wore clothes she knew were flattering. She brought a novel. It was eight, so there was a crowd, but space was found for her at the bar, just as she'd planned. There had been some gamble—a night off, a new job, maybe he was ugly or unappealing in some way he wasn't in memory, or gay, or married and honest. This had something to do with Asher Jaffee, as so much of her life now seemed to. The thing their night at the Philharmonic had been moving toward, the thing it was lacking, was sex. Brooke had some kind of fidget or urge she couldn't explain. Maybe it was to do with whatever the pricker had put into her body. Maybe it was simply being human.

"You're joining us for dinner." The ceremony of a place mat, a napkin, a glass of water on a coaster, a menu.

She ordered a martini and studied the menu like she'd never before seen one.

"What can we get you this evening?" He had command over his eyebrows, a gift, communicating his interest either in her or in a substantial tip. He made everyone he spoke to feel they were the only people on the planet.

"What do you recommend?" She wasn't asking but playing.

Whether he recognized her even he didn't know. "You're a gin martini type. You're a steak frites type."

"I'm hungry tonight." Somehow she did not need to raise her voice to be heard over the din. "What if I want a first course?"

It was a sidewalk game of chance. Possible to win big, possible to be humiliated. "A Caesar salad." He crossed arms against chest, showing the body to its best advantage, chambray shirt pushed back over veiny muscles, a peek of a youthful tattoo you couldn't quite make out.

"Correct." This was a remarkable performance. She felt the falsity and the conviction in every syllable. It was this way with men; you had to pretend for it to work.

"They make us tell you that it comes with anchovies on top." He didn't want to imply that she was not adventurous.

She ordered that. He would consider the palate an important measure of something. A grin like a boy's, self-satisfied, maybe a little dumb. He left her with her book. He presented her salad. He refilled her water. She finished every bite. There was another ceremony delivering the sharp knife, clutched in a napkin so he wouldn't dirty it, more water, the steak. He had to clear space to accommodate the oval plate. He brought dollhouse-size jars of ketchup, mustard, mayonnaise.

The char yielded to the serrated blade. Blood pooled into grease. Impossible to read when the food demanded both hands. She ate. She looked from the plate to the room to the window to the wall to the faces. People intent on their conversations, their spinach salads, their crème caramels, trying to spear the Luxardo at the bottom of their Manhattans.

She was caught unawares by the glass of wine he brought. "Just trust me on this one."

She tasted it, put the glass down. "You've earned my trust." The whole room felt like sex, the place full of lovers and spouses and one couple whose babysitter fell through, their seven-year-old watching cartoons on an iPad while his thirty-dollar hamburger went cold.

"I appreciate a clean plate." He whisked away the mess.

"Did your mother insist on it?" She took a sip of water. There was something filthy in the sentiment, some wicked twist, perversity. She felt something beneath her skin. There was nothing wrong with her, or at least this part of her was in working order.

"Every night!" He laughed and put a hand on his belly, jiggling it, though he was lean, muscled, and knew it. "I'm going to give you a minute. Then we'll talk about dessert."

On the way to the bathroom, a balding man put his hand on her wrist as she passed. "Could we get another round—the cabernet and a vodka soda?"

Brooke looked at the man, just a generic man, a redness to his face, his hair nothing, his eyes less still. His date was a man much younger, with a strong jaw and superhero hair. "I'm sorry?" Why was her instinct always to apologize? It was to do with being a woman, it was to do with being Black. It was a necessity and she hated it.

As the man repeated his order, Brooke interrupted. "I don't work here." She withdrew from his touch.

He began to say something ("I'm so—"), but Brooke walked away before he could finish his apology. Walked, not stormed. She had seen the Black waitress, a light-skinned girl with braids to her neck. They looked nothing alike. In the bathroom, she breathed to return herself to that pinch of anticipation. She would not let this distract her from her mission. She would not be reminded just how the world worked, not right then. Brooke washed her face, didn't worry about her smell, which would be the same as his, as everyone gathered in that close room, butter, herb, fat, flame. It would be better, more honest, than smelling of perfume and breath mint. She saw herself in the mirror and she was beautiful. God, she was beautiful. She was an animal and, like one, knew just what she wanted.

The customers beside her had left. He had folded her napkin, refilled her water, righted the place mat. She opened the book.

"So?" The eyebrow, again, provided the punctuation. "Something sweet?"

It was all but done now. She should buy him a drink, she said, a thanks for the wine. He poured them each one of those whiskeys that taste of smoke. It had to mellow, and he'd be back when it was ready to sip. Victory. She read. He returned, stood on his side of the bar, and they clinked their glasses, and they made their introductions. His name was Estes and she didn't remark upon its oddity as most people would have. He liked this.

He brought the bill, but asked her to stay. His words: "Stick around, if you would?" He was off at nine, he said. The couple with the child departed, father toting sleepy junior. There was a changing of the guard, the untying of an apron at the waist, and Estes was relieved.

The summer trees were so thick with leaf that the moon didn't seem quite bright enough. She could feel its tug on her the way the waves did. Maybe volition didn't matter, people just a collection of impulses, life like the board game that shared its name, with a finite number of paths.

They kissed in the back seat of an SUV driven by a quiet Bangladeshi. She could smell meat on her coat, her hands, Estes's neck, his chambray shirt. He held her hand as they climbed the steps. She unlocked the door and had the passing thought that he could rape her, kill her, abduct her, that Alex and her mother and Kim and Eeyore would be so sad.

His nudity enhanced his beauty. His body was strong and downy, his movements confident, every choice marked by an inquisitive "Okay?" She said yes without words. She didn't want him to seek consent. She wanted him to overwhelm. She stopped seeing the familiar bed, the bit of mess left behind so it wouldn't seem like she was compulsive, like that deliberate imperfection in beadwork so you don't anger God by daring to make something flawless. It took longer than she'd expected, his focus not flagging even once he'd ejaculated, politely onto himself instead of her bed.

A glass of water, nude in the kitchen, and he asked if he could shower. This was more intimate than anything they'd done to each other. He'd worked all day; she'd tasted the sweat on his chest. They kissed at the door, with real affection, or maybe appreciation, with no nicety to revise the transaction into something else, no phone numbers exchanged, no talk of plans. She bolted the door, the final

word, the true farewell, but also that was her habit. She was returned to herself. She would shower, drink water, go back to the
bed, the meaty smell dissipating but still present. Again, in that
alternate scenario in which she was raped, killed; surely Asher Jaffee
would offer a reward, surely he'd want justice.

It had been—not easy, but direct. A series of steps, a specific
goal. She'd barely even thought about it, or, maybe more importantly, hadn't told herself how consciously she was thinking of it.
Wouldn't it be as easy with Asher, and wouldn't the satisfaction last
longer? Was tonight but a rehearsal for something she could barely
bring herself to say that she wanted? She had simply used the man
called Estes, who was now a dull, warm sensation, and by tomorrow
would be forgotten, a ghost.

T hey called this rite *sit-down Chinese*, family vernacular to distinguish it from a Wednesday night of sugary chicken picked directly from the cardboard container and bickering over the last shrimp curled in the dun, thick noodles. This particular restaurant was a destination for minor celebrations, like positive parent-teacher conferences and ninth-grade Alex's comic triumph in *You Can't Take It with You*. Though they were only four, Maggie badgered the hostess into seating them at one of the round tables, because she thought a lazy Susan festive.

"This is a special place for us." Maggie filled and handed around little cups of weak oolong.

"She's heard all about it." Alex draped an arm across the back of Rachel's chair.

"I'm glad I finally got the invite!" Rachel was, as ever, happy to be along. All the more so at a Chinese dinner, where no one would notice that she was not drinking alcohol, which was a part of why Alex had proposed this destination.

Brooke had her elbows on the table, cup in both hands. "Manage your expectations," she said. The food was run-of-the-mill, beside the point, but Brooke knew that Rachel's excitement had nothing to do with the menu.

"I happen to think the salt-and-pepper shrimp is excellent," Maggie said, misunderstanding the jest, feeling defensive.

Alex agreed. "We're definitely ordering that."

Rachel, almost daughter by law, asked Maggie how she had been, something the children would not have done.

"It's been a lot." Maggie was grateful for the girl's interest. "You know that we lost Alex's auntie. I've been working on a memorial service."

Rachel made an appropriately grave face.

"That reminds me to remind both of you. We're doing it at Auntie Sayo's. But you know how she is with planning. So it's mostly fallen to me. But never mind. I've got so many people coming— girls we knew at Barnard, some of the people from *Vogue*. Just be sure you have something to wear. Brooke, when we were at Theory, we got you that black suit. I thought that might be nice."

Alex came to their defense. "Mom, we're in our thirties. You don't have to dress us."

"Old habits. I just want things to go perfectly." A pause as though for a tear to well. The party logistics had helped distract Maggie from her anger over her dear friend's death. The world should not work this way, but maybe if she exerted control over her life that world would leave her alone.

"I'm sure it'll be great." Brooke dipped one of the oily wontons into the bowl of orange sauce. She heard the crunch in her ear as she asked, "When is it?"

"Next Saturday, the nineteenth. Auntie Sayo's place, remember, not ours. My place is hardly big enough." A wry laugh at her own expense.

Brooke looked heavenward and the cheap reddish light looked back. "I have some bad news. A schedule conflict."

That Saturday, Ghalyela's scholars would present their culminating performance. It was something of an open house, a chance for prospective families to see what the Throop School was all about. It was an advertisement, effectively, for the session Ghalyela ran those final days of summer, when parents most needed something to do with their children. That weeklong course was a part of Throop's commitment to the community and, sliding scale or no, it was also one of the school's biggest infusions of capital. That, Brooke had said, was until the Asher and Carol Jaffee Foundation entered the picture.

"What could possibly be more important than Auntie Paige?" It was one of those questions to which no answer was possible, none required, none sought.

Brooke explained that she had decided this was the moment to introduce Asher Jaffee to the Throop School. Jody was skeptical that he would bother, that he would trek in from the country to go to Brooklyn, but Brooke had faith. Let him see the children dancing, a sight that would move even an impassive heart. It was the key moment: Asher's first look at Brooke's project, the final step in Brooke's work. Here, she would say, are the souls. All that would remain was the ask: save them. *Asher, let's give these people a million dollars.* "There's so much riding on this. I've already got Asher to commit. You know he doesn't work weekends, not even Fridays, so this was a big favor for me, for the school."

"I don't understand what I'm hearing." Maggie thought this gentler than admitting that she did not understand Brooke herself. "How can this—your auntie. This is a celebration of her life. She loved you. She adored you. You loved her!"

Brooke didn't think it quite as simple as that. "I did. I think maybe she'd understand. That I'm doing important work—"

"Important work is curing cancer. It's feeding the hungry. It's immigration law. Nuclear nonproliferation. This is just an elaborate scam by one man to dodge the estate tax. How can you not see that?" Maggie's tone was urgent.

Alex knew that his mother had gone too far. "I'm sure Brooke can manage both. Right? What time is the memorial?"

Brooke ignored this. "Mom, you don't know anything about it. I've tried to tell you—some of the things we're doing. It's like what you said. Oysters cleaning the waterways. Children learning to care about art. It matters. What I do, it matters, to the world but also to me."

Softer now, Maggie continued. "I'm glad you've found work that you like. That you find meaningful. I know that teaching wasn't for you. But how can you put that work ahead of your life? This is real. This is very disappointing to me. I won't be the only one. Allison will be there. Sayo. Kim. Your brother and sister-in-law." She pointed at Rachel, who frowned down at her empty plate.

The task was always keeping up with her friends, her brother and sister-in-law, everyone else. "The show's over by four. I'll take a car, I can be in the city in an hour. But I have to do this." Brooke was resolute.

"See?" Alex always saw the brightest side. "It's settled."

Maggie disagreed. "None of us *have to* do anything, Brooke. We choose. We decide who we are, the sort of person we're going to be. I've tried to teach you that, now I have to just let you be." She was disappointed.

If Brooke listened, she could hear the heartbeat thrum of the light overhead. She could make out the traffic, ever present as the ocean. There was a whisper of air recirculating and somewhere distant the crackle of their dumplings being fried. "I'm sorry if I'm a disappointment."

Maggie was stung. "I never said that." But she knew that she didn't need to specify. She knew just what she had said, and knew how it would have sounded.

"We're not fighting." Alex thought that saying it made it true. "It's all sorted out."

"You did say that." Brooke didn't want to go back through it. "I know it. I'm not you. I'm only me. Trying to make my life. And I'm doing that. You don't see it, and you don't understand it, and you don't respect it, but I am doing it."

"This job, Brooke. It's only about money. It's not about service. That's about human communion, about feeling, about some genuine aspiration for something. This is just money. Moving money from him to other people." Maggie wanted her daughter to understand, but comprehension was indifferent to how badly it was desired.

Brooke didn't know how to make her mother understand. Perhaps it couldn't be done. This was private, a crusade. "I will come. I'll be late, but I will come." She ate another wonton.

Rachel, meaning only to be kind, decided to fill the temporary silence. "Brooke! Tell me what's going on with your apartment search."

Brooke sat back, considered this woman she did not know at all. "Maybe later. First why don't you bring Mom up to speed on your big news?" Brooke laid a hand across her own belly, flat and taut, satisfied.

T he school had no air-conditioning. The auditorium was unbearable, but the gymnasium was vast enough to be almost pleasant. The wood floor was a peeling green. Backboards attached to the ceiling could be lowered by winch. There were sun-faded photographs of souls long lost to adulthood, grinning with basketballs. The acoustics were punishing. Children, like some species of animal, jockeyed for dominance by shrieking. There were girls whispering in private conspiracy. Boys huddled in groups, watching something on someone's big brother's cellphone. Asher seemed so old, because this was the first Brooke had seen him surrounded by the so young. But Asher felt alive. The school smelled just like the one he'd attended.

Brooke had some impulse to take pictures. She had hoped for cookies and juice, a vantage of Asher surrounded by Black girls in kente sarongs, holding up a handwritten banner communicating welcome. Some balloons. A trace of joy. No, none of that. Ghalyela took a different perspective. An honored guest deserved her hospitality but not her scholars' humbling. These Black children did not have to acknowledge a white man for allowing them to exist. Remember, they hadn't sought his help, and he would offer not salvation but investment. Ghalyela wore her customary white, no makeup but a theatrical smile. "Sister Brooke." The endearment sounded like a measure of trust that it wasn't.

"Asher Jaffee, Ghalyela Jefferson." Brooke hoped to wed these two strangers in some profound union. It was funny, or anticlimax, to introduce them to each other.

"Pleasure." Asher, who would indeed have made a good statesman, held the hand of the woman dressed like a benign witch, all-seeing.

"Such a great pleasure, Mr. Jaffee. I'll say Brother Asher." She indicated the cavernous space, crowded with mothers and aunties, the fathers who had been corralled into attendance. "You are in for a treat."

A pervasive camaraderie. He felt he belonged—yes, even him. In every room such as this was some white grandparent. "I'm looking forward to a show."

Ghalyela deposited the guests of honor in metal folding chairs, reserved per the white pages Scotch-taped to their backs. On the court, some teenage boys, barefoot, bare-chested, were sounding tentative thumps on their djembes.

Alissa McDonald descended the bleachers, Mohammed racing to that mountain, nodding greetings to everyone she passed. "Brooke Orr. Great to see you again."

Brooke had her hands tucked under her armpits as though cold.

"Alissa. Nice to see you." The near echo of her words was a measure of Brooke's disinterest.

Alissa, born candidate, would not waste an opportunity. "You must be Mr. Jaffee."

So many handshakes in every day. "Nice to meet you." It always sounded sincere.

"This is Alissa McDonald. She's running for local office." It was a matter of pride: Brooke would not be this girl's sister. Sisterhood was a tool, and Brooke would be the one to wield it.

"City council," Alissa explained. "And as such I needed to meet the man interested in investing in this community. Just the kind of thing I'm hoping to facilitate."

The woman's Brooklyn pronunciation put Asher in mind of his own mother. "For the record, credit goes to Brooke. I'm excited to see what's got her so excited."

"Community is everything. That's why I'm focused on local office."

Asher had a soft spot for a delusional go-getter. "I appreciate the ambition." Anyway, he had to be nice to her, lest he seem racist.

"I'm going to shoot my shot. If you're interested in supporting a progressive candidate who is committed to a community-driven approach to local politics. Working with the citizens on the ground to create governance that's more representative of actual opinion and need. I'm that candidate. It's an off year, it's a special election, the party machinery is very powerful. There's a lot of support and money behind the designated favorite. And I am definitely not that person." She could deliver this spiel with a straight face. She'd go far.

"The foundation does not support political candidates," Brooke interjected. She hated Alissa, her entitlement, her self-satisfaction, her familiarity with a man she'd only just met.

Alissa rebuffed with a smile. "Mr. Jaffee, your support would mean a big difference to us. Now we've met. I'll stay in touch." Then the woman was gone, absorbed into the crowd.

Asher could sense Brooke not rolling her eyes. "You don't care for her."

"It doesn't matter." Alissa hadn't managed anything yet, only acted as though it were inevitable that she would.

Ghalyela strode to center court to the jangling of her cowrie anklets. The unpleasant feedback of a cheap microphone. One more thing Asher's grace might rectify. Asher's money could buy everything they'd ever need. "Ago!"

Many of the assembled knew their part. "Ame!"

The response was too half-hearted for Ghalyela. She repeated her call once, twice, five times, and smiled as the voices coalesced into unison, Asher's and Brooke's included, once they figured out what was being asked of them.

The teenagers with drums had organized themselves into a line. They wound across the court, steadfast. Some in the crowd picked up the rhythm with feet pounded on glossy floorboards. Dancers, several girls and a lone bucktoothed boy with blond locs, emerged. They stomped and thrust. A few grinned and others frowned in childish concentration. The drums shifted and the dance followed. The percussion contained pride, bravery, introspection, triumph. There was a narrative, too elusive to follow, like opera. Adults took shaky cellphone video for housebound grandparents. Brooke couldn't even remember which was the child called Sistine. They were, every one of them, an accomplishment as grand as that chapel, as anything Mozart had come up with. Surely Asher Jaffee would see that. There were jubilant cheers. It was either one performance with several encores or many planned interludes. After thirty minutes, there was more applause, brief remarks by Ghalyela, and the assembled were directed to the tables to enroll in the after-school program scheduled for that fall.

There were Girl Scouts with order forms, a frowning Trinidadian woman selling bake and sorrel, and two young entrepreneurs, fraternal twin sisters, pushing homemade shea lotion redolent of vanilla. There were proud parents cradling bodega carnations, little siblings holding on to oversize helium balloons of congratulation. Brooke gripped Asher's arm as they slipped through the good-natured crowd, like a bride on a father's arm. He seemed diminished and in need of her protection. She was pleased to be the one providing that, to walk beside him.

The day's heat smacked them. More alive than he'd felt in a minute. "That was rousing!" The primal drums echoed the thrum of a healthy heart. His still was. Thank Christ. The whole show was a wish, and he was the one who might grant it.

Christopher, reliable Christopher, was parked illegally in the lane reserved for school buses. They stood beside the gleaming, sturdy car.

Brooke could see that Jody had been right; a story had been decisive. The story of Asher Jaffee, savior. "I'm happy you were able to be there." Now this business could proceed. Now she could ask him, or recommend to him, or however you preferred to think of it.

He looked at Brooke's face, saw beneath its attempted impassivity. Those children were a ghost of a Brooke he'd never meet. We wish that, of the people we truly love, to see them as they were before we knew them. "Were you moved, Brooke? You're a stoic. I almost said cynic, but that's not quite right, is it? This was your idea."

You couldn't help it! Angel children, rehearsing for life itself. "I'm excited that you're excited. I suppose it's time to talk about a gift."

"I showed you Mozart and you showed me this." Asher squinted in the sun. He could touch her but he could not reach her. What a world. You still learned something, saw something for the first time, no matter how old you were. This girl had done something for him and he was grateful. "It's a job well done, I'd say."

"Thank you, Asher." His pride filled her up. There was nothing like it. He was her father in this moment, a person who did not exist. She could do anything.

"We'll talk about it next week. But I don't think it's premature to celebrate. Where are we going?" He was not done with her. He wanted only to sit beside her, tell her more things about himself, ask more things about her, drink, feel the way that she made him feel.

She pulled her black blazer closed, though the day was astonishingly hot. Her funereal best for her beloved Auntie Paige. She had somewhere to be. "Where are we going?" It was the right question. She had no sense of her own destination. Asher would help Ghalyela. Surely Brooke would see some reward, too.

He couldn't take her to the club, of course. And he'd taken her to Jean-Georges. "We'll go to the Carlyle. They have a nice bar."

Christopher held the door first for Brooke, who slid across the seat, familiar now. She relaxed into the Bentley's chill. She leaned her head against the high seat and was able, from the back window, to glimpse the blue sky. Paige's memorial service had started but an hour ago. The guests would linger two hours more at the least.

It did not happen during the drive over the bridge and up toward the grand hotel, it did not happen as they were being shown through the dim room to a small table, it did not happen during her first potent and sweet Manhattan but her second one—that was when Brooke understood. She was in that elegant place, listening to Asher tell a story about the time he met Margaret Thatcher, and Brooke hadn't even looked at her watch, she had simply known that she would not run out to Fifth Avenue, wave arms for a taxi, direct a disinterested driver to Kim's mother's apartment. She could not be in two places at once, she could not be two people at once. So she would be this person. She ordered a third drink and Asher walked her to the bellman and insisted that he put her into a cab. Brooke did not look at her phone, which was all text messages and missed calls from the people who knew her best, but stared out as the buildings slipped slowly past and reflected that Paige, unique among her aunties, an iconoclast, a presence, a woman to admire, might have understood.

Eileen, in menopausal flush, seemed impervious to the powerful air-conditioning. The rest of the foundation women went about in blazers and pashminas, slouched as though trying to preserve some of the body's warmth. Asher noticed none of this. He set the temperature in every room. He controlled the weather. And now the frost in his office was a direct result of the man, leaning back in the chair, hands cradling his head from behind, perilously close to the Philip Guston behind his desk, lost in a bad mood.

"This isn't the business I want to be in, Eileen." He could not hear how petulant he sounded.

The Asher and Carol Jaffee Foundation was trying to dispose of one of the Jaffee Corporation's last remaining holdings: dozens of parcels of land across this most charmed nation. Old warehouses, abandoned malls, parking lots. It had been the boon that made Asher Jaffee rich, but now was just collateral that no one wanted. This had

been Jody's brainstorm: deed each to the nearest local community college. A sweeping investment in accessible higher education. It would
go further than some never-visited room in an Ivy League library. It
might change lives. Asher just wanted to be nice. Why was it so difficult?

While these holdings were not useful, they were valuable. The
idea was the schools could develop, sell, whatever they wished. They'd
take these off Jaffee's hands and get richer themselves. But there
were complications, as there inevitably were, of taxes, and rules, and
many boring other matters. Eileen repeated something that one of
the lawyers had said on the conference call just ended.

Asher rubbed at his blue eyes the way people who wore glasses
did when they took them off. "Don't need to hear it again. Anyway,
I'm not going to have this whole thing undone by some tax bill on
an Indiana warehouse."

Brooke piped up. Why else was she in the room? "Maybe—if it's
a donation. There must be some way to have the state forgive these
things. In the interest of the gift." Brooke could make it make sense.
If the government would listen, they would understand.

In this moment, Brooke reminded him of first Barbara and now
Carol. This was how they spoke of the money that he manipulated,
commanded, conjured. They imagined their proximity to him gave
them the right. But it was silly, like talking to a child. Carol, lately,
had almost badgered. She felt that things would be so much simpler
if she knew there was a certain number she could count on. You
know, *after.* She could manage the upkeep of the house. She could
keep the staff on. She didn't understand that numbers were uncertain, liable to change, to grow or shrink. But Asher loved her and

Asher relented. His irritation wasn't directed at Brooke but at his wife. "I don't know if telling the state tax authority about my good intentions is going to get anyone very far."

He had to be wrong! There were tax exemptions for charitable giving. He had those lawyers and advisers, but perhaps they had failed to look at the matter the right way. "I just think—you're doing good work, if there were someone in the government who understood that. A liaison or something at the IRS."

God, incredible how she sounded just like Carol! Carol, daughter of a coupon-clipping *homemaker* and a man who ran a St. Paul hardware store, lamenting that she'd no idea how she'd sleep worrying about how to keep up the tennis court, the personal trainer, the insurance on the art, for the next twenty, thirty, however many years she outlived him by. To hear her tell it, the whole enterprise of their life was a burden. How could he put some cause, however noble, over his own wife's peace of mind? "That's not how it works." He was curt with Brooke because he could not be with Carol. But these women didn't understand what he did! He dared her. "Email the lawyers. Collate these numbers. Dig into what we can do. You'll see quickly that you have no idea what you're talking about."

"I think that's a nonstarter." Eileen wouldn't let Brooke be punished. This had nothing to do with her staff. "I'd like to bring in Jeremy. He's the one I mentioned to you last week—"

His patience was at an end. "I'll give them some time but we are making this gift next year."

"The crowning achievement." Eileen italicized the words just so. She heard in them his triumph and her own. She saw them on her CV. She saw her retirement. She saw that, as architect of this gift, she could be an even more expensive consultant than Jody. Eileen was repeating the story that Jody had spun. "I'm fairly certain that it'll be the single largest gift to the nation's community college system."

"Let's look into that *fairly*, Eileen." She was writing her résumé; he was drafting the obituary. "I want credit. I want a splash."

"I'll study the language." She was tired, but couldn't be tired. There would be more of this. "We'll make sure people understand the scope of what you're doing."

Asher turned his attention to his protégé. "What about you? You and Jody have been huddling together for weeks. What are you cooking up?"

Brooke thought those dancing children spoke for themselves more eloquently than she ever could. "You saw the show," she reminded him. "You liked what you saw."

"Asher mentioned." Eileen tried to assist. "It sounded like you were impressed."

That. He had forgotten it. There were important things to be done. "Sure. Cute. Sweet. Let's get a check out—"

Brooke felt something in her throat. "We have a full presentation for you. A proposal. I'd like you to see our thinking. We're hoping for a significant gift."

"You haven't made any promises." Eileen barely glanced up.

She wasn't a child! No promises. But dreams. A triumphant story. "Nothing like that. But they have ambition. We were thinking maybe—a headquarters. A place to call home. We're just in the early stages yet." She wanted them to hear the whole grand vision, to be impressed, to be moved.

"I thought we were talking about graham crackers and art supplies?" Asher shook his head. A headquarters? He liked a go-getter but he had sent her out on a lark. It was a flirtation. It was a way of giving her a reason to live as she had given him one. It was tit for tat. It was his gratitude but now the matter was decided.

"We'll discuss it with Jody—" Eileen said.

"Ten thousand dollars," Asher said. He remembered every sum ever mentioned in his presence. "That's what you said. When you were at that school? They wouldn't give you ten thousand for an art program. So, here it is. Justice." It was his gift to her.

A million dollars for oysters. Ten thousand for the souls of Black children. "We were talking about—"

Asher was done with this. "Eileen and I do have other things we need to focus on."

"In fact, we should go." Eileen stood. She was done talking. "Brooke and I can hammer out next steps. I'll get a meeting with Jeremy, and we'll give the team a timeline."

Natalie forever hovered on the periphery. She sensed the end of the meeting and swept into the room like a stagehand, papers in her arms and prompts for Asher Jaffee. So they were dismissed. Brooke couldn't even catch Asher's eye. She followed Eileen into the hall. Never mind. She needed a new strategy. But she would demand, from Asher, another chance. She had that right, at least.

A conspirator's whisper from Eileen. She beckoned Brooke to follow, closed the door to the little office. Eileen made a jocular face, like an adult who's never spent time with one trying to amuse a child. "He has his days."

Brooke didn't want to be disloyal but—"What was all that about?"

"I told you that this is what it's like, this sort of work. One man's whim, ultimately. It's not for the faint of heart. The real estate gift is, in some part, maybe largely, though you never heard this from me, about easing Asher's various tax liabilities. He's trying to clean up a mess that's been neglected for years. It was Jody's idea and it's a good one. You know the vice president's wife teaches at a community college? Asher thinks the whole thing in line with the administration's goals. So he calls the secretary of education. Prematurely, but never mind. The secretary is excited and for some reason suggests to Asher that this might be his shot at the Presidential Medal of Freedom."

So much for virtue being its own reward. This was who Asher was, a man like any other, with his small vanity. Yes, give him the Presidential Medal of Freedom! Did he not deserve it?

"The thing is, Asher wants it from Obama, not Hillary. So time is of the essence. Of course, the IRS and the lawyers won't care about that. It's just how it's going to be."

More importantly: "Jody and I have put together a thoughtful proposal. He went to the school with me on Saturday. He loved it." Brooke recalled Asher's old body in some not quite conscious sway as the drums filled the room. He had looked so happy. He had told her he was proud. "I was anticipating a more significant donation." He was only in a mood. She could try again. She had seduced that bartender, she could do anything.

"For more context." Eileen figured there was no point in discretion. "Asher has decided to move one billion dollars out of the foundation."

They had won him over, against her advice! "The Ford Foundation."

Eileen shook her head. "It's for Mrs. Jaffee. They've altered some of the estate planning." Her pause held what she could not say. "This is how it goes. He's changed his mind, or she has. It doesn't matter. We still have a lot to do, and we still have a lot of money to give away."

He had said that he was giving it all away before he died. But would anyone fact-check that after he had shuffled off? The ten thousand dollars Asher would give to Ghalyela would barely make a chip in his net worth, in Carol Jaffee's inevitable inheritance. And it would accomplish none of what Ghalyela hoped to. "We were working toward a much more ambitious number."

Eileen's heart had been broken a million times over. It came with the job. You had to remain, nonetheless, an optimist. "You heard him." Eileen softened. "Maybe he'll forget. Or maybe he won't. I wouldn't push it."

Brooke left Eileen's office and went back to her own. Jody had printed the presentation, a tidy stack atop Brooke's otherwise empty desk. The cover image was a smiling girl. Was that the child, Sistine? It didn't matter. Had she been a different person, Brooke would have shoved these off her desk, let them scatter on the floor. She turned the pile over. She had promised Ghalyela the world, and the world cost more than ten thousand dollars.

Brooke allowed herself a moment of self-pity. The Subway Pricker had got her and maybe she'd thought that meant something. She was chosen, she was the elect. Somehow she'd made a muddle of her life. She'd failed at a mission that had come to mean a great deal. She had missed the moment to honor Auntie Paige. Her mother was furious over that, but what was worse was her general, parental disappointment. Alex and Rachel were furious that she had disclosed their pregnancy over dinner, misunderstanding strategy as impulse. Brooke had only wanted to use information for the desired effect, something she had learned from Asher. Maybe he, not the pricker, was the one to blame. She had tried to live as Asher Jaffee advised and it had come only to all this.

There was, however, still the question of Andrea from Chase and whether she'd permit Brooke to buy, with some imaginary money, the apartment on Twenty-ninth Street. Maybe Asher hadn't been persuaded by Ghalyela's dancers and drummers because he was reserving his grace for Brooke herself. Maybe what Brooke wanted most was still possible.

Brooke hid in her office much of the morning. She was certain to see Asher if she ventured out, because he was everywhere, and she was uncertain that she wanted to. But an office was not a home, and she was not a teen free to sulk in the bedroom. Naturally, when eventually she did leave, she came across Asher and Carol Jaffee, cozy and side by side on the living-room sofa. Brooke had never met Carol but had seen her photograph so many times that she had come to feel something for her.

"There she is." Asher had been looking forward to this meeting. He thought it would absolve him of something, for Carol and Brooke to occupy the same room. It would clarify his real loyalty. "I was just telling Carol what a bear I was. I said you must be avoiding me."

"Don't be silly." Brooke held out a hand. It was time for her to perform. She would not disappoint. "Mrs. Jaffee."

"Carol, please." She had midwestern manners. She seemed nice.

Asher was at ease, his two women together at last. "Sit with us! Mrs. Jaffee was just checking up on me."

"I was in the neighborhood." Carol was happy her husband had work that gave meaning to his days. These were, she understood, numbered. But, she reasoned, everyone's were. Her name was on the letterhead but this was his passion. "Natalie told me Asher had a free hour so here I am."

"I think she's worried about all the fun you and I get up to around here." He felt license to flirt with his wife right there, testament to his innocence, his goodness.

Carol had heard him say this girl's name. It was one of a thousand names she heard from him in a day. Like most spouses, she had learned how to half listen. Carol never worried about her husband, and never mistrusted him. "You must have fun. You should see him at the end of the day. Bouncing off the walls. An overexcited kid."

"They go home the same way. Thrilled to be away from me." This was what he believed. "I'm a slave driver."

Brooke ignored this turn of phrase, distracted by something different in Asher's grin. She saw it was smug. He wanted the attention of President Obama as surely as she wanted his attention. "We're worn out after keeping up with you. Your relentless demands." *Give Sister Ghalyela one million dollars*, she wanted to say. *No, five. Ten. Twenty.* She deserved it. Souls cost money.

"This one likes to tease me, Carol. I'm like that comedian, what's his name? I get no respect!" His smile seemed put on.

"Brooke, you're enjoying your time here? I can't believe we haven't met. I guess we were gone on our extravagant vacation." Carol felt guilty, as she knew the rest of the staff well. "But never mind. We're back! And we'll have the chance to get to know each other a bit at the party."

No need to be anything but honest. "I love it." It was the truth after all. This job had given Brooke a sense of herself, a mission, a purpose. "I love it here. What party is that?"

"I'm not paying her to say that." Asher's jokes seemed more ridiculous, played for Carol's attention. "And it's Carol's birthday party. You haven't heard?" They shared that secret of the Frankenthaler, paid for, insured, and hidden away in a room the servants had pledged to keep Mrs. Jaffee from entering.

"Just a little something, at our place in the country. We're going to bring out everyone. Old friends. You and the rest of the staff, naturally. And the folks who have received gifts from the foundation." Carol pretended not to, but she loved a party.

Still a comic routine: "I've given them thirty-two million dollars already. I need to give them canapés, too?"

"That sounds lovely." Brooke had been inside that apartment in the city. Maybe being inside the house in the country would complete this revelation or whatever it was.

"Asher, stop joking. Brooke, is this what he's always like?" Carol knew, naturally, just what he was like.

Brooke understood this as an assertion of ownership. They were married. They were in love. Brooke looked at Carol more closely. Was there something coarse about her, something cheap, something unworthy of Asher Jaffee, or had Brooke simply come to believe that what existed between her and Asher was sanctified? Could Carol understand that? Was she afraid? She should have been.

Kim said they would christen the apartment. A private ceremony, a portent for the years to come. She bought a gingham blanket you'd use at a storybook picnic, ordered enough Thai appetizers for ten: fried parcels of pork and dough, chicken on wooden skewers, glassine rolls. Just some bites and then a movie down the street. In her head it was charming, an anecdote they'd repeat for years. But the apartment was cold, the recessed bulbs overhead unforgiving. Voices carried with nothing but right angles and bare surfaces to absorb them. The decorator had not yet brought in a single thing. There was nowhere to sit but the floor, and after the age of thirty, that was exercise, not rest.

Matthew perched on the step down into the living room, spring roll in fingers like a cigar. The restaurant had sent chopsticks, which he could never use, and Kim had no forks in the house. "At least you remembered to bring cups for the wine."

"I thought it would be cute. I'm sorry, guys." Kim had dribbled plum sauce onto the brand-new blanket. She was prone to this kind of thing—her adventures came up short, her plots unraveled—and knew it was a kind of incompetence for which others could mock her.

"It's fine," Brooke reassured her. The apartment was grander than Brooke had remembered but also less welcoming. It wasn't a matter of its lack of sofas, rugs, tables.

The place would always be cold, indifferent, too good for them. It was an error, a waste of millions. Nothing like the place on Twenty-ninth Street, nothing like Asher Jaffee's aerie, nowhere Brooke would want to live.

"It's not." Kim was disappointed in herself. "But I've got plans. So we're doing that long sofa just there, past where Matthew is. And I was so particular about the coffee table that they asked me to sketch something and it turned out that they love it. So we're doing something custom based on my drawing. Anyway, I was thinking of doing an upholstered wall over there. Like emerald green, a cut velvet? So soft."

Matthew chewed thoughtfully and tried to imagine these touches. "Sounds nice. I need to see it."

"I have a whole folder of inspiration. Tear sheets. Colors, fabrics, fixtures. Once you start looking at a space there are so many elements involved. I'm really starting to feel like this is something I could do, you know? Like there's so much I want to try in this house that it won't ever be possible. There's only nineteen hundred square feet here! I guess that's the appeal of this job, you can work out these ideas for your clients." Kim trailed off.

"I like this for you," Brooke said. "I always ask you for outfit approval. You do have great taste."

"I know you think it's stupid. But I'm excited."

Matthew's eyebrows crawled up in surprise. "Let's not do that again."

"I didn't say it was stupid." Brooke couldn't believe that her opinion mattered this much to Kim. But she wasn't going to pretend to find meaning in this work—helping rich people buy ottomans and choose paint colors.

"I suppose nothing could compare with your job these days. I can't believe you missed Auntie Paige's memorial for work." Kim was less meek than she seemed. She'd been planning to lob this observation at Brooke all week.

Brooke had ignored her phone that night. She had made excuses the next day. She chose not to feel bad about what had already been done. She loved Paige but had chosen the living over the dead. If her family didn't understand that, it was not her concern.

"What did you miss?" Matthew's mouth was full. "What did I miss?"

"It's nothing." Brooke was too busy. The grief had never really arrived and maybe the guilt wouldn't, either.

"Our auntie's memorial service—" Kim explained.

"I've got a lot going on." Brooke hadn't bothered telling anyone about the Subway Pricker selecting her. She would not explain herself, not even to Kim. She was filled with some purpose, could feel it in her blood. She was a woman alone, not merely tough but indefatigable. There was some tingle on her skin, some heat rising; it almost felt like anger. It was not just Kim; no one understood her. When her phone's screen lit up, it seemed somehow to underscore this point. Brooke rose out of her crouch. "I have to take this." She walked away from her friends, not noticing the meaningful glance they were sharing, to the small terrace. The door leading out was heavy. There was less breeze than she had expected and the sound of a siren far below her. "Hi, Andrea."

Andrea at Chase had been dissatisfied with what Brooke had shared. She wanted to see more. "Good evening, Brooke. I'm sorry, I know it's the end of the day—"

"It's not a problem. Or maybe there is a problem, but I'm not certain I understand what it is." Brooke crossed one arm against herself and looked out at the city. She tried to sound like Alissa McDonald, to sound like Asher Jaffee, to sound like someone who refused to accept how the world worked.

"There's a lot we require before we can make a loan of this size. It's all standard." Andrea's nonchalance meant that she didn't think Brooke was hiding something.

Brooke knew otherwise. The whole point was that standard was not for her. She felt like shrieking, even if Andrea was not to blame. No one was. Everyone was. Underwriters were impartial or people could only be judged by the numbers. Brooke, despite everything, was only her numbers. The grade point average, the permanent record, the credit report: it was never a secret, the extent to which data determined your life. The right person could extrapolate your life span from your zip code and body mass index. Could Andrea at Chase Bank look into the monitor of her PC and divine when Brooke would die? "I understand. These things are standard. These are rules. That is what governs all of life. We agree to rules. Most of us. There are some, though, you know, who do not obey, who are not asked to observe them. There are those who are lucky, who are— what's the word? It's *blessed*. There are those who are blessed. There are those who do not live among the rest of us. You might say, even, that they distract the rest of us with their rules, their decrees, their standards. That people like you, people like me, are so busy trying to adhere to them, to conform to them, to obey, to fall into line, whatever you want to say, that we don't notice, we don't see, we don't pay attention, to how these things do not apply universally. That there are exceptions made. That grace is granted. That some other way of life, some better way of life, is possible, if you simply demand it."

Brooke did not notice whether Andrea at Chase was still listening. She was. She wasn't taking notes because there was no procedure in place, nothing to do with this new information.

"I'm not interested in standard anymore, Andrea, I'm done with standard. I never agreed to these terms. That my existence, my happiness, my future, my—I don't even know what the right noun is— would be determined by math, independent of my input, not taking into account anything of interest. What if I'm good? What if I am a good person? Can a number show you that, and can we answer why it can't?" She could hear how she sounded. She did not care. "I am a good person. That is the answer, one answer, to a question that no one is asking because it's irrelevant." She demanded it. A better way. A bit of grace. Dispensation. She deserved it, but that didn't matter, either. Brooke demanded it!

In the old days you could slam down a heavy plastic receiver and feel something. She pressed the button to end the call, and it was anticlimactic. She put the phone in her pocket and went back inside.

"Who were you yelling at?" Matthew looked laughable, hunched on the step in his work drag—J.Crew shirt tucked in at his waist, trousers just the right length to reveal a peek of striped sock.

Brooke loved that he could disguise himself thus, vanish into that office, with its dull corporate cool, and pass as one of some poorly defined *them* that she considered inferior. "I wasn't yelling." She laughed. People always misunderstood conviction as something else.

"You were yelling." Kim began to giggle, in part because Brooke had laughed, in part because she didn't know how else to respond. "What's going on?"

"I'm under a lot of stress, if you need to know." Brooke sat back down on the floor, in what they used to call Indian style. You couldn't say that anymore. Her kids at Endeavor called it *crisscross applesauce*. She was not hungry. She did not want her wine. Brooke felt like she had just run a race but also like she could run another. Did these people—her oldest friends—understand nothing?

Kim was serious now, regretted her teasing. "Something is going on. First Saturday, now you're all—what is—"

"I just want to have my life in order." She said it icily, as though it were Kim who was preventing it. "I want to buy this apartment. I want to do a good job at my job, my job doing good. My mother thinks it's a joke. She thinks it's a scam. She thinks I'm a secretary."

Matthew finished chewing. He tried to sound reasonable, like an adult with a toddler. "I want my life in order, too. That's what everyone wants. And my mother has no idea what I do." And what did he do? He read emails and looked at spreadsheets. He helped a bunch of art directors order eggplant parmesan for dinner. "You're feeling sorry for yourself."

"I think I should just ask him." Fuck Andrea at Chase Bank. "I think I need to act. The universe gives to those who ask. At least I'll know."

"Ask who? Ask what?" Kim was perplexed.

Brooke went on. "I mean, it makes sense. I have a need, he has a

solution. That's my whole job. Ask him for money. That is his purpose in life. Give money away." Brooke looked at Kim, who would
never know, truly know, what it was to need something that she did
not possess. Brooke couldn't envy her, she loved her. But God, to be
so free. "Something is different. I think he's waiting, honestly, he's
waiting for me to say something to him."

Matthew understood what this was. Brooke was determined to
see this through to its end and he thought the end was sex. "What
if he's waiting to make a move. What if his whole strategy is to
wait—twenty-first century and all—for you to make that first move.
Then he's the victim, the object, I don't know. It's possible."

She shook her head, almost pitied Matthew his naïveté. "It's not
that. There are other things between people. We have—Asher would
respect me if I explain it right. Tell the right story. He wants to change
the world, make it better. He has to see how he'd be making the
world better, for me, that this is in keeping with his larger vision,
his plan."

What did Matthew know of the dealings between men and
women? It all baffled him. "You don't need to sell me," Matthew
said. "You need to sell him." This was so much simpler in his own
life. He never had to pretend that a transaction was anything but
that. Brooke was beautiful. She was alive with something, it was apparent to anyone. There was something happening but Matthew
didn't know what it was and didn't know how to be useful.

"I wish I knew who he was, or what we were talking about," Kim
said. She felt left out.

"Money is bullshit, but it's the thing. It's the one thing. Makes
the world go round, as they say. So why is it—why can't we say it,
why can't we admit it, that it matters, that it's maybe the only thing

that matters?" Brooke did not expect either of them to answer. "It's right there for the taking."

Matthew tried to see things her way. Advocate for the devil. He could help. "Maybe you tell him, it's an opportunity to invest. Not a company, not a fund, but a person, his protégé." It almost sounded reasonable, it almost sounded plausible. "That's what you tell him."

"And he wants to get rid of it. Can't enter heaven with it. Can't take it with you. I'll be helping him. It's mutually beneficial. I am his legacy." She was his daughter. She was his life's work. She was his ambition made flesh, she was Jaffee in a Jiffy!, she was his most beautiful accomplishment, she was his salvation as much as he was hers. "Things used to be different, you know. Higher wages. Cheaper education. Cheaper everything. Greatest Generation because it was the Great Society and everything was underwritten. You married a man with a job and he stayed at the same company for half a century and retired with a pension. That was life! I have every advantage you can. I have cash in the bank, I have health and education, it doesn't matter. The cost of things makes no sense. Value is determined by rooms full of guys trading things. It's abstract. We used to say *the American dream* was a home, but now a home is just some weird commodity. We said that so much that we believe there's some moral advantage to it. Owning a house. Owning a thing. But that doesn't make you a better person or a person at all. We are people." If there was no ethical superiority in being rich, what was the problem in asking for money? "I can't stop myself wanting things." She saw this as a fundamental part of being alive. Everyone but the Buddha himself.

Matthew did, in some secret part of himself, understand her. This was a private thing, a reckoning, an ecstasy or a possession. "You have to do what you have to do."

T
hey assembled at Grand Central like a little family.
Eileen had brought her husband. Jody had brought
her wife. Kate had brought a boyfriend, a hirsute
Kevin. All of them in their festive best, it was one
of those moments Brooke usually swore would never come to pass:
she felt conspicuously alone. Why hadn't she asked Matthew along?

"Where's Natalie?" Brooke wondered. Not the same without her!

"She's already out in Connecticut," Eileen said. "I'm sure she's been
there all day."

Grey, whom Asher fretted was the man of the house, met them
at Greenwich Station. Grey competently piloted a van large enough
to accommodate ten. Brooke wondered whether this vehicle belonged
to Asher (it did) and what it was used for besides ferrying visitors to
the Jaffee home (nothing).

There had been much discussion about what the Jaffee house
would look like. Subjects for office banter in a workplace of so few
people were in short supply. They passed one another in halls, rode

up and down together in that silence that always prevailed in elevators. That they had so little to say to one another, Brooke and Jody and Kate and Eileen, revealed their embarrassment, maybe affirmed that they were just a delusional few, trying to make a change in the universe. Maybe that was every workplace.

Off the unassuming Riversville Road was a short driveway, obscured by hedges and gate. Beyond this, the vast house was curled up beneath a thicket of trees. The unpaved drive circled around an island of fanciful plantings and a fountain. It was a white board building with a red door and black shutters, something suited for the English country, a fantasia made more absurd by the pool, the tennis courts, the guesthouse, a stone-cottage garden folly, by being in America at all. It was tasteful. The main house crouched so low you didn't realize it was vast. The place unfolded from the entry point, branching here and there like a spilled liquid. There were barrel windows and French doors opening to a flagstone path. The garden was a tangle of purples and yellows beckoning to butterflies and bees. Inside, the floors were now parquet, now checkerboard tile, now floral carpet, now rugs from Iran. There were fireplaces, antique tables, a piano, and masterpieces: the Francis Bacon, the Childe Hassam, the Mary Cassatt, the David Hockney. There was a Warhol *Liz* and a Fairfield Porter that depicted an interior rather like the room that held it, dusty light and a striped sofa. Later that night, the Frankenthaler would be unveiled. The crowd would applaud. Carol would weep.

Asher emerged with the patriarch's joy at seeing the whole clan. He had instructed them to arrive before the rest of the guests— Carol's oldest pals, their foundation's partners at other nonprofits, various state and federal apparatchiks, the Orthodox brothers who took a tidy tax break for free rent on the suite of rooms at 256 West Thirty-sixth Street. Time for a private toast, a little peek. No, a full tour wasn't possible (the Realtors pegged it at nineteen thousand square feet) but the greatest hits: the Lucian Freud, some Korean ceramics, the chair in which Kennedy had rocked Caroline, which required the story of how Asher had bought it at the Onassis estate auction ($442,000). Everyone *ooh*ed and *aah*ed over the things and the stories behind the things. Vicarious grandeur, but not splendor, the ceilings low, the rooms designed for real lives. They each imagined themselves living there.

Natalie had been to the house many times, but she followed this tour, because it was for foundation staff and she was one of them. But she was more, too, which was why she broke off, periodically, to field questions from Christina, one of the household staff, the person charged with throwing their parties. Watching Natalie and this woman confer, Brooke saw that the determined look on Natalie's face was pleasure, as close as she'd get to a smile. Natalie kept pausing to offer instruction to the black-clad servers bustling around them. Service gave meaning to Natalie's life.

The apartment on Twenty-ninth Street would have fit snugly inside the room in which she stood, wouldn't it? This was an illness. There was some itch in her limbs. What was a party, Brooke thought, but a compulsion, some animal instinct, people no different from ants, swarming and manic with unknown purpose.

The door opened and closed. The day was hot and uncanny. It was summer but Asher called and people came, grumbled privately on the schlep from Sag Harbor. *We love Carol!* The intimate scale of the rooms meant the party felt crowded immediately. People huddled in groups, by the fireplace, by the Steinway, in the ballroom, on a window seat. They talked about Obama, they talked about taxes, they talked about the Subway Pricker, still at large. They talked about home renovations, and children heading to college, and the Subway Pricker, who had struck again. They talked about war, and the climate, and the Subway Pricker, fascinated, as the rich always are, with the ugliest aspects of reality. They spoke of these things with remove, with bemusement, the horror over the war, the climate, the Subway Pricker feigned, because it would never come for them. What else was there to talk about?

Brooke slipped away from a chat with a nervous man from the governor's office, in search of a powder room. One of the women in black trousers showed her the way—down that hallway. There was a Basquiat hanging outside of the bathroom. Brooke peed, washed her hands, picked the dust from her own black pants.

She returned to the party, and with that synapse or pheromone some possess, she saw the other Black people—Sister Ghalyela, accompanied by Alissa McDonald, who at that very moment had herself divined the presence of a Black person, Brooke, and gave a subdued wave.

Any conversation with them would turn Brooke into a liar. They would see these many rooms full of beautiful things and ask again about the gift Brooke had promised to the Throop School. Ghalyela Jefferson would be vindicated, Alissa McDonald insulted. Brooke would be revealed: a liar, a phony, a pretender, ineffectual as any secretary. Brooke gave a tentative wave back, jittery with a sense of mission. She would find Asher Jaffee, she would bring the subject to her apartment on Twenty-ninth Street. This was her moment.

A short hall took her to a bright room with a swinging door. Here had congregated the other Black people at the party, one face familiar: Christopher, Asher Jaffee's driver, suited and tied as always. She greeted him more warmly than ever she had, knowing that the four women who stood around him, neither glasses nor plates in their hands, must be his wife and daughters. "Hello, Christopher."

"Miss Orr." He gave the same nod he always gave. "Please meet my wife, Abeba."

The oldest woman of the quartet had a guarded smile that did not show her teeth. She wore a scarf because she was devout. Her daughters did not, though their dress was modest. These girls were American stunners, all, tall from a youth of whole milk, absurdly shining skin and dimples inherited from their father.

Brooke offered party pleasantries. She had some impulse to play hostess. "You're not drinking? Or eating? There's so much food. You must help yourselves."

Christopher would never permit himself to look uncomfortable. He only smiled. "A beautiful party for Mrs. Jaffee."

She sensed he was ill at ease nonetheless, and tried on modesty, for his sake. "It is," she agreed. "A lovely celebration. I feel so honored just to be here."

"Amina, this is the woman I told you about." He addressed himself to his oldest child. "Miss Orr is Mr. Jaffee's right-hand woman."

Brooke demurred. "I don't know about that, Christopher."

He knew, though. "Every day, I take you so many places. Meetings and business and all of these things. The driver sees everything, you know. It is wonderful. Your parents must be very proud of you."

Brooke let this pass. "Amina. It's nice we've met. What do you do?"

She had her mother's taut smile. "I'm a nurse."

"Of course." Too late, Brooke remembered. Asher would not have forgotten this fact. "Your father mentioned that. You know, Mr.

Jaffee is very interested in health care. As an area of giving. Is there an association of nurses? Or maybe there's a scholarship opportunity. I know he'd like that. Do something to train the future nurses of America. Christopher, have you ever talked to Mr. Jaffee about that?"

The man made a face that said he hadn't quite heard or understood.

Amina laughed, a musical, hearty sound, unrestrained. "My father and Mr. Jaffee do not discuss these things."

It made perfect sense to Brooke. "But, Christopher, you should. You know Mr. Jaffee is—"

Amina interrupted. "My father's name is not Christopher. Mr. Jaffee does not know that. I see you do not, either. But his name is Christophe. He is from Yaoundé, where we speak French, where this is a common name. His father was a judge on the Cour Suprême. But to Mr. Jaffee, to you, I see, he is Christopher, the man who drives his expensive car."

Christopher said his eldest daughter's name with the paternal foreboding that was the same in every tongue.

Brooke knew that these people would know that she was blushing. "I didn't realize. I'm so sorry."

"No." Amina agreed with her. "You didn't realize."

"You should join the party," Brooke said. "I know Mr. Jaffee will like to see you enjoying yourselves. I saw a Basquiat painting! This house is incredible."

"We will wait here until it is time to sing happy birthday," Amina said.

"You're a guest," Brooke said. "You have every right." Brooke wanted to tell her the story of how Asher Jaffee had saved Natalie's elderly mother. That was the sort of man he was. But to Amina, Brooke knew that he would only ever be the man who didn't know her father's name.

Amina had everything she needed. She had her life in order. She had a sense of who she was in the world and was happy. "We are fine here. Celebrating together, the five of us."

The woman had nothing to fiddle with, nothing in her hands, and did not seem to mind this. The room was hers, it was her father's, it was her family's, and Brooke was the one who didn't belong there. "You'll excuse me." She wanted a drink.

There was another room, this without much in the way of furniture and not a single person inside of it. It felt like trespassing. In the adjacent room, wide and sturdy, as though reserved for dancing, was a bar. The bartender, a short man with a shaved head, was the only other person there. He smiled at her, offered his wares.

She asked for a whiskey on the rocks and idly entertained going to bed with him. "Maybe no one knows you're back here."

He handed her a fat tumbler, wrapped in a black napkin. "Always a logjam. People linger up front. Then they realize how many rooms are open. That there's more than one bar." He had served at many of these parties.

She couldn't hide away like Christopher—Christophe—and his women. She smiled her thanks. There was a flurry behind her, more people emerging from yet some other room. The woman of the house, trailed by the party planner, two other people, and reliable Natalie. Carol was in a frenzy. Reared on midwestern potluck, Carol now had to direct these Kabuki productions. "There's no one back here! This bar hasn't been touched." Maybe this imperiousness was inevitable when you'd spent three decades with four billion dollars.

You can't take the Midwest out of the girl, but you could add something into the mix.

The bartender busied himself, knowing better than to address the lady of the house.

Brooke prepared her face. What would be required? A broad smile? A feeble hug? An air-kiss of reunion?

"You." Carol pointed at Brooke. "Go circulate up front. Tell the guests there's a bar back here. Room to spread out." She kept walking, a head of state flanked by his generals, a queen and her retinue. They were gone in that hoofbeat of expensive shoes on expensive tiles. The bartender looked down at his work.

Brooke had worn a cashmere shell, black, and trousers, tapered a bit to show off her new Louboutins. She thought it gave her the look of a gallery attendant, or someone who worked at Christie's. But she supposed it was also how you might characterize a waitress. Unless you looked closely—and Carol had been in a rush!—you wouldn't see the fine heft of the top, the sharp lines of the trousers, the flawless leather of the thousand-dollar shoes, all paid for, at least temporarily, she intended to pay him back, by Asher Jaffee.

An impulse. A joke. Natalie found profound joy in a life of service to this man. Maybe Brooke would, too. Good enough for Christophe not Christopher, for Andrea from Chase, for Ghalyela Jefferson, for the various people who were not invisible at all but exerted real control over life, or over Brooke's life. Someone, possibly one of the black-clad women flanking Carol, had left a tray, silver and laid with a black cocktail napkin, on one of the tables. Brooke picked this up. She could feel the eyes of the bartender on her back but did not look his way, clicking down the hall into the next room, the tray balanced on her right hand, and went to work.

A woman with red hair smiled in apology and Brooke offered the tray with a deferential nod. She set down her lipstick-stained flute and continued her conversation. Brooke put a thumb on the glass's base to keep it steady. She gathered crumpled napkins from the mantel. She put the rubbish on the tray. There were more people in the next room. She recognized Tony, one of the suits from the Ford Foundation, holding forth in front of four people she did not know. She wondered what had become of Tessa, the woman hit by a car the day Asher had taken her to see the Frankenthaler. She wanted to ask but instead kept her head level, her smile unworried. Two more empty glasses were deposited on the tray. It was not burdensome. She realized, moving through the room, that music was playing. Where was it coming from?

"I'll take another Seven and Seven, thanks." Tony did not look into her eyes.

Oh, they had met, many times! An electric thrill in disappearing into thin air. "Of course, sir. Can I get anyone anything else?" She thought the *sir* a nice touch.

She went back to the bar in the empty room. "Seven and Seven. White wine. Sparkling water, with lemon."

The bartender wanted no part of this. "What are you doing?"

"What I was born to do." She walked behind him and tossed the napkins into his garbage can. How could she explain it? She had asked for too much from the world. She had not realized that this was an option: to give in to it. She wanted to help? Then serve. She wanted to be alone? She already was. She wanted to exist unseen? That wish had long been granted! Brooke had only to enjoy it. "Where do the dirties go?"

He was a bartender. He did what was asked. He poured the drinks in silence. "You can leave these here." He put the used glasses into a tub beneath the bar. "But the dirties go back toward the kitchen."

She didn't introduce herself because who she was no longer seemed to matter at all. Brooke or? Her name itself was a question. She delivered the drinks. There were so many rooms, so many people, mostly strangers. She knew Mayor Bloomberg but he didn't know her, so she didn't need to worry about being recognized. The round tray in her hand, draped with a square piece of cloth, was magic, a force field, a talisman. She had felt so beautiful, leaving the house in her expensive shoes and perfect clothes. This feeling was better. It was true power, stalking these rooms unnoticed as a house cat, a boring painting, another antique gewgaw. Brooke collected empty glasses. She righted a knocked-over flute. She cautioned a woman to watch her step on the tile then realized it was Laurie Anderson. "It's a little slippery there, ma'am." She loved it, the taste of

---

that *ma'am*. Laurie Anderson smiled appreciation, eyes disappearing into squint.

Brooke may not have known her matrilineal heritage but maybe all Black women in America had in their veins the knowledge of where the kitchen was. She unloaded more glasses into bus tubs on a long table. She peeked inside. Several people at work, the hiss of grease in a pan, the clang of aluminum against marble.

The cook was looking at her. "Crab cakes," he said, as if she were stupid.

Brooke walked briskly. She didn't want the food to get cold! It wasn't difficult. Before they were pressed to admit their hunger, Brooke looked them in the eye and said, "Crab cakes?" A feline woman in a cheongsam asked whether the food was nut free. "Indeed!" Brooke told her, with the conviction that they were. Just a guess. Soon her tray was balled-up napkins and spent skewers.

Another of the servers, a girl with a long ponytail, looked at Brooke, tentative and nervous. "I have to pee," the girl confessed.

"That's allowed, isn't it?" It had to be! They were only human.

"Can you cover the foyer? Christina asked me to—"

Brooke's face said, *Say no more.* They swapped her clean tray for Brooke's soiled one. Men paused their stories to request drinks. A bangled hand rattled an empty glass in the air and Brooke fetched it. A man whose English seemed unsteady inquired after the toilet. Brooke walked him two rooms over and pointed down the hall. "It's by the Basquiat," she said.

Time sped up. Brooke was exhilarated. It was as though she were in someone else's life. She had never understood that what she most craved was erasure. What a joy to no longer be a person, with her stupid needs, her small problems, her body that required a trip to the bathroom. Now, she was just a task. Smile, soothe, serve. If anyone who knew her saw her, she did not see them seeing her. She was a new woman at last, after all these weeks of trying to be one. She did not exist. That, it turned out, was all she had ever wanted.

"I owe you," the girl with the ponytail said, later. "If you want to go catch a smoke, you can. I've got it here."

There was no reason for nerves—she was a guest, free to step into the garden and smoke. It sounded alluring, it sounded wonderful. Invisible, even cancer couldn't find her. People fit themselves into groups of two, three, four, talking seriously about various matters in the summer haze. Evening was tiptoeing in. The lawn so vast, studded with benches, topiary, hedges, plantings, that it had an institutional quality. People could never fill it up. Some distance from the house—considerate—a man in a navy tie was smoking a cigarette. What would Mayor Bloomberg say?

Brooke cadged a Marlboro, and he seemed disappointed that she did not linger to flirt. She ventured out onto the vast lawn, from a distance a field of perfect green, though as she walked on it, tentative in her heels, she could see the gaps between the grasses, the black earth beneath. She stood beneath a tree and smoked and looked back at the house. She would go inside, and find Asher, and ask him what she had meant to him. She would ask him where the Frankenthaler painting was hidden. She would not bother to ask him for more money for Ghalyela, because Brooke knew that she had never cared about sisterhood at all. She was interested only in her own, private happiness.

She stubbed the cigarette out, determined to extinguish it, fearful of causing a fire. Imagine destroying this tree, this lawn, this beautiful mansion, these perfect lives. She strode back into the house, followed the crowd into the ballroom. Asher stood on a little raised platform, Carol by his side, proud in her reign. There was tremendous, awed applause as the Korean prodigy Chae-Yeong Kim took the stage with her three-million-dollar violin.

The staff used this opportunity to restore order. Brooke observed the beautiful choreography of their preparations as they kindled the chemical fires beneath chafing dishes, set out stacks of plates, fiddled with utensils. Brooke, a ghost now, did not warrant reproach from any of the servers who might have wondered why she was not helping.

All of the lights were on in implicit welcome and Brooke followed these upstairs like a misled summer moth. The long hallway was wide enough that it was punctuated, every few feet, by mahogany armoire, overstuffed chair, console. What was inside those drawers? Who would sit on a chair in this empty hallway? Maybe some nights Asher needed a rest after climbing the stairs. She didn't like to imagine it. She pushed open a door. It was a bedroom, grand but not sufficiently grand to be the master bedroom. No, *primary*. A gingham check on the bed. The copper lamp on the bedside was switched on. She studied the titles in the bookcase, considered the view, those trees near the house now illuminated by floodlight, those farther distant fading slowly into shadow. Who would sleep here tonight?

She opened other doors. An office, maybe Carol's. Photographs of Asher and Carol with George and Barbara Bush, with Ed Koch, with F. W. de Klerk, with Robert Mugabe. There was a painting by Whistler. Brooke didn't have to wonder whether it was real. Would the Frankenthaler be hung in this very room? There was no space for it! There was a desk, stacks of paper, a little malachite box, a brass-handled letter opener (women like Carol had *correspondence*), a pair of reading glasses, a carafe of water. Brooke sat and imagined being lost in some business there, in the pleasant quiet of the Connecticut night, the rest of the world somewhere very far away.

She could hear footsteps in the hallway. She did not worry. She went into the bathroom adjoining the office. She locked the door behind her and sat on the edge of the tub. She didn't need a Whistler. Who cared about Whistler? She didn't need to mix with politicians and madmen, didn't need fine furniture, booty from history, a black-clad staff, a ballroom for speeches. But this she coveted, this lovely little bathroom, white tile, stainless steel, soft light, a potted fern.

Brooke ran the bath. She slipped off her top. She unhooked her bra. Her body was fragrant with honest sweat, tinged with the stink of cigarette. It was like the nights of her now-concluded youth, leaving Kim and Matthew in the bar and showering the beer and smoke from her body in the bathroom of her childhood. She'd be happy to be alone but also regret not being with them. She wanted it both ways, everyone did. Brooke hung her trousers on a well-placed hook on the back of the door. She put her underwear in a tidy pile on the counter. The water ran very hot. She turned it down. She slipped into it as you might a swimming pool on a hot day. She sank into it, over her ears, the whole world vanishing but the roar of water into water. From there she did not hear the sound of three hundred voices in unison, singing "Happy Birthday."

She had made mistakes. She had misunderstood something, possibly everything. But she could not shake the sense that she was on the verge of the solution to some problem she couldn't even articulate. Brooke could not return to whoever she had been before she had met Asher Jaffee. So she would become the person who owned the apartment on Twenty-ninth Street. She still understood that it was right there for the taking and she would never be able to live with herself if she did not try.

Brooke sat in the tub until the water grew too cold. She dried herself thoroughly. She no longer smelled of sweat. There was a rose-scented lotion and she worked this between her fingers, up her ankles, over her shoulders, between her breasts. She put her clothes back on and hung the towel to dry. As she opened the door, steam escaped the confines of the little room. Her eyes adjusted to the shift in light; the small bright bath, the larger darker room, Asher Jaffee, handsome in his suit, arms crossed across his chest, a strange look she'd never seen on his face, Natalie behind him, a crow's intelligence in her hard eyes.

What are you doing—" He wasn't sure how to complete the thought.

Still, Brooke knew the answer. She was in the process of becoming who she had always meant to be.

Natalie was triumphant. She had been preparing for this moment. "You see, Mr. Jaffee."

"I don't know what to say." Asher had at last shut up. Asher had, after all his years, been surprised.

Natalie did. "I've had suspicions. And I saw her. Standing on the lawn with a cigarette while you were speaking. I followed her up here. The bathtub running? I didn't know what to think. That's why I— well, you had to see it for yourself."

Flushed, Brooke ran a hand across her damp head. She was still proud of her expensive clothes. "Now you've seen for yourself, I guess." She laughed a little.

Asher collected himself. "Natalie told me she has concerns."

"What are those?" Brooke sat on a chair with a needlepoint seat. She wanted to hear the case against her.

"I read that letter. A fraudulent. A lie. Exaggerating your salary." Natalie's impassive eyes contained some pleasure. "Mr. Jaffee, I don't like to bring it up now, but I took the liberty. I pulled the corporate-card statements. Saks Fifth Avenue. And the car service. So many trips, I don't know where, some place in Brooklyn."

"What about the toilet brush, Natalie?" Brooke was placid. Maybe a secretary was to be feared, after all. "But that was an honest mistake. I didn't know. I just printed the receipt. I didn't mean to." Brooke didn't say that all those trips to Ghalyela had been the official business of the Asher and Carol Jaffee Foundation. There was no point. The world had fallen out of alignment. But when? Maybe the answer had to do with generational allegiance: it was either September 11, or the day George W. Bush became president, the day news anchors had to explain what Clinton had done with the cigar, the day man stepped on the moon or said that he did, the day the Japanese strafed Pearl Harbor, the day Gavrilo Princip took aim, whenever. Brooke shouldn't be thinking about the future and she shouldn't be thinking about the past. She should be thinking about this moment.

"I'm sure I don't know what you're talking about. But I can't see anything funny in this. Making a mockery of Mr. Jaffee's charity, walking around his home as though you belonged here." Natalie was trembling. She would have something to talk about for the rest of the years of her small, mean life.

Brooke knew, though, that she did not belong there. Anyway, she was not interested in being prosecuted. "Natalie, would you leave us alone?"

"I certainly will not—"

Asher put a hand on the woman's bony shoulder. "Please go back to the party. I don't want Mrs. Jaffee to wonder where I am. Please tell her something." He knew Natalie would come up with the perfect lie.

"Of course, Mr. Jaffee." Natalie did not even look at Brooke. All this over what—some money? She felt ill.

Asher sat on the edge of the daybed. He made his *I'm listening* face.

Brooke could give him her pitch. She had worked it out beautifully:

So much of what we're doing here is preparing for the future. The future of your money, the future of these organizations, even, forgive me, a future that you yourself will not see. That's why you took me to the Ford Foundation, that's what you said to me the other night, after we heard Mozart. You want to enlist the future me in maintaining your legacy. And you're prepared to reward me, accordingly, to take care of you after you're gone. So there we are. You want to take care of me, please do. I want you, not the foundation, but you, to invest in me, in the same way the foundation invests in its partners. It's a small sum, a rounding error, in the context of your giving, of your estate.

She saw now that this was the wrong approach. Her destiny was not the entitlement Asher Jaffee enjoyed. If she wanted to enter heaven, she would have to earn it.

Asher went on, filling the silence. "Natalie is saying—fraud? I can't believe that. What have you done?" He gestured at her and himself with his pointer fingers, chummily. "This is a special thing we have." There was something on her face he couldn't parse. Maybe he'd never been able to read her at all.

"I've mentioned before that I want an apartment." Did he understand? "It's not enough money, not right now. Going forward—" She could sense that he wanted her to stop.

"You're asking for money." He had more money than anyone should have. It was immoral. Mostly he pretended not to feel guilty or strange. "You want a raise." So he would give her one. He knew that Natalie had misunderstood. He knew that Brooke would not have done something bad. So she had—taken a bath in his wife's office? Hadn't he done worse in his life?

This wasn't working. She *needed* his money. "I asked you for one million dollars for the Throop Community School. For those souls. And you said no. Fine. I need an apartment. For me. You're Asher Jaffee. Everything is possible. You're a man. A white man! Everything is possible for you."

Asher Jaffee shook his head. "Don't turn this into the battle of the sexes," he said. One million dollars for who? "You have a goal. What's the word, even? I was going to say *moxie* but this is a whole other level. You want me to buy you an apartment?"

"I want you to secure something for me. A future." She told herself there was nobility in it. She believed this. Salvation itself.

"I'm not sure what that means. What's to stop you from asking me—pay for my wedding, send my kid to private school, I want a house in the country—"

"You've not been listening. All these weeks. I'm marrying this apartment, if it helps you to think in those terms. It's all falling apart out there." She gestured toward the windows, the dark night beyond. "The bees are dying. Someone's pricking women on the subway. Remember that? It's all anyone talks about. I thought it was nonsense but I understand it now. The poison. It's in me. You don't understand because you don't have to."

"Because I'm a man?" He knew that she couldn't help thinking this way. It was generational. Women were angry. Maybe they were right to be.

"Because you have everything in the world," she said. He could help Ghalyela, he could help her.

"Money doesn't buy happiness." A lie, often repeated.

"So why are you giving Carol a billion dollars before you die? You promised that for good. You told me you wanted to save souls. And I found some that need saving. I'm honest with you, so please be honest with me."

"I lost my child, Brooke!" He was moved. He was angry. "The one thing in my life that mattered to me. And I'm not talking about my wife. You're not my wife. Do you understand what we're doing here?"

"I understand we're trying to get you the Presidential Medal of Freedom before you die," she pointed out. "I understand we're trying to settle your tax bills. I understand your wife doesn't want the whole lot to go to poor kids in Brooklyn. I understand everything. And I know what you could do for me. I thought there was some feeling there. I thought you liked me. I thought I would ask. It's what you would have done. You asked me, *Who is going to take care of you?* I decided it could be you."

He wasn't angry. He was almost proud of her. "It must be difficult to hand out my money. But we're addressing need. Not want."

"It's not want. It's survival. This is the world." That Frankenthaler downstairs, that Philip Guston on Thirty-sixth Street. A codicil in his will and her problems were solved. "All your money, all your sophistication, this is what it won't get you. A sense of how the world works for most of us."

"You make me sound like a monster," Asher said. Did she hate him or love him? The question every parent had for their child.

"I know you're not. I think, in fact, that you love me. I know that you're just a rich man with a guilty conscience, nearing death's threshold. But I know that, too, that you love me."

He could admit it. "Fine. Maybe, possibly, another reality, another life."

"You put your hand on my head. Didn't anyone ever tell you not to touch a Black woman's hair without her permission?" She felt alive.

These problems had solutions. "You could sue me," he said. "Get your apartment." A nondisclosure and a settlement and this baffling woman would be satisfied.

"You could fuck me," she returned. There it was, plan B, the one she should have led with, herself as servant, ready to abet Asher Jaffee's dreams. "Give me a child. A beautiful, caramel-colored child. The one thing you don't have, right? An heir. You could take care of her, instead of me. I'll even call her Linda." She ought to have seduced him, allowed the hand on her head that night to guide her where it would, to provide for him what little it was in her power to provide anyone. She should have served but had only just learned that was her destiny. Truly, she had never been so impressive a student.

He had thought it, and she had sensed that. That was not his fault. It was biology. It was destiny. And it had only been a passing thought, how her skin, how Black skin, might feel against his. There was nothing shameful in it. He had done nothing wrong in thinking it. It was she who had violated something by saying it. He was too disgusted to come up with words to dismiss it.

"I'm prepared to give that to you," she continued. "The rest of my life. I don't want to be a mother but if that's what the world wants from me, why don't we do it this way? I would give it absolutely everything I have. An heir, a child, that's your only chance at immortality." She could see the imagined baby dissolve.

"Please get out of this room." There were tears in his eyes. He hated this, he hated her. "Please get—"

She stood up. She smiled. "I was never here." No longer waitress, Brooke became a ghost, a spirit slipping into the wild. She felt herself come apart, she felt the pleasure of her own dissolving.

The unhurried click-clack of her expensive shoes on the wooden steps drifted up to the high ceiling. That suggestion of festivity— distant music, distant laughter, distant food smell, distant light— lifted the soul. It hurt a bit, didn't it, to have to leave the party? But she hadn't even noticed this Diebenkorn over the console in the foyer. Maybe that happened when you had everything; you started to see nothing. A shame. The painting was a stunner. One more masterpiece and not even a bench provided for reflection, visitation. Another day, Brooke might have liked to sit and stare, try to enter it, find its soul. But the painting belonged to Asher and would be forever indifferent to her. So it went. So it was.

She pulled open the door and found the night was now cool. The warmth of the bath and the heat of her shame provided some comfort. These, too, would dissipate, drift away, forgotten, in only minutes. Here there was no music and no crowd chatter. Outside was the delirium of chirping insects and the cold light of the stars. True what was said: there were so many, once you got out of the city. What a world, as Asher Jaffee might have said.

Where was she? Oh, she was nowhere. The gravel shuffled beneath her leather soles. They were hard to walk in and she no longer needed them. Brooke freed herself from them, held the shoes in her hand, then reconsidered, left them where she stood, like an evangelical's vision of the body taken in the Rapture, expensive shoes left behind, pointless in paradise. She enjoyed the exquisite near pain of the rocks on her tender feet. Her fine skin on the sharp stone was the only sound in the vast night. Dressed in black, Black herself, Brooke merged into the very air, faded into nothing, or perhaps everything was her now. There were pinpricks of light set into the landscaping, but by the time she reached the driveway's end, these were at her back, pointlessly illuminating sculpted hedges. Now her eyes could adjust, comprehend the darkness. Now she saw, perhaps for the first time in her thirty-three years.

Brooke hadn't paid any attention during the drive from the train station. She hadn't left a trail of breadcrumbs to follow as children in fairy tales knew to. She had no idea where these paths led. She didn't know whether to turn left or right. But the yellow lines on the road reassured her. There was something to show her the way. She would follow that road anywhere. She would end up back in New York City, or she would not. It didn't matter. The road would trace hills and snake around bends and through the night, and it would lead, somehow, to herself. That is what she would find. Nothing bothered her, not in that moment: not the perfect quiet, not the utter dark, not the chill, not the realization that she was alone in the world. Weren't we all? Nothing to fear in that. The human condition. She was there, in this moment, breathing, miraculous, alive. She was free.

ACKNOWLEDGMENTS

Thank you to Julie Barer, Louise Erdrich, Sara Friedlander, Lovia Gyarkye, Eleanor Kriseman, Idra Novey, Kiley Reid, Danzy Senna, David Tamarkin, Jessica Winter, and Charles Yu.

Thanks to Riverhead: Nora Alice Demick, Alison Fairbrother, Bianca Flores, Ashley Garland, Jynne Dilling Martin, Sarah McGrath, and Glory Anne Plata.

Thank you to Lynn Steger Strong.

More than thank you to Marley Trigg Stewart.

Thank you to David Land, though that hardly seems adequate; I owe you everything.

Sincere apologies to Sylvia Plath.